I0589384

Code Bravo

Michael Milford

and

J.C. Pollari

This project was partially supported by the generosity of friends, family and people I have not even met.

Major Kickstarter Supporters: Peter Milford, Sean DiLizio, David Roebuck, Jasmin Craufurd-Hill, Michael Brand, Katherine Leben, Julie McKay and Andrew Allwood

For Ethan and Rachel

Prologue

0 minutes left

Will heaved himself up another rung of the rattling metal ladder, his heart drumming in his ears.

Every muscle in his body screamed. His foot slipped, and he banged heavily into the metal framing. He cried out, as pain radiated sharp and jagged from the knife wound in his side.

He had to get higher. There was no time.

Clenching his teeth, he forced one foot up, then the other. Grab, pull, repeat.

Then his hand hit air. A platform.

Was he high enough? How high did he have to be?

It didn't matter. It was too late now. He had seconds, if that.

He tugged at the suit balled under his arm. It flapped open, the wind catching at the arms and legs and cracking the thin synthetic fabric like a whip. His hands were shaking, but he gritted his teeth and shoved one leg and then the other in. Gingerly, wincing against the burning in his side, he encased his arms in the rustling fabric.

He stepped to the edge of the platform.

In the blue-black dark he could just make out the mountainside dropping away far, far below. Nothing but space and turbulent air between him and jagged rocks and scrub.

And in the distance: the twinkling lights of Brisbane city. Where Eliza was.

He swallowed, his eyes suddenly prickling. He swiped a hand, steeling himself.

He'd done all he could. It was no longer up to him if the city survived.

He glanced down at his watch. The luminescent display read 7:00 PM.

Everything seemed to still, like the world was holding its breath.

Then a column of light shot into the air. Pain shot through Will's skull: too bright.

Too *close*.

He felt the beginning swell of heat, a deep pulsing of subsonic sound that rumbled in the chambers of his body rather than being truly heard.

The ground swam below him. He had no choice. Forwards was the only direction left for him.

His heart shuddered, a staccato thrumming in his ears. He raised his arms, poised on the edge of the platform as if tied to a cross.

And he jumped.

The wind whipped at his hair and whistled past his

ears, and then began to roar. He was falling, the tower at his belly, headfirst towards the ground.

And he was gaining speed.

Too much speed, too fast.

The top of the mountain pulsed. Birds and bats rose screaming into the air.

Suddenly, the wind caught in the taut fabric stretched between his arms and legs, and the wound in his side screamed as the wingsuit finally, *finally*, started to work.

A deep, ear-splitting rumbling replaced the growl of the wind. Below him, the scrub collapsed downwards as the ground crumpled, the very earth disintegrating from beneath roots and trunks and tangled branches.

And then he was clear of the imploding mountaintop, and he was accelerating, arms and legs taut with the effort of remaining steady. His breath rushed in and out, in tiny, amazed gasps. He was still alive.

He was *still alive!*

He risked a look down, at the dim outline of the trees and rocks he was skimming over.

His stomach flipped, a sick punch in his gut.

And he realised that he didn't have a parachute.

Chapter 1.

73 hours and 43 minutes left

Will's eyes narrowed as he looked across the shopping centre at the banners plastered over the jewellery store windows.

Late Night Shopping Super Sale. Take 50% off the marked price, and then take a further 45% off that.

"Bingo," he said, a grin spreading over his face. He nodded towards the huge, gaudy banner still being hung by a shop assistant. "I told you."

"It's not going to work," Eliza said, not looking up from her phone, her slim fingers flicking over the virtual keyboard. Light from the screen flashed on her black-rimmed, rectangular glasses. "No one's dumb enough to fall for it."

"Not even Carl?" Will said.

That made her look up. He followed her gaze and saw her pause, motionless, as a hulking boy the same age as them stood up from behind a counter.

"Shouldn't he be out looking for smart people to antagonise?" she said, raising an eyebrow.

"His dad owns the store," Will said, and if it were possible, his smile grew even wider.

"Okay," Eliza said, and she blanked the phone screen. "I'm listening."

Will turned, his back to the store, and lowered his voice. He ran his hand through his hair, brushing it from his eyes. "Okay. So your job is distraction. See the other assistant?"

He saw Eliza's gaze shift, past his shoulder, beyond him to the shop, and she nodded.

"Keep her away from Carl. Make up something believable."

Eliza still said nothing, her eyes turning back on him, impassive. She fiddled with the end of her plait, her dark wavy hair bound, in some kind of complicated pattern that made no sense to him, over her left shoulder.

He swallowed. "This is the best I can come up with since the online money dried up," he said. He cleared his throat. It sounded like he was whining, but he needed her on board. "And it's a one-time deal. Tonight only!"

"Okay," she said, and he relaxed, letting out a breath he didn't know he was holding. "I'm in."

He grinned again. "I knew you respected great ideas."

She rolled her eyes. "Okay, so, I'll be buying a watch for my boyfriend?"

"You did hear me say believable?" he said, raising his eyebrows.

She shoved him. Though she was tiny, and way shorter, she'd always been able to hold her own against him.

"Ow," he said, with a pained gasp of a laugh. He staggered backwards. It was only half for effect.

"Men find me desirable," she said, raising an eyebrow again, and emphasising the word *men*.

"Lucky them," he said.

"Cash," she said, holding out her hand. "If you want it to be believable, I need to actually buy something."

"Okay, okay." He yanked his wallet from the pocket of his jeans and rifled through a wad of crisp notes before handing a couple to her.

As she tucked them into her purse, he dug in his other pocket and pulled out a large black button attached to a small plastic box with a thin cable.

"Is that a hidden camera?" Eliza asked, her voice turning dubious again.

Will nodded. "Just some insurance." He replaced the middle button of his shirt with the camera and awkwardly tried to feed the cable down into his pocket again.

"Here," Eliza said, rolling her eyes. "Some secret agent you'd make." She tugged the box from his fingers and with quick, deft movements, arranged it under his shirt against his skin.

"Don't tickle!" Will protested, as her fingers brushed against his ribs.

"I'm not tickling you," she snapped. "Hold still

and don't be a baby."

She pulled her hands away and he raised an eyebrow quizzically at her, patting his shirt down.

She shook her head. "Can't see it."

"Let's do this," Will said, a grin spreading again.

Eliza's cheek tugged up, the little resigned half-smile that he knew she couldn't help, and her dark brown eyes glimmered. It just made him grin broader. She still played it cool, but he knew she got the same thrill out of this that he did.

Will watched as she entered the store, and waited until the other assistant approached her. Eliza led the other girl towards the front window, so that the assistant's back was to Carl, and over her shoulder, met Will's eye with the barest of nods.

Hand in pocket, Will wandered in, his finger silently flicking the switch on the camera box.

Carl's back was to him as he approached the counter. He turned around when Will cleared his throat.

"Hey, Carl," Will said, smiling, meeting Carl's gaze.

Carl hulked over him. Will wasn't that much shorter, but Carl's bulk made him seem like he filled the room. They'd scuffled once after a rugby match got heated. Both had ended up with a black eye.

There were a few seconds of silence as Carl glowered. Will waited, his smile growing wider, seeing the cogs slowly clicking over behind Carl's eyes as he realised that Will was a customer and he'd have to serve him.

"What do you want?" Carl said, his face twisted in a scowl.

"My older brother sent me to pick something up for him." Will said, as if Carl's tone was polite rather than borderline threatening.

He pulled out his wallet and plucked out the thick wad of fifties and hundreds, and tapped it casually on the benchtop, while peering into the cabinet of rings between them.

From the corner of his eye, he saw Carl straighten, the scowl softening. He even tried a smile, a parodic impersonation of a pleasant salesman.

Will had to clench his teeth to hold back the burst of laughter. This was perfect. Going exactly to plan.

"He needs a ring to propose to his missus, but he's off working in the mines," Will said, wandering down the length of the glass cabinet, still tapping the wad of cash. His story wouldn't stand up to any scrutiny – apart from anything else, he didn't have a brother – but Carl didn't know that, and he had several hundred distractions being waved around in front of his face.

"Right, right," said Carl, trying not to look at the money. And failing.

Will spotted a ring, and his stomach flipped. Perfect. That was the one.

"Let me have a look at that," he said, tapping his finger on the glass above the prize. "The big one. Two carat diamond."

Carl glanced at him quickly, then at the money, then at the case. "Yeah. Okay," he said, and with fat fingers better suited to a rugby ball than the tiny key he was using, eventually managed to get the case open.

He grabbed it, the massive diamond set in sparkling gold dwarfed by his hands. He went to hand it to Will, and as he did, the price tag swung around, and they both saw it at once. It read *$35,990*.

Carl paused, hand in the air between them. Will saw those sluggish cogs churning again, trying to work out if Will was playing him.

More distraction needed.

Quickly, he yanked his wallet out and extracted a second, even thicker wad of money, and Carl visibly relaxed.

"Don't drop it," Carl said, his voice caught in some weird battle between being professional and showing Will how little he thought of him. Kind of made him sound like a frog, more than anything else. Will nodded, placed the cash on the bench and tweaked the ring from Carl's fingers. He twisted the ring in the light, not really looking. From the corner of his eye, he could see Carl's eyes glued to the money. On the other side of the shop, the other assistant was locked in animated conversation with Eliza, a variety of metal-banded watches looped around both girls' wrists.

"Perfect," Will said, and he met Carl's eyes again, setting the ring down. "I'll take it. Paying cash, obviously."

He scooped up his bundle of notes. "I guess you'll have to clear that with your boss over there," he said, nodding at the other assistant.

Carl's eyes narrowed. "She's not my boss," he snapped. "I'm going to be running this store in a couple of years. I don't need her permission."

Slamming the cabinet door shut, Carl locked it and stood up. He poked the ring into the box and slid it into a small paper bag, stalking back to the register.

Will followed. His heartrate was starting to pick up. This was it.

"Don't forget the discount," he said, nodding at the banner at the front of the store.

"Of course," Carl said, his voice taking on a sneering quality now, like Will was telling him something extremely obvious.

Carl looked down at the register and ran his finger along the buttons. Will followed his gaze, scanning the labels printed on them.

Half-price.

Members' Discount.

5% off.

10% off.

The discount buttons ran in five percent increments all the way to ninety-five percent off.

Will waited. He forced himself to breathe, to keep the same calm smile on his face.

He saw Carl glance towards Eliza's assistant, a shadow of doubt flitting across his features.

Bingo again.

"If you don't know what to do, I'll go ask her," Will said, shifting towards Eliza and the other girl.

"It's fine," Carl snapped, his scowl returning.

"Just trying to help," Will said, holding his hands up.

Carl shot him a glowering look, then reached across the counter and snatched a brochure, opening it to the page showing the discount. He pecked out the digits *35990* into the register, and hit the *50% off* button.

Will watched, heart thumping, as Carl ran a finger along the *"take a further 45% off that"* part of the text. His brow furrowed, and then he poked the *45% off* button savagely.

Nothing happened.

Will felt light with relief. Carl obviously didn't know it, but it looked like Will's research had been right. The point of sale system could only apply a single discount. Carl had to enter the discount in one go.

And he had no idea how to calculate it.

"Look, I'm going to miss my movie. Can't you just get her to do this?" Will said, letting a bored annoyance flow into his voice. He glanced at his watch and once again made to move over to the other side of the store, but Carl growled out something that sounded like "wait".

"Okay, okay, settle down."

Carl's jaw clenched spasmodically as his eyes

flicked between the register and the assistant who was now moving to the other register with Eliza.

"Look," said Will, his tone carefully disinterested. "It's just ninety-five percent off isn't it? I mean, fifty plus forty-five is ninety-five, right?"

Carl paused, then entered *50 + 45* into the register. The screen flashed *95* back at him.

"Looks right," Will said.

Carl repeated the calculation, with the same result. He glanced at Will, his eyes scanning, those cogs grinding, but Will kept his face expressionless.

Turning back to the register, Carl sighed loudly and entered *35990* in again. And then he pressed the *95% off* button.

1799.5 appeared on the screen. And Will whooped with triumph in his head.

"Eighteen hundred dollars," Carl said.

Will flipped out the wad of notes and with fast flicks of his fingers, counted out the price onto the counter, before Carl could think too much about the amount.

Then he had to watch Carl slowly recount them.

Twenty agonizing seconds later, Carl dumped the notes into the drawer and hit the *Sale complete* button.

The register started noisily printing the receipt. From the corner of his eye, Will glimpsed Eliza leaving the shop, a small bag swinging between her fingers.

"Here," Carl said, shoving the receipt into the tiny bag sitting between them.

As he did it, the door to the store's back room squeaked open, and a heavyset older man in a suit emerged.

As Carl turned to see who it was, Will swiped the bag off the countertop, and walked briskly from the shop, his breath catching in his throat.

Eliza was waiting outside, just out of sight, and she raised an eyebrow, questioning.

"Done," Will said, and a grin split over Eliza's face.

They half-jogged from the gallery of shops towards the food court packed with people out for late night shopping. Only then did they stop behind a large pot plant and look back.

"Any second now," Will said.

Back in the store, the man in the suit was talking to Carl. He wrapped an arm around Carl's shoulder, as Carl brandished a receipt. The man took it and examined it for a few seconds.

Then his arm slipped off Carl's shoulder.

He stepped back and smacked the receipt with the back of his hand. Carl moved to a register, typed in some numbers then gestured for the man to look. Shaking his head, the man typed in his own set of numbers.

Even from a distance, Will and Eliza could hear the rising voices in the store.

"Looks like dad's not happy," Eliza said.

"That's what happens when you blow $8100," Will said. He felt breathless, adrenaline coursing through his bloodstream.

Moments later, a panicked-looking Carl burst out into the shopping mall amidst crowds of shoppers. He ran a few metres up the mall, then in the opposite direction, craning his neck to scan the crowds.

Eliza grabbed the back of Will's shirt, tugging him further behind the pot plant, and he had to stifle a burst of giggles.

"It's not funny," Eliza said, but she was starting to laugh, low and quiet, too.

After a few long moments, Carl turned back and re-entered the store, his every movement dragging with reluctance.

"Also not happy," Will said, getting his laughter under control.

"I kind of want to hear his dad yell at him," Eliza said, grinning. "Does that make me a bad person?"

Leaving the pot plant behind, they drifted through the food court.

"I reckon I can pawn it for eight grand, no problem," Will said, jamming the tiny bag containing his prize into his jean pocket. "That leaves us more than six grand up."

"He's going to kill you at school tomorrow," Eliza said.

"Me? What about you?"

"Unlike you, I have years of good girl credit built up," Eliza said. "No one could possibly suspect me of being involved."

"Hmm," Will said. She was right. They were all in

Year 11, Carl included. But although Will and Eliza had ended up in all the same classes – Math B, Math C, Information Processing and Technology, Physics, Chemistry and of course, English – Eliza was the top of all their classes, while Will only did the very minimum he needed to do to pass. And sometimes not even that. Years of that kind of behaviour was why he'd been surprised that she was, actually, still kind of cool, underneath all the excellence awards.

"Well, that's why I have this, isn't it?" He tugged the camera from his shirt. "Apart from being an upstanding young citizen, what other shining personal qualities does Carl have?"

"An ego the size of Western Australia?"

"So which do you think Carl would rather – put up with some grief from his Dad, or become a worldwide sensation on YouTube for being a dumbass?"

Eliza smiled, slow and broad, her white teeth gleaming. "We're going to go to hell, aren't we?"

Chapter 2.

The expanse of concrete that was the Port of Brisbane was covered by shipping containers and a huge warehouse that opened towards the water. Cranes towered over the ships lining the wharf and rows of container trucks.

In a back corner of the warehouse, Senior Sergeant Drake Wessley shoved his shotgun around the end of a shipping container and fired.

His jaw clenched as hundreds of rounds ricocheted off the container walls. Rusty metal fragments rained down on his head.

"Sir. Sir!"

Drake glanced at the sergeant sheltering behind the other end of the container. He was all that remained of the nine-man team Drake had accompanied to the port inspection.

Drake dredged up the man's name from memory – Smith. Terrance Smith. His brain seemed at once to be on overdrive, taking in everything around

16

him, while simultaneously blocking out everything earlier than ten damn minutes ago, when this disaster of a situation had begun.

"Handgun mags?" Smith said, panting.

Drake withdrew a mag from a pouch on his belt and tossed it to Smith.

"Last one – make it count." He realised he was shouting to overcome the ringing in his ears. "They're wearing vests – I hit one with three rounds in the chest and he didn't drop. Go for the head."

Smith nodded, reloaded, and fired two rounds.

Immediately, return fire hammered Smith's end of the container.

Drake risked a look around his corner. Crates set alight by gunfire filled the warehouse with smoke. At the warehouse entrance, Drake could see the refugee boat they'd been sent to inspect sitting in its dry dock.

Two gunmen stood by the boat talking to someone out of view, their weapons stiff in their hands.

Drake swallowed, and leaned out further. There was a third man on the boat deck. He passed a metal crate down to the two others, and they loaded it into the back of a white van.

Drake flinched as a reflection high up in the crane blinded him. A fraction of a second later a bullet snapped over his head and smashed into the concrete floor behind him.

He jerked back into cover.

"Sniper on the crane," Drake said, and Smith

nodded, his face white. "Whatever they're loading: it can't be good. We have to stop them leaving."

"How?" Smith said. "I've got less bullets left than bad guys, and they've got bloody assault rifles."

Sneaking another peak around the corner, Drake saw the man on the boat deck jump down and jog to a black ute in front of the van.

His mind flicked over the possibilities. Hold tight and wait for help: bad guys get away. Charge the van and truck: sniper nails them before they get close.

"We've got another problem," said Smith, pointing at a line of tanks inside the entrance to the warehouse. Each tank had a red *HIGHLY FLAMMABLE FUEL* warning painted on the side.

Another gunman was crouched by the tank, unscrewing a massive valve with both hands. He lurched backwards as a torrent of brown liquid spewed forth, then leapt into the back of the ute, which screeched into motion.

The fuel flowed steadily into the warehouse.

Towards the burning crates.

Drake's nostrils flared as dizzying fuel fumes wafted over them. He glanced at his shotgun, and swore. "You reckon you've got any chance of hitting that sniper?"

"Sure. This baby's accurate to half a klick," Smith said, patting the barrel of his handgun, but the look on his face didn't match the forced confidence in his voice. "Maybe the sniper's cleared out too?"

Holding his shotgun by the barrel, Drake stuck the

butt out the side of the shipping container.

It exploded into kindling.

"Nope," Drake said, brushing splinters from his shirt and dropping the remnants of the weapon. "Did anyone in our squad bring long arms? Like a sharpshooter, for example?"

"Not exactly. Benson had an M4, but... they got him," Smith said.

The team had made a fighting retreat into the back of the warehouse, using crates and shipping containers as cover. Drake could see the carbine lying beside Benson's body about ten metres back. It was a short run under normal circumstances but a death sentence under sniper fire.

"I can cover you," Smith said, following Drake's gaze.

"Right," Drake said, and swallowed. "When I break cover, you open up. Keep his head down long enough for me to grab it and get back."

Smith nodded, face drawn.

Drake took a few deep breaths then burst forwards.

Sound exploded behind him as Smith started to fire steadily. Drake skidded, scooped at the rifle with his left hand and pushed off the ground with his right.

A bullet hissed past.

Drake forced his legs to accelerate, and dived the last metres back into cover. He shoved himself off his stomach and panted, his back against the container.

"No holes, sergeant." He patted himself down and

grinned. His heart raced, thudding in his ears.

"How do you feel about crispiness?" Smith said grimly, pointing. The fuel was lapping at the first of the burning crates.

Drake pulled the magazine from the carbine, and his grin vanished. Empty. "Better get ready to run."

"Might be one in the chamber?"

Drake checked. Desperate hope mingled with dismay. "One shot," he said.

He glanced over the rifle. The scope was intact. But he needed a range to dial it in. "You haven't got a laser rangefinder, have you?"

"Sure," Smith said. "Would you like the basic or the deluxe version?" He kicked at the shell casings by his feet. "All the tactical gear's back at base."

Drake sighed. It seemed like a lifetime, but until ten minutes ago, this had been a standard intelligence operation. Inspect the refugee boat. Take some photos. Report back. The biggest opposition such operations normally faced were inept government officials. And rats.

"Could be three hundred, could be five – hard to tell," said Smith, glancing out from behind the container. He was exposed for less than a second, but almost instantly, a bullet punched into the concrete where his head had been.

"Something tells me *he* knows what the range is," Drake said, his teeth gritted. His brain churned, dredging up training years old. He could estimate the range using a familiar object near the sniper. But as he ran the M4 scope over the crane, all he could see was metal scaffolding and ropes, and, just barely in the fading light, a black-clad bump that was probably the sniper's head.

Nothing obvious he could use. He put the rifle down and rubbed his eyes. The smell of fuel was making his head throb.

A bullet hit a floor grate and sent sparks flying into the fuel. Drake winced, expecting the burst of flame that would fry them like sausages, but miraculously, it didn't ignite.

"Whatever you're planning, sir, we have to do it now," Smith said, his voice tense.

Drake clutched his face, trying to ignore his growing headache. A bullet clanged off a nearby metal pole and restarted the ringing in his ears. A moment later he heard the much fainter crack of the shot.

He dropped his hands sharply. "That's it," he said. "Smith – how many rounds you got left?"

Smith checked. "Two."

Drake nodded once. "Right. When I say, stick your head up and fire one round."

Drake pressed a button on his watch twice. The display showed *0:00:00*.

"Okay… GO!"

Smith stood, sighted briefly, shot off a round and then ducked. Drake waited for the flash from the sniper rifle and then pressed the button. A fraction of a second later the shipping container clanged loudly. Then, after what seemed an age, Drake heard the faint

21

snap of the sniper's shot. He pressed the button again. The display read *0:01:17*.

"One more," Drake said, and Smith nodded.

This time the responding sniper bullet passed overhead and smashed into the back wall of the warehouse. Now the display showed *0:01:24*.

"Double check this math for me," said Drake, stabbing buttons on his watch. "Sum of 117..." Another button press. "And 124?"

"241," Smith said immediately.

"Okay, about 1.2 seconds for the sound of his shot to get to us. Sound travels at about 340 metres per second, so..."

Drake scrunched his eyes shut and muttered to himself.

"It's 408 metres, sir," said Smith, after barely a second.

Drake raised his eyebrows.

Smith shrugged. "I spend a lot of time at the racetrack."

"Let's hope you're right," said Drake. Twisting the scope, he dialled in the range. A second twist adjusted for the angle of the shot.

He looked at Smith and swallowed hard. This was it. Their only chance. "I'm going to need four or five seconds to get lined up on this guy, so you're going to have to keep him distracted."

Smith nodded, his face pale.

"Try…" Drake hesitated. What he was asking Smith to do was dangerous. Very dangerous. But they had no other choice. "Try making a run for that pile of crates."

Smith crouched, readying himself in a sprint position. "Ready," he said.

"Be careful," Drake said, and Smith nodded, eyes on his finish line. "On three."

"One," Drake said, his voice dropping low. Smith tensed, his muscles visibly bunching beneath his uniform. "Two… THREE!"

Smith exploded forwards, zigzagging erratically.

Drake rolled sideways into a crouch, bringing the M4 up and dropping his eye to the scope. The crosshair raced up the crane as Drake counted off the stairway platforms. When he hit the third platform, he arrested the upwards movement of the rifle and nestled the butt deeper into his shoulder.

The sniper fired again, the flash lighting up his hiding spot.

There was a muffled cry, and Drake gritted his teeth. He held steady, focussing on shifting the crosshair until it lay centred on the sniper's head.

He breathed out, his eyes unblinking.

And squeezed the trigger.

He kept his eye at the scope, imagining the bullet flying through the air.

There was a beat of stillness.

Then, silently, the sniper's head snapped backwards out of sight.

Drake's heart yammered. Had he made the hit? Or was the sniper taking cover?

Then, finally, he saw it. The sniper's head, slowly lolling forwards to hang limply off the edge of the platform.

Relief washed through Drake.

"Smith," he called, but there was no answer. Heat spiked through him, and he dropped the rifle, scrambling for the crates.

"Smith!" he called louder, and skidded around the corner of the crates. His voice sounded too loud in the silence now empty of gunfire.

Smith was lying with his back against a crate, blood spreading out from where his hands were clutching his thigh.

"You got him?" Smith said, his voice low and tight with pain.

"Got him. Let's get the hell out of here." Drake crouched down beside the sergeant. "Can you walk?"

"Just a flesh wound," Smith said, but as he tried to get up, he crumpled around the injury, his face white.

"Come on," Drake said, and wedged his arm under Smith's shoulder, hauling him to his feet.

Together they staggered around the burning crates and bodies, towards the warehouse entrance. A rush of fresh air hit Drake in the face and he gasped it in, his head spinning after the petrol fumes.

Then there was a *WHOOMPF* behind them.

Drake glanced back. The fuel had reached the first burning crate. And a wall of flames was roaring towards the tanks.

"Damn it," Drake grunted, and he jerked Smith

into a limping, shambling run. "Move, move, move!"

They cleared the entrance. The flames were licking at the first tank as they stumbled past. Drake glimpsed the top of a ladder on the dock edge. There. That might save them.

He forced every remaining ounce of energy he had into his muscles, almost lifting Smith off the ground. Seconds – that was all they had.

They were almost at the ladder when Drake glanced back again. The tanks were practically wrapped in flame now.

Drake yelled, tightening his hold on Smith, and charged over the edge of the dock.

Legs still windmilling, they plummeted towards dark water.

There was an immense *crump*, and intense heat seared Drake's back. A sheet of fire shot out over their heads, licking tongues reaching down for them.

But then the water was there, and with a shock that tore Smith from his grip, Drake plunged into ice-cold blackness.

He was suspended in the depths, his punished lungs screaming for air. He twisted, trying to find which way was up. A vision of surfacing into a raging inferno flickered over his mind, but when he finally breached the surface, the flames had dissipated.

He sucked in fresh air, his vision swimming. An orange glow was raging above the dock, far above him. Where was Smith? He spun on the spot, relief filling him when he saw the dark shape of the sergeant's head bob above the waves.

For a few glorious moments, the dead police and the aching pains in his bruised and battered body were all forgotten. They were alive. Alive! His brain seemed to be frozen between exaltation and some kind of shock. How had his normal day at work turned into this – this action-hero, gun-toting, exploding-buildings madness?

He swam for Smith, grabbing him before the man could disappear again beneath the surface.

"You think it was drugs?" Smith said, a grimace visibly twisting his face even in the shadowy twilight.

"Not sure," said Drake. He rolled onto his back, wrapped his arm around the sergeant's chest and kicked out with his legs, heading for the ladder. The joy of just being alive was quickly wearing off, and his brain was kicking back into gear. Into reality. "Whatever it was, there was a lot of it – that van's tyres were rubbing against the frame."

"And those guys were equipped," Smith muttered. "Assault rifles, tactical gear."

"Yeah. Not exactly your typical drug dealers."

The sergeant lapsed into silence, his eyes clenched shut. Drake swam on, his brow furrowed, his eyes staring intently into the evening sky. He had never known an Australian drug crew to shoot it out with police. Yet these gunmen had just killed seven federal police to protect whatever had been in those crates.

And now they, and their cargo, were loose in the city.

Chapter 3.

"Did you tell Jeff you're staying here?" Eliza asked, stashing the diamond ring behind a book on her bookshelf.

Will plopped into the half-retro, half-just-old single armchair in the corner of Eliza's room. He raised one eyebrow. "Really?"

Eliza scooted back on her bed, crossing her legs and leaning against the wall. She raised her hands, palm-out. "Just checking."

"As long as I show up at school and don't drink, do drugs or murder people, he doesn't care," Will said shortly, tugging a magazine from the jumbled stack beside the chair and flicking it open to a random page. He knew that Abby, Eliza's mum, probably had texted his uncle Jeff telling him that Will was staying anyway.

"Toss me the camera and I'll download the footage," Eliza said, pulling her laptop onto her knees and flipping it open.

Will grinned, dropping the magazine back onto

the pile, and threw himself onto the bed beside Eliza, slumping back on his elbows beside her.

There were a few moments of silence while her fingers whizzed over the track pad. Then the video was playing on mute in an editing program, the shot focussed clear on Carl's face as he struggled with the register.

Will laughed, low and devious.

"Why don't you use these skills in school?" Eliza said, also grinning. "You'd never beat me, obviously, but you could easily smash the others in our classes."

"Meh," Will said, shrugging.

Eliza rolled her eyes. "You could get really good results if you put in even the slightest amount of effort."

"I did once, and they just thought I'd cheated," Will said, and Eliza barked out a laugh. "So I stopped. And what's the point of effort anyway? I'm already making bank." He nodded towards the bookshelf where the ring was stashed.

"Oh, I don't know, maybe prepare yourself for a life *not* of crime?"

"I'm no criminal," Will said, his voice taking on a haughty air. "I just take advantage of beneficial situations."

"Like online gambling?" Eliza said, her tone becoming taunting, her eyes still on the laptop screen.

Will scowled. A month ago he'd been busted by the police for online gambling using… innovative methods.

"You're just lucky that you've got Jeff," Eliza said. "If I'd been caught: I'd have been grounded until graduation. And maybe even longer, if they could manage it. Jeff didn't even punish you."

Will shrugged. His uncle had just talked to some guys he knew in the police, and that was the end of it. He'd barely even yelled.

"He's been more bi-polar than usual, lately," he said, his voice dropping low.

Eliza paused in her video editing and glanced over at him. "Any clue why?"

Will shook his head, his eyes back on the screen. It wasn't the kind of thing that he and Jeff talked about. Why Jeff seemed overly happy, jovial and joking around one minute, and distant and abrupt the next, was beyond him.

Of course, Will knew that Jeff loved him. And had done – was still doing – the best he could, raising a kid that wasn't his. When Will had come to him, Jeff had been in his late-twenties and full party mode. And that had all been cut abruptly short by... Will.

Sometimes he thought it would have been better if, maybe, Jeff had ever had a girlfriend. But somehow, though he'd never say it, even to Eliza, Will suspected that it was part of Jeff's way of punishing himself for what had happened. That there was only one role that Jeff was entitled to now, and that was being Will's guardian.

"Okay, done," Eliza said, finishing the edit on the video and hitting the render command. She glanced at

Will. "At least Jeff's usually around," she said. "It's been two months since Dad was home." Eliza's dad, a management analyst for some company defined by a bunch of words like *corporate* and *conglomerate* and *international*, travelled constantly.

Will nodded. "Yeah, I guess." He smiled for her sake, but it didn't go all the way down. Abby had been his mother's best friend. And when his parents died, Abby had made it clear that he was as good as blood, and he was always welcome in their home. But it wasn't really the same. Will was like an island, really. He'd always been alone. But sometimes he still caught himself wondering what it would be like to have parents that went away and travelled so much that you missed them being around.

*

The next morning, with Will's ring in her pocket, Eliza sat beside Will on the early bus. The plan was to drop by his house and grab an experimental report that was due in their physics class today, before ducking into the pawn shop to collect Will's profit.

"I can just hand it in late," Will muttered, yawning, running his hand through his sandy-brown hair, the short waves messy. Probably un-brushed. Eliza repressed a sigh. He hadn't stopped whinging since they'd gotten up. In fact, he probably had been whinging in his sleep, since she'd reminded him at midnight before bed.

"You'll appreciate me one day," Eliza said, not looking up from the phone in her lap. Jasmine, a girl also in their physics class, had just texted her in psychedelic freak-out mode because she'd lost the checklist of what was meant to be in the report. So of course, Eliza was the default backup checklist. She finished typing *CALM DOWN JASMINE* and started on the list that was embedded into her brain like a blueprint. "Like when you're not getting expelled for being incomplete in every subject."

"Hmm," Will grumbled. "Hey. Check it out." He tapped the window.

Eliza glanced up. The bus route hugged the base of Mount Coot-tha, the stubby mountain overlooking the city. "Yes, that's a mountain, Will."

He rolled his eyes. "I mean the wing suit guys."

"Oh." That was vaguely more interesting. Figuring Jasmine had survived this long already without the checklist, Eliza leaned over Will to peer upwards through the glass.

As they watched, a bright red speck trailing smoke flew down the side of the mountain. A second later, a grey blob exploded in the air above the speck and blossomed into the familiar shape of a parachute.

"They use tiny jet engines on their legs to give them the thrust they need, because Coot-tha's too low for unpowered jumps," Will said. "See the smoke?"

"Hmm," Eliza said, still watching. "The things you know about things that no one cares about."

Will jerked his knee and she yelped as it smacked her rib.

"Oops," he said, and grinned, the morning light

31

catching in his green-blue eyes as she drew back, scowling.

"What happens if the engines fail, then?" she said, her voice sulky.

"Splat, I guess," Will said, and he widened his grin, baring his teeth at her like he was some kind of predatory animal. She rolled her eyes, and went back to solving Jasmine's problems.

Five minutes later, the bus dropped them at the entrance to Will's street. Nestled in the bushland at the end of the cul-de-sac, Jeff's modern brick house was a hundred metres from the nearest neighbours, but with the vegetation, it might as well have been kilometres.

The front door had a high-tech electronic keypad next to it. Will punched a sequence in.

"Eight-digit passcode," said Will, as the door chimed. "Take you weeks to try every combination."

"What are you, a piano virtuoso?" Eliza said. "More like a year."

"Whatever," Will said. He grabbed the handle and pushed hard. Eliza glimpsed the metal bracing running along the sides of the door as it swung open.

"Uncle Jeff," Will called. His voice echoed. Eliza shivered. It felt cold, too still. Not lived in. She followed Will to the kitchen, the stark, almost bland décor of the place striking her as always. Jeff was some kind of freelance security analyst, she knew that much. Will didn't say much about Jeff's work, because he didn't know much either, beyond that he worked on contracts for the government and multinational corporations.

"Is he working?" Eliza asked, her voice sounding too-small in the cavernous space. There was a reason they gravitated towards hanging out at her home. Because it was… well, a home.

"He could be in his study," Will said, but his voice sounded uncertain. Eliza nodded. Every time she'd ever been here in living memory, Jeff had emerged bleary-eyed and distracted from his study.

Will flicked a light switch, but the room stayed dark.

"Is your power out?" Eliza asked, opening the fridge. Nothing but shadowy darkness around a few cola cans, take-away containers and condiment bottles, though a wash of cool air trickled out. "The door thing's still working."

"It's on a different system," Will said, his voice sounding strange. Flat, kind of muted. He strode down the hallway, and she followed. Eliza realised her heart was pounding. The silent house, and the shadowy lack of power: it was creepy.

Will froze, beyond her, at the end of the hall. "Holy crap," he said, his voice low.

"What?" she said, but before he could answer, she reached Jeff's study and saw for herself.

Thousands of sheets of paper littered the floor. The drawers had been pulled out of the filing cabinet and desk in the room and upturned. A computer case lay ripped open, its cables spilling out. Intricate spaceship models had been ripped apart and scattered across the room.

"What the hell happened?" she breathed.

Will's face was stiff, and he pulled his phone from his pocket with jerky movements. He dialled a number, and after a few seconds, there was a ringing sound from beneath the clutter of papers.

Gingerly, Eliza stepped over the broken plastic and strewn wires, and brushed aside the papers. Beneath, there was a small, black mobile.

She reached out for it, then hesitated. Was this a crime scene? Should she touch anything?

She glanced back up at Will, but the doorway was empty. Heart racing, she grabbed the phone, and ran after him.

He was standing in the doorway to the garage.

"His car's gone," Will said, his voice flat. "He doesn't go anywhere without his phone."

"Maybe he forgot," Eliza said, but it sounded false, pointless, even to her. Tentatively, she reached out, putting her hand on Will's arm. "He probably wasn't even here, when they…"

She trailed off, and swallowed hard.

"Yeah," Will said. He was still staring blankly, into the empty garage.

"We need to call the police," Eliza said. Will didn't answer. She shook his arm, and finally, he looked at her. A pang went through her. In the semi-light his eyes were shadowed. Flat and empty.

"What?" he said.

"I'm going to call the police. Okay?"

"Oh. Yeah."

She tore her eyes away from him. From his face that looked like someone had just slapped him. And she dialled triple-zero on her phone.

Chapter 4.

57 hours and 53 minutes left

"A routine inspection?" Drake shouted, slamming his fist down. "My team was killed by a dozen guys in combat gear. Their blood is on your hands."

He paced across the interrogation room. The room stank of stale coffee. He'd snatched no more than three or four hours sleep in twenty-seven hours straight. And for the last three he'd been stuck here, answering the same questions over and over.

"Why wasn't your team in a state of readiness?"

"Where was your backup?"

And again and again: "Did you recognise the attackers?"

"Why the hell would I recognise them? They were wearing balaclavas!"

"Okay Drake, settle down," said Ronnie, Drake's boss, an older moustached man who was leaning against the wall.

Drake froze, and swung around to face the female officer who was questioning him. "Hold on. Are you

36

saying I *would* have recognized them without balaclavas?"

"No, we're..."

Ronnie leaned forwards, and tapped her on the shoulder.

"Take a break, Jessica," he said. "Get some fresh air."

A flicker of disappointment crossed her face, but she stood stiffly and left.

Ronnie waited until the door shut. "I know you're emotional, Drake. Believe me, I understand why. But you've got to keep you head if we're going to get these bastards."

"Then why aren't we out *doing something*?" Drake snarled. The adrenaline of his escape had long since worn off. Now he was just frustrated, angry, exhausted, and sick of this crap. He just keep seeing the faces of his team flicking past like a newsreel. How many families were destroyed tonight? How many husbands and wives and children getting the worse possible news, while he was cooped up here being *grilled*?

Ronnie crouched by the table. Drake watched, as he reached under. There was a click.

"I've known you ten years," Ronnie said, reaching for the camera attached to the ceiling. "And I believe you."

The light blinked out on the camera.

"What I'm about to tell you," Ronnie continued. "Is between you and me, got it?"

Drake nodded, pinching his thumb and forefinger to the bridge of his nose, forcing himself to calm down, to concentrate.

"For a year now, one of our intelligence guys, Jeffrey Roberts, has been working undercover for a new drug cartel," said Ronnie, collapsing into the chair opposite Drake. "Global outreach, well-financed, slick sort of operation."

"I know Jeffrey," Drake said. "Worked with him on the embassy bombing. Quiet, but a good analyst."

"Well, he had the cartel fooled. Last month he helped them import a shipment of drugs. He gave them navy patrol schedules, all that. All vetted by us, of course."

"Coming in by sea: risky," Drake said, leaning forwards. "They'd have to know the navy boys would pick them up a long way offshore."

"Well," Ronnie said. "A week ago, Jeffrey identified an inbound refugee boat as the one carrying the shipment. We were prepared to deal with the whole matter offshore, but when the navy found the refugees: they were all dying. More than a hundred. Too many for the offshore medical centre. They towed the boat to the nearest port with a major hospital: the Port of Brisbane..."

"...where my team was ordered to inspect it," said Drake, nodding slowly. "Clever, using our own processes against us. All the cartel had to do was pick it up from the port. Except we got in the way." He leaned back in his chair. "What time did the boat get

38

in?"

"4:30 PM yesterday. With your team ordered to inspect it an hour later." Ronnie paused, his eyes on Drake. "An order that maybe a dozen police here would have heard."

Drake stilled. The pieces clicked together, one by one. "You think we have a traitor."

Ronnie nodded. "Whoever took out your team knew they had a limited window to strike before their cargo would be in police hands. And they came in guns blazing, because your team was pre-empted."

"Maybe they got lucky," Drake said cautiously. "We don't know for sure it's one of ours. And Jeffrey – did they mention a police source to him?"

"I'd ask," Ronnie said, his voice suddenly weary. "Except Jeffrey was killed late last night in a car crash. Drink-driving. Perfect bloody timing, don't you think?"

There was a beat of silence, then Drake sighed. "Jesus. How long before we get external backup?"

"The feds are mobilising. But you know as well as I do, our best chance is to nail these guys now, while the evidence is fresh. Once the feds arrive…"

"It'll be a circus," Drake muttered.

Ronnie nodded. "And you'll be on your own, Drake. We can't risk anyone else catching wind. That is, if you're up for it."

"They murdered seven of our people," Drake said, his voice low.

Ronnie nodded slowly. "Then Jeffrey's your

starting point, specifically, his home office."

Drake nodded.

"And, unfortunately, next of kin hasn't been informed yet," Ronnie continued, grimacing as he pulled a sheet of paper from his pocket. "No living parents. An older brother deceased ten years ago. But he's legal guardian for his brother's kid, William. Sixteen years old. Lives with him."

"Great." Drake stood, another wave of tiredness hitting him. "Breaking the news. Just what I need." This was the part of the job he'd always hated. But the risk of bringing someone else on was too much. Besides, he needed to get a look at that home office.

Ronnie clapped him on the shoulder. "That's the spirit," he said, but Drake just grunted.

Chapter 5.

57 hours and 45 minutes left

The semi-trailer reversed into the industrial park warehouse, its tray empty. Inside, four trucks, their trays already loaded with containers, were parked beside a white van and black ute. Two men rolled a steel drum inside, their shirtless torsos dripping with sweat.

Danial watched the men heave the drum upright and position it beside the others. Another man, carrying a small metal crate, followed them inside. The sinews in his arms strained as he placed the box on top of the steel drum.

"Last one in place," he said.

"Good," said Danial, his face expressionless. "Let's get it loaded."

His men grabbed the doors, and leant against them. They clanged shut, the sound reverberating through the warehouse.

"Clear," one of the men yelled, after shoving a bolt through the door and twisting it into the locked position.

A gantry crane hummed to life, its drum reeling in cables attached to the four corners of the container. It rose, and the semi-trailer reversed slowly, a slow beeping echoing in the cavernous space.

There were shouts behind him. Danial spun: at the warehouse entrance, a police officer was scuffling with his men. Curses floated through the air as they held the officer back.

Then he caught sight of Danial.

"You! What god-awful mess did you make at the port?"

Danial strode towards the entrance, his movements lithe like a cat.

"Detective Riley, what a pleasure to see you," he said, waving the guards off before holding out his hand.

"Get your bloody hands off me," Riley snapped, then stumbled as the men withdrew. He ignored Danial's proffered hand, instead straightening his uniform with jerky little movements.

"We were protecting our investment," said Danial, withdrawing his hand. "We couldn't afford to lose this shipment."

"Protecting?" said Riley. "You *imbeciles* killed seven police!"

Danial's men tensed around Riley.

"The port was supposed to be clear," said Danial, waving his men back. "You were to make sure we had a whole night to unload. Instead your cops turn up after only one hour. They fired upon us. What would you have us do?"

"They weren't just cops," said Riley, shaking his head. "There were federal agents in that team. They're going to come after you with everything they've got."

Danial's eyes narrowed. The men they'd ambushed at the port had regrouped surprisingly quickly for local cops, and fought tenaciously. "And what were they doing at a boat inspection?"

"I don't know, I don't know," said Riley, the words tumbling out. His eyes darted to the trucks.

"Maybe they were tipped off," Danial said, softly.

"Not by me," said Riley, taking a step back. "Maybe that analyst squealed before you took care of him."

Danial fixed his stare on Riley. "He didn't know anything." He glanced back into the warehouse. The last container had been loaded and was being bolted down. "Anyway, none of this matters," he continued. "The shipment will be out of our hands and distributed to our buyers very soon."

"It better be," said Riley, his voice steady again. "And because of the mess you left me with, my fee's gone up. The risk goes up, the charge goes up. Two-hundred thousand. In cash." He waved at the containers. "With this much product, that shouldn't be a problem."

Danial smiled. "That is reasonable," he said. "Of course, we don't have the cash with us now. It'll take me a couple of days."

Riley's eyes narrowed. "Don't try to screw me, or I'll put so much heat on you, you won't even make it out of this warehouse."

"Don't worry," Danial said, manoeuvring Riley towards the entrance. "I will make sure you are rewarded for your efforts. Now, we're leaving. Might be wise if you do too."

Riley took one last look around, muttered something inaudible and headed for the entrance. Halfway there, he stopped and turned.

"One more thing. The report I filed on the analyst last night – a cop from my station pulled it this morning."

"You assured me that you dealt with it," Danial said. Heat flushed through him, but he kept his voice smooth and cold. "Is that not what I'm paying you for?

"No one's going to think twice reading that report," Riley said, but his face was turning pale and blotchy. "But you better hope you left nothing incriminating at the port."

"Who?" Danial barked. "Who pulled the report?"

"Senior Sergeant Drake Wessley."

"Is he a threat?"

Riley shook his head, too fast. "I'll keep an eye on him."

Danial said nothing, and Riley swallowed.

"Make sure you get me my money," Riley added. Then he turned, and hurried to his car.

Danial waited until he'd driven out of sight. Then

he turned to face his men.

They were in a semi-circle, all eyes on him. The warehouse was silent apart from the scuffling sounds of his men shifting their weight from foot to foot.

"You all know what you must do," Danial said. "I know we will succeed."

After this long together, there was no need for ceremony. His men dispersed, heading for the trucks, the van and the ute.

The building filled with the rumbling of diesel engines. As the first truck started to pull out, Danial strode towards a small table at the edge of the warehouse. As he walked, he reached into his pocket and pulled out a crumpled photo of a smiling young boy. Running his fingers over the photo, he brought it to his lips and kissed it.

Two minutes later the giant roller doors at the entrance shuddered shut, cutting off the sunlight. In the darkness, four candles spluttered fitfully, wax leaking onto the table beneath. The boy's photo leant against one, his face seemingly alive in the flickering light. A spinning top pockmarked with jagged holes rested against the second. Near the third candle lay a water pistol, its plastic barrel melted and distorted. A doll sat against the final candle. It had long lustrous hair and wore a bright red dress, but its legs were charred black.

Chapter 6.

57 hours and 29 minutes left

Drake turned his car, eyes fixed on the blue sedan in his rear-view mirror. It had pulled out behind him as he left the police station, and now it was still following even after driving a closed loop of the block.

He slowed to a crawl and waited. The sedan made no attempt to change lanes. Drake looked for the bump under the rear-view mirror where the camera was located on unmarked police cars, but there wasn't one.

"A little paranoia never hurt anyone," he muttered, flicking on his lights and slowing to a stop. He unclipped his handgun and got out, approaching the driver's door of the sedan.

It was a woman, in her thirties, and she was rolling down her window. His eyes flicked over her, quickly cataloguing a description by habit. Blonde, but well-dyed. Carefully-styled hair and clothes. Professional make-up. Polished, poised.

He frowned slightly. Actually, she looked kind of

familiar.

"Please step out of the vehicle," he said.

"You're Drake Wessley," she stated, as she got out.

"Do I know you?" He frowned harder. She was definitely familiar. But from where?

"Melissa Green," she said, flipping a card from some hidden pocket and giving it to him in one smooth movement. "Senior journalist at Channel Eleven."

His stomach sank, and he clenched his teeth as he gave the card a cursory glance. Great. That's where he recognised her from. Some flashy current affairs program.

"I'm following up on the incident at the port last night," Melissa said. She had her phone out, one end pointed towards him. "I understand you were involved." Her tone was steely.

"No comment," Drake said, his voice a growl. "I've no idea what you're talking about."

"Lot of cuts on your face for *no idea*," Melissa said.

He ignored her and turned, walking back towards the cruiser.

"My sources say your people botched the operation and the targets got away." Melissa's voice rose, and he heard the crunch of her heels on the bitumen.

"If you keep following me, I'll arrest you for obstructing the police," he said, rounding on her. His head was starting to throb. He was way too tired for this.

She didn't back down. "Perhaps you can comment on why there has been no investigation announcement despite there being multiple police fatalities," she said, her voice harsh.

He met her eyes. Surprised, he actually saw anger there, a flinty determination.

"Or is this another cover-up?" she continued. "Like the death of Jeffrey Roberts." Her voice became caustic. "Why has there been no official statement yet regarding his *accident*?"

His mind swam. "I don't know what you're talking about," he repeated flatly, and turned back to the car, slamming his door behind him.

She followed, her fingers clasping the window frame. He hit the button and the window started to slide upwards.

"Oh, and one more thing," she said, her face stiff. "Did you find any drugs?"

He kept his finger pressed down. She jerked her hand back at the last minute, and then there was blissful silence again as the window closed her out.

Reporters. Couldn't stand the parasites. He gunned the engine, and didn't look back, as the spinning wheels left her in a cloud of dust.

*

"I think the cops are here," Eliza said. "Finally."

Will nodded, and led the way to the heavy security door. His mind reeled, the possibilities flicking and being squashed at high speed. He didn't know

48

anything yet. Everything could be fine.

At the door, there was a single, tall, stocky officer. Will frowned. Only one?

"I called two hours ago," Eliza said, from behind Will's shoulder.

"William Roberts?" The officer said, ignoring Eliza.

"Yeah," Will said. "You are…?"

"Drake. Senior Sergeant Drake Wessley," the man replied. Will's eyes flicked over him. The man had a dozen cuts sliced into his face and his eyes were bloodshot and shadowed. Frankly, he looked terrible.

"Can I come in?" Drake said, and Will nodded, stepping back.

Drake strode into the house, his hand reaching out automatically to flick the light switch.

"Power's out," Will said.

Drake stopped, and turned back towards him. "Just the two of you here?"

"Yeah," Eliza said, before Will could answer. "Look, what's going on? There's been a break-in, the whole place is a crime scene. You need your guys down here to find out – "

Drake held up a hand, and she fell silent. Will swallowed. He was starting to get this kind of unreal sort of under-watery feeling, like everything was happening in slow motion.

Drake sighed. His hands clenched together in front of him. And he looked at Will.

"I'm afraid I have some bad news, William," he

said, and everything churning inside Will spun to a stop. His breath caught in his throat, but Drake wasn't done. He knew Drake wasn't done. It wasn't done until the whole world had been torn down. Again.

"Your uncle Jeffrey was killed in a car accident last night," Drake continued, but Will heard his voice as if through thick treacle. Like he was speaking from really far away.

"No," he said, the words coming out little more than a whisper.

"What?" Eliza's voice beside him was breathless, and he suddenly felt heat on his side, the hard grip of her hands on his arm.

"I'm sorry for your loss," Drake said.

"Oh my god," Eliza said, and suddenly her voice was filled with tears. She sobbed. He felt the shake of her body against his.

"That can't be," Will said. His voice sounded flat, like another person was speaking using his mouth. "I just saw him yesterday morning."

"I'm sorry," Drake repeated. "He lost control of his car and collided with the side of a tunnel near Belmont."

"Oh, god," Eliza said, sobs twisting her words. "Oh, Will, I'm so sorry." She twisted towards him, wrapping her arms around his neck.

Automatically, he put an arm around her, but he felt stiff, disconnected. Over her shoulder – she was so short, her arms were pulling him down like an anchor – he glimpsed a photo of him and Jeff on the fridge door. One from years ago, when Will was only a little kid. Outdoors somewhere, probably on one of Jeff's attempts to get him into some kind of sport as a way of distracting Will from his grief. And now, suddenly, he was that kid again. The little kid who took months – or years, even – for the shock to wear off and the brutal reality to set in, that he was entirely, completely alone.

"You said there was a break-in?" Drake was saying now. Eliza drew away from him, her face red and blotchy.

"Yeah," she said, her voice thick. "The study."

"Jeffrey's study?"

The scenes of destruction in Jeff's study flashed back into Will's mind. "They trashed it," he said, woodenly.

"I'll show you," Eliza said. She pulled away from Will and he dropped his arms limply to his side. She met his gaze, her eyes puffy, then led Drake down the hallway.

There was a beat of silence. Will stood, leaning against the kitchen counter, cold frozen ice forming inside him. The study. An accident? It couldn't be. Why was the study trashed, if it was an accident? Jeff didn't drive crazy. He never drove crazy. And why the study?

He pushed off from the counter, his mind clicking instinctively, automatically, into problem-solving mode.

"A hard drive," Eliza was telling Drake when Will

got to the study. She was crouched beside the gutted computer case, on its side on the floor.

"They didn't take anything else?" Drake asked.

Eliza shrugged helplessly, her eyes flicking over the mess of paper and miscellanea in the room.

Will stepped inside. "This has to be connected to… to Uncle Jeff, right? To what happened to him?"

Drake paused, glancing back at him. He had a fan of papers in his hands, and Will glimpsed dense text and a map of the Australian coastline with lots of red lines drawn across the ocean to points on the coast. Gently, he put the papers down on the desk. "What happened to your uncle was an accident, William," he said.

But Will saw something there, some flicker in his eyes. "I don't believe it. Why would there be a break-in, and then… and then, *he dies*?" His voice cracked. He was suddenly aware of his heart pounding, hard and fast, in his chest.

Eliza moved towards him, reaching out to grasp his arm.

He shook her off. "Right? This must be connected?"

Drake didn't say anything for a second, and then he sighed. "Do you know where they broke in?" When neither Will nor Eliza answered, he waved his hand. "Broken window, unlocked door, that sort of thing?"

"The windows are all barred," Will said. "And front and back door are both coded."

Drake nodded. "Right. Let me double-check."

He disappeared back into the hall. Will went to follow, but Eliza caught his arm.

"Will," she said, her voice small, but strong. "Will, hang on. Just… just take a second, okay?"

"I'm fine," he said, but he kept his eyes focussed on the floor. On the papers. He knew if he looked at her, saw the pity in her eyes… he just couldn't. Not yet.

She was silent for a second. "You'll stay with us, right?" she said finally, her voice shaking. "You can't… you can't stay here."

The word *alone* went unsaid, filling the space between them like an inflating balloon.

"Yeah," he said, his voice rough. "Yeah, sure."

Drake reappeared. "No forced entry, that's for sure. Did anyone other than you and your uncle have the code for the doors?"

Will shook his head.

"What's the code?" Drake said, already striding back towards the front door. Will followed, Eliza letting go of his arm.

"19541998," Will said.

"Good. I can check the log," Drake said. "These things always have them."

He punched the code into the solid back door. "Nothing here for…" His finger flicked quickly over the touch-screen display. "Weeks."

"We never use the back door," Will said.

Drake said nothing, and paced through the house

53

to the front door. "Ha," he said after a moment, his voice low. "Last night's log."

Will scanned the information on the display.

LOG OPEN 10:05 PM.

LOG OPEN 10:20 PM.

"Did your uncle normally head out late at night?" said Drake, tapping the screen.

"No," Will said. It made no sense. 10:00 PM? Jeff would be lucky to still be awake at 10:00 PM. "When he's not working, he barely leaves the house."

"Friends dropping over?" Drake said.

"Jeff doesn't have any friends." Will stared blankly at the screen, his heart thudding.

"And it wasn't you." Drake said, a statement, rather than a question.

"He was at my place last night," Eliza said, her voice still thick.

"Right," Drake said. His brow was pinched together, a deep crease caught in shadows. "Okay. Well, William, I need you to come down to the station to do some paperwork. But before we go, where does your uncle keep his drinks?"

"The fridge," Will said flatly. He felt like he was going crazy. Like none of this was making sense. Like he was unmoored, floating adrift.

Eliza glanced between Will and Drake. "There's some cola cans," she said.

Drake shook his head. "I mean alcoholic drinks. Spirits. Wine. Beer."

Will struggled to make this fit, with the dead

electricity, the trashed study. With Jeff. With Jeff being... *dead*. Why was Drake asking about alcohol? "There are none," he said, his voice dull. "Jeff doesn't..."

His voice caught in his throat, and he swallowed hard. Tried again, his eyes staring blankly at the dead space between Eliza and Drake. "Jeff didn't drink."

Chapter 7.

56 hours and 55 minutes left

"Here," Eliza said softly. "Use this." She hooked an old backpack from the mess at the foot of Will's bed, and set it open on the bed beside her.

Will nodded mutely, back to her, in front of his open closet.

Eliza blinked away tears. Drake was outside on her phone talking to her mum, organising temporary guardianship and whatever else became necessary when... someone's world collapsed. Eliza had called her to tell her the news just minutes before.

She saw Will reach for something – jeans, maybe – from the neatly folded piles. *Jeff*-folded piles. Will was never that tidy. His hand shook, and he hesitated, before tugging the pile towards him.

It tumbled to the floor, Will stepping back like he couldn't work out what was happening. The sometimes-awkward way he normally moved, like someone unsure of their body's relationship to the space around it, was exaggerated, stiffer.

Eliza swallowed, and dashed a hand across her eyes.

"Here, sit down," she said, and she took his arm, pulling him backwards to sit on the bed. His whole arm was trembling.

"Sorry," he said, voice flat.

She didn't answer, stooping to pick up the clothes and shoving them back onto the shelves. "These okay?" she said after a moment, holding up two pairs of jeans.

Will looked between them, and her heart twisted. His face was like one of those masks the drama kids wore, the lines carved deep. Frozen, in a kind of stunned rictus. The smattering of freckles, normally almost invisible, stood out against skin that was too pale. His eyes flicked between the pants, as if unseeing.

He was in shock. It was written all over his face. The unreality of choosing clothes, making decisions: she could see it was too much for him. She had to choke back tears again. How could anyone picture a future for themselves now, from this horrible point forward? Even at the most basic level of imagining the clothes you might want to wear tomorrow, the next day, or the one after?

"Will," she said, abandoning the jeans and sitting back next to him. "I'm… I'm so, so sorry."

The words felt so inadequate. Stupid, even as she said them. Her parents – damn, even all four of her grandparents, were all still alive. Like Will, she'd been only five when his parents had died. Then, and to this day, she was completely incapable of comprehending the kind of grief that he'd lived with, day in, day out. And that he was forced to deal with it all again? How was that fair?

Will nodded, his hand brushing his hair back out of his eyes, an automatic gesture, one he did habitually dozens of times a day. She took his hand between hers as he lowered it, and squeezed it tight. She had nothing to say that could help. But he had to know there were still people in the world who were warm and breathing and… *here*.

They sat like that in silence for some minutes, before Will spoke.

"Some part of me is always half-prepared for this," he said, his voice so low it was almost a whisper.

"For this?"

"For terrible news. Some part of me is… always waiting for it."

He paused, his eyes on the floor. The messy floor, scattered with shoes, books, computer parts.

"I was afraid of the telephone for years," he said, finally. "I… I still get chills when I hear the phone ring in your house."

Eliza swallowed. Her mum had had the same chintzy ring tone on their cordless for as long as she could remember. Some theme song from a show cancelled long before Eliza was born. Will was being babysat at her house that night. *The* night. Her parents on duty with the kids while Will's mum, Karina, followed his dad John, and Jeff, to a party. The last party they'd ever attend.

He barked a low, cold laugh. "I mean, I was five. I probably can't even *remember* it happening, not really. All made up."

Eliza blinked as tears spilled over. She didn't bother trying to stop them. Will had stayed with her family then, too, while Jeff was in the hospital. The survivor, that time. And though eventually Will had left, moved in with Jeff, they'd grown up together. Her mum had taken them both to soccer every week. Her dad had taught them to ride their first bikes, matching ones in different colours that they got the Christmas after it happened. Sleepovers, beach days, camping trips: they'd done it all together.

When they'd started high school, there'd been a few years of weirdness. Will had always been prickly and abrupt with people, everyone except her, and her mum and dad, and Jeff – mostly, at least. And could you blame him, with what had happened? But then, when high school started, they just kind of... drew apart. No fight, nothing like that. Just both focussed on their own pathways through the trauma of high school, and being cool, and constructing the face that you wanted the world to see. For a while, all those prickles had started turning on for her, too. But when, eventually, she'd realised that underneath he was still the same boy she'd grown up with, it was like those years had never happened. They'd just picked up where they left off.

"It doesn't feel real," Will said, and she heard tears in his voice too, now. "Just like… it's some horrible dream. And I'm going to wake up. But at the same time, I know it's not. Because you never wake up. It just keeps going." His voice cracked.

"Oh, Will," she whispered, and slipped her arm around his back. His head was bowed forwards, his whole body slumped like he couldn't manage the weight of it all.

There was a soft knock at the doorway, and Eliza glanced up, the dark shape of Drake wavering beyond her tears.

"Everything's organised," Drake said. "Your mum will collect you both from the station when we're finished."

Awkwardly, he held Eliza's phone back out to her, and she took it, fingers trembling.

"I'll meet you in the car,' Drake said, his voice stiff. She nodded, glancing back to Will's motionless form as he disappeared. Why had they sent only this stolid, impassive officer, to deliver the bad news? The fresh wounds all over his face notwithstanding, he looked like he'd rather be sticking pins in his arm than comforting two distraught teenagers.

"Are you okay to go?" she said, squeezing Will gently. She could feel his ribs through his thin t-shirt.

"Yeah. Sure." He stood, then wobbled, and she grabbed him, gripping his arms.

"Will," she said, and finally, he looked at her, and met her eyes. A pang twisted through her, deep and raw. He looked… broken. Hollow, like the inside of him had shattered and crumbled away. She swallowed. "If you can't do this now, I'll tell him."

He shook his head. "I'm okay. No, I want to do it. Get it over with."

He pulled his hands away, not roughly, and forced a smile, the movement cracking the mask, and she let him go, everything in her aching, a mirror to his pain.

Chapter 8.

56 hours and 40 minutes left

Will stared out the window of the police cruiser as the building signed *Queensland Police Headquarters* swung into view. Eliza was in the other window seat, the backpack filled with clothes she'd shoved in there before they left between them.

Eliza beside him, he followed Drake up a lift, through the reception and down a corridor to a windowless room with a desk and four metal chairs.

"Have a seat," Drake said. "Back in a second."

Will did, the cold metal sucking the heat from his flesh. He shivered, and Eliza looked at him, her face twisted in a frown again. He forced a quick smile at her, and she pursed her lips, but said nothing, slipping into the chair next to him and fiddling with the ends of her hair.

Drake returned, clicking the door shut behind him. Sinking into a chair opposite, he slid a folder onto the table.

"This is the official crash report," Drake said,

opening the folder. Papers, photographs and a pen spilled out, the pen skittering across the tabletop. Drake shuffled the pages back together, hurriedly slipping a photo to the back and clipping it all together. But not before Will glimpsed it: a burnt out car, crumpled against a concrete wall. Nothing left but a skeleton of metal.

Will's breath caught in his throat, and he swallowed hard.

"A patrol car found the wreck just after midnight. Your uncle had a blood-alcohol level five times the legal limit," Drake continued, not looking up from the report.

"No, that's wrong," Will said. His heart thudded. "Jeff doesn't drink anymore. He used to, but he doesn't now."

"Are you sure?" Drake's eyes narrowed. "Maybe just not around you?"

Flames seared through Will.

"I'm sure," he ground out, between clenched teeth. Drake opened his mouth, but Will cut him off. "My parents are dead because my dad decided to drive drunk. Jeff *doesn't drink*."

Drake looked at him, his eyes shadowed. Will glared back. How dare this *cop* say that about Jeff? He clenched his hands into fists, but before he could speak again, he felt a soft warmth on his arm. Eliza's hand was firmly on his.

"Will's dad, John, and Jeff used to party a lot on the weekends," she said, her voice wavering. "They used to drink a lot. When we were five, John was driving home from a party, with Will's mum, Karina, and Jeff, in the car. He crashed. Jeff was the only one who survived the crash."

Will took a deep breath. "Jeff hasn't had a drink since that night," he said, trying to keep his voice steady. "He's spent my whole life paying for how my parents died. He'd... he'd just never do it, okay?"

Drake cleared his throat. "Well, I didn't know that," he said at last. "But these tests are never wrong, at least not by that much."

"Your lab guys could have screwed up," Will snapped, and he reached across the table and yanked the report from beneath Drake's hands. A problem. This was what this was. And he could solve problems. That was what he always had, no matter what else happened.

Drake flinched, made to pull it back, then sighed, lifting his hands up in an *I-give-up* gesture.

Will's eyes flicked over the page. *Preliminary Coroner's Report* was written at the top, and beneath it, the alcohol reading: *BAC 0.25.*

Will swallowed, and flicked the page over. Here there was an overhead sketch of skid marks running along a road and into the tunnel wall. *30m* was scrawled next to the marks. Below the sketch was a formula:

$$v_{end} = \sqrt{v_{initial}^2 - 2 \times g \times d_{braking} \times (f \pm G)}$$

"They use that to calculate the speed at impact,"

Drake said, his voice weary. "From the initial speed..."

"...gravity, the length of the skid, the road gradient and the friction coefficient," Will interrupted. He ran his fingers across the next line on the page.

$$v_{end} = \sqrt{80^2 - 2 \times 9.81 \times 30 \times (0.7 + 0.1)}$$

$$v_{end} = 77km/hr$$

"You a fan of physics, then?" Drake said.

"My mum's a physicist, at the university," Eliza said, leaning over the report. "She drilled us on road trips when we were kids instead of playing eye-spy. Jeff's car was new, right?"

"A couple years old, I believe," Drake said. "Why?"

"Well, did the air bags deploy?"

Drake leaned forwards, brushing Will's hand aside and flipping the report pages, twisting his head to read upside-down.

"Nope," he said, ignoring Will's glare. "But airbag failures kill hundreds of people every year."

"Unless it didn't fail," Will said. "How'd they work out this?" He flipped back to the formula and stabbed the initial speed with his finger.

Drake sighed, and tugged the report back towards him, spinning it around. Pages turned, and then he flipped the report again to show two grainy greyscale photos of a car. *10:54:17:00* and *10:54:18:00* were printed at the bottom right of each photo. A photo on the facing page showed two police officers at opposite ends of a yellow measuring tape stretched along the road. *22m* was written below.

"A security camera clocked the car just before the tunnel," he said.

"So according to this," Will said, flicking back to the skid calculations. "Jeff was driving at eighty kilometres an hour, braked hard for thirty metres and still hit the wall at seventy-seven kilometres an hour."

He squinted at the page and then jabbed the formula. His heart thudded in his ears. "Except he didn't. They've done a NASA."

"What?" Drake said, frowning and peering at the formula.

"Mixed up the units," Eliza said. Her voice rose as she leaned forwards to the report. "NASA mixed up miles and kilometres. Whoever did this – "

"Used kilometres and metres in the same calculation," Will finished. He fished in his pocket for his phone, dimly registering Drake snatching the report from in front of him and standing up, the report held almost to his nose.

"What's the right numbers?" Eliza said, her phone already in her hands.

"Give it here," Will said, waving his hand to Drake. He knew this was bull. He *knew* it! He looked up, meeting Drake's eyes. Drake hesitated for a fraction of a second, and then wordlessly, passed the report back to Will. As he did so, the pages with the security camera photos slipped out of the clasp, spinning across the table.

Will's eyes jumped to the formula, and started

reading it out, while Eliza typed with one hand. With her other, she grabbed the pen.

"Don't write on it," Drake said with a groan, and he whipped out a notebook before Eliza could scrawl on the report. Will ripped a page out and slipped it across the table to her. One hand still flying over the calculator on her phone, Eliza wrote three more lines.

$$v_{end} = \sqrt{22^2 - 2 \times 9.81 \times 30 \times (0.7 + 0.1)}$$
$$v_{end} = 3.6 m/s$$
$$v_{end} = 13 km/hr$$

"That's why the airbags didn't go off," Eliza said, leaning back and tapping the last number.

Will's heart raced. "So Jeff's car nudged the wall and then *blew up*?" He looked up at Drake.

Drake's face was stiff, his eyes on the grainy photographs. The page was pinioned between his thick fingers.

"There's something else," he said. Slowly, he spun the page around until it was facing Will and Eliza. "I think there was somebody in the back seat of his car."

Will peered at the photo. "There," he breathed. There was a blurred shape in the back seat behind Jeff, only visible in the first photo. "What hack signed off on this crap? Screwed-up math, and missing that there's a second person in the car?"

Drake pursed his lips, and flipped to the start of the report. A signature was scrawled on the line marked *Primary investigating officer*.

"Riley," he said. "Narcotics detective."

Will's mind spun. "So if this passenger was in the crash, shouldn't he have shown up in a hospital somewhere?"

Drake nodded, his eyes shadowed. He was still staring at the name on the front cover. "I can check admissions records from last night," he said, after a pause.

"Well, I hope he's injured or dead," Will said, his voice dropping low.

"You *hope*?" Eliza said, and Will glanced at her. Her face was pale.

"It's better than the alternative," Will said, looking back at Drake.

Drake's face was steely, his eyes locked on Will. But before he could speak, there was a knock on the door.

"Will, what are you saying?" Eliza said, her voice shaking.

"His guys," Will said, pointing at Drake. "Stumbled on the crash more than an hour after it happened. No call, no tip off, not a word from anyone."

"You're saying someone *walked away*?" Eliza said. "And left Jeff there to die?" Her voice caught. *"Why?"*

Drake turned away, opening the door.

"I have no idea," Will said, his teeth clenched together. Drake was talking, the words inaudible, to someone Will couldn't see beyond the door. "But I bet someone around here does."

As he spoke, Drake turned back around.

"Drake?" Will said, rising slowly from his seat. "Why would someone want my uncle dead?"

Drake raised his hands, placating. "There's sure to be a rational explanation for this," he said. He glanced from the report on the table, to the door, then cleared his throat. "Look. I've got to go."

He stepped forwards, and gathered up the papers back into the folder.

"No. Wait!" Will said. His voice pitched higher. "Jeff – I've got to know – "

"I'm sorry, William," Drake said.

And then he was gone, the door clicking shut behind him.

Chapter 9.

56 hours and 22 minutes left

"What's going on?" Drake said, jogging after Ronnie down the hall. Ronnie waved a hand, and Drake pursed his lips. Not where ears might be listening, then.

When they got to Ronnie's office, he shut the door carefully behind Drake.

"Take a look at this," Ronnie said, his voice grim, flipping the open laptop on the desk around to face them.

A grainy black and white video played. The camera panned across a row of mechanical and auto parts warehouses, all of them looking run-down and half-abandoned. Suddenly, a large truck emerged from the biggest warehouse and lumbered into the street.

A shipping container was loaded on the back. Seconds later, another truck followed. Then a third, and a fourth and a fifth.

And then, a white van. Followed by a black ute.

Drake winced.

Ronnie met his gaze, his face lined deep. "The partial we ran on the number plate you got hit on this," he said. "One of our graffiti-prevention cameras."

"Where?"

"West End industrial park."

Drake leaned past Ronnie and pressed a key. The video reversed, until the fifth truck backed into the frame. Wisps of smoke froze above the rear wheels. He squinted at the screen. The tyres were jammed against the rims. "Riding real low," he said.

Ronnie nodded. "Should be half a foot clearance in those wells for a truck that size. You didn't see these trucks at the port?"

Drake shook his head. He rubbed at his temple, the exhaustion knotting into a pounding ache behind his eyes. "And that van wasn't big enough to carry enough product to overload one truck, let alone five."

"Looks like the shipment you intercepted wasn't the only one," Ronnie said. "I'd wager they've been building up a supply before they make their move."

"There's twenty-odd-million people in Australia," Drake said. "Unless that's marijuana, there's no way they can distribute five truckloads of drugs, not in this country anyway. They must have a few tonnes in each of those trucks."

"I used to drive trucks like this when I was in college, deliveries for the supermarkets," Ronnie said, his eyes narrowing. "Tonnes of potatoes, carrots, all sorts of veggies. But our trucks didn't ride that low.

They're designed for heavy loads."

Drake squeezed his eyes shut, ignoring the pounding. "Right. Well, let's work it out then." He tugged his notebook from his pocket and sank down in one of the hard, uncomfortable, you're-about-to-be-told-off-by-your-boss chairs in front of Ronnie's desk. "How much would you load up on any given night?"

Ronnie stared off into space for a moment. "Well, three hundred boxes on a good night. Maybe ten kilograms for a typical box."

Drake scribbled it down. "And how much lower would the truck ride?"

Ronnie screwed up his face and scratched at his chin.

"Estimate," Drake said flatly.

"Okay. Maybe… a couple of centimetres lower."

"Right. Well, these trucks are flat up against the rims – a good fifteen centimetres of movement." He peered at his calculations. "So they've got, what, maybe fifteen, twenty tonnes in the back of each truck."

"No way that can all be hard drugs," Ronnie said. "Maybe liquor. Something heavy."

"Any other cameras pick up where they were going?"

"Not yet. Got to pull tapes from half-a-dozen companies who are a whole lot less cooperative when things have to be done discreetly."

Drake scowled. "Great. Well, nothing else for it

but to start somewhere," he said, tugging on his jacket with a little too much force. "Maybe, just maybe, they left something behind."

*

Drake parked the unmarked police car a block short of the warehouse from the security video. With slow, steady steps, he approached the building.

He hesitated as he reached the closed roller door. Backup was at least five minutes away. And a lot could go wrong in five minutes. Steeling himself, he unfastened his holster, pulled out the Glock and moved towards the door. This wouldn't be another dock situation. He couldn't be that unlucky twice in as many days.

He crouched, and tugged at the door with his free hand. It screeched, sticking at waist height, and he shuffled underneath.

Quickly, he swept his gun from side-to-side. Then breathed out. Empty.

Except for a table on the far wall.

His footsteps echoed through the cavernous space. Shadows pooled around the table, the lumps on top indistinguishable in the gloom. Holstering the pistol, he strode towards it, blinking, trying to adjust to the dim light filtering in through the high, dusty windows.

As the shapes resolved, he slowed. Bright colours: red, yellow, blue. Things not meant to be in a place like this.

A chill rippled down his spine, and he tugged out

his phone.

"Any leads?" Ronnie's voice scratched from the speaker.

"They cleaned up shop," Drake said. He reached forwards, taking one of the objects and turning it over. "No-one here."

"Nothing left, then?"

"Not exactly," Drake said, and gently, he placed the bizarre object back in its place, in the makeshift shrine.

Chapter 10.

50 hours and 15 minutes left

"Will, you okay?"

Will started. Eliza, at the door. He looked down. His hands were under the bathroom tap, had been for... he didn't know. He'd just been standing here. Staring into space.

He twisted the tap off, dried his hands on the bright pink towel beside the basin.

"Yeah. Coming," he said. His voice sounded distant and strange.

Eliza was standing opposite the door when he opened it, her arms wrapped around her chest. Her dark brown eyes were red-rimmed. "Mum's ducked out to get some take-out," she said, her voice low.

Will nodded. He felt drained, numb. When Abby had arrived to collect him and Eliza from the station, everything had gone to hell. Abby striding towards him, her arms outstretched, the red in her eyes: he'd been undone. Hadn't stopped crying the whole way back to Eliza's, plus several gallons more besides wedged between Eliza and Abby on the couch in their too-familiar, too-homey living room.

"Do you want to, I don't know, watch something while we wait?"

He shrugged. "Sure."

She nodded. There was a pause, then she reached out and put her hand on his arm. She forced a crooked-smile, and he tried one back, but it felt like a grimace.

Ten minutes later, they were side-by-side on her bed, something playing on low volume on Eliza's laptop between them. Will stared into space, the colours flicking over his retinas without getting any further than that into his brain.

"It feels so unreal," Eliza whispered. "I just can't believe that..." She trailed off, and he heard her breath catch.

He nodded stiffly. "Yeah."

"Jeff has always been so..." Eliza started again. "I don't know. *There*, I guess."

Will stared at the screen. She was right. Jeff didn't travel for work, not like Amir, Eliza's dad. Jeff didn't go on holidays. He didn't even have *friends*. He was just either working, or mooching about the house.

"He was like the fridge, or, I don't know, a couch," Will said.

Eliza glanced at him, her eyebrow raised.

"Like... just... always around but not really doing anything," he finished. As he said it, some kind of half-laugh, half-sob burst unexpectedly from him.

"Oh…" Eliza said, and then she was half-laughing, half-sobbing too. "Yeah. Uncle Jeff, the couch."

The half-half sob-laugh turned entirely into sobs, and he leaned back against the wall, one hand up over his face, his eyes squeezed shut. He felt movement, the sound of the show being shut off, and then Eliza's arms were around him.

He leaned into her, his face buried in the thick dark curls spilling over her shoulders. The darkness behind his closed lids pulsed around him.

Alone. He was *alone*.

"I'm here, Will," she murmured into the crook of his neck. As if she'd heard his thoughts.

He wrapped his arms around her narrow shoulders, and held on, as if by doing so he might feel, somehow, less adrift in this sea of black. She *was* here. She was the only thing he had left now. His only family. Preppy, goody-goody Eliza who underneath all the teacher's-pet and academic façades had still been the same girl he'd grown up with. Eliza, who had shocked him when he discovered she liked all the same lame-slash-awesome things that he liked. Who was willing to help him con football jocks out of thousands of dollars. Who came up with far better schemes than he ever had on his own. And who got away with them, because she had way too much credit banked in her good-girl account to ever be even a suspect.

Finally, his tears slowed.

"Here," Eliza said softly, drawing back from his arms and passing him a box of tissues.

There was a moment of silence as he tried to pull himself back together.

"It's all just so crazy," she murmured, as he scrubbed at his face. "An accident, but none of the details match up… and Jeff, drink-driving?" She paused, the silence filling with everything they'd seen in the report. "And… what if it was… murder?" Her voice dropped to a whisper.

Will nodded. "His life was so… boring," he said, sucking in a hitched breath. "Things like this don't happen to boring people."

"The police will get to the bottom of it," Eliza said, but she didn't sound so sure. "They'll tell us what's going on."

Will glanced at her, saw the doubt in her eyes. Heat rushed through him.

"Yeah. If Drake deigns to speak to us," he said, his voice rough. "Not cool that he just *left*."

Eliza nodded, a frown puckering her brow. "Maybe a lead came in."

"Or he got told to stop talking to us."

"You think he's involved? Or his boss, or whoever, is?"

Will paused before answering. "I'd like to know why he looks like he's been dragged over a cheese grater."

There was a sudden sharp rapping on the door.

Eliza glanced at Will quickly, frown deepening.

"Abby forget her keys?" Will said, and Eliza shrugged, pushing forwards off the bed.

A few moments later, he heard murmuring, and then Eliza's voice rising. His heart jumped, and he slipped off the bed, jogging down the stairs after her.

Framed in the doorway, there was a woman. Eliza had one hand on the half-opened door, the other on the wall. Blocking.

"Do you have no sense of decency?" Eliza's voice was snappy, high-pitched.

Will frowned. The woman trying unsubtly to push past Eliza was in her late thirties but carried it well. Real well. Hot, could be an adjective used to describe her, if she wasn't trying to accost his best friend.

"Hey, back off!" he said, his voice deepening as he strode towards the door.

Her head snapped up. "Will," she said, sounding slightly breathless.

She looked vaguely familiar. For a brief second, he wondered if he knew her. Not many people called him Will. The rest of the time, usually because it involved a teacher telling him off or the principal ordering him to the office, he got called William.

"I *said*, you're not welcome here," Eliza snapped, pushing back on the door.

"Look, I just need to talk to you – " she huffed out, heaving back against the door from her side. "About Jeff. About your uncle."

As she said this, Will reached the door. He froze as he grabbed the door above Eliza's hand, about to lend his strength to forcing whoever this was back out. Again with the nicknames. Everyone but him and Eliza's family called Jeff *Jeffrey*.

"My name's Melissa," the woman said, as he hesitated. "Melissa Green."

"She's a reporter," Eliza snapped, her eyes fixed on the woman.

"From Channel Eleven," Melissa said.

"He doesn't want to comment – "

"I'm not looking for a quote," Melissa said, rounding back on Eliza.

Will put his hand on Eliza's shoulder, and she glanced at him. Her face was twisted in a scowl, but she stepped back from the door. "What, then?"

Melissa stumbled as the door shifted, then righted herself, tugging at her neat dress suit. "First of all, I'm sorry about your uncle – "

"You didn't even know him," Will ground out, heat flashing over him. There was a flash of emotion across Melissa's face, and she sucked in a sharp breath.

"I'll get to the point then," she said, her face blanking. "You can't trust the police. Whatever they've told you: it's a lie."

Will glanced at Eliza. Her face was pale.

"And you would know?" he said.

"There's a traitor in the police force," she said. Her voice was harsh. Angry. Almost... desperate. "You uncle... he called me," she continued. "A week ago. He was scared. Of the police he was working

80

with. He'd been working on a covert operation, something to do with international drug rings. But something had spooked him."

"Why'd he call you?" Will interrupted.

"I was the one who took down Gregory Hearsh," she said, quickly. Will shook his head, nonplussed. "The corrupt judge. Anyway. It doesn't matter." She took a deep breath. "Jeff was supposed to meet me last night, but he never showed."

"I don't understand," Eliza said. "He's an analyst. He worked mostly from home, right, Will? He wasn't in the field. What was he scared of?"

Melissa's eyes were stony. "He thought his life was in danger."

Will ran his fingers through his hair. "No," he said, thoughts whirling. This made no sense. "No, it was an accident. He... he crashed the car. And killed himself."

There was a long, fraught pause.

"Who do you think we can't trust?" Eliza said. Will glanced at her. She was staring at Melissa. "Do you know who the traitor is, then?"

"You can't trust any of them. Any one of them could be the traitor. Or more than one."

"Drake helped us," Eliza interjected, and Melissa started.

"Drake Wessley?"

Will and Eliza both nodded.

"So I suppose you know that he was involved in a shoot-out last night," Melissa said, eyes burning. "At the port. An inspection of a drug boat they'd just brought in."

"No," Will said, glancing quickly at Eliza. The cuts on Drake's face. They were from a shoot-out? With drug smugglers? He saw the same shock on her face.

"Drake was with a team of elite forces," Melissa continued. "He was accompanying a team of federal police. Nine of them went into the warehouse, and gunfire breaks out. Drake and one other officer make it out alive. The other officer's in intensive care. No other survivors."

"What?" Eliza breathed.

"But then, when the rest of the police got there, they didn't find anything. No bad guys, no guns, in fact, no sign of any reason for a firefight at all," Melissa said, her voice grim.

"What about the drugs?" Will said.

"Nada," said Melissa. "All gone. If they ever existed." She paused, her eyes meeting Will's. "Whatever your uncle was involved in, Will, it's serious," she said. "And now, you're involved too. Whether you like it or not."

Chapter 11.

"So a doll: that's all they left behind?" Ronnie grunted, slamming his office door shut.

Drake rubbed his eyes. He'd been filling out paperwork for hours, waiting to get Ronnie alone. He tugged the charred, blackened doll from his pocket and tossed it to Ronnie.

"A doll," Ronnie restated, holding the evidence bag like it was contaminated.

Drake kept pulling objects from his pockets, piling them on the desk, each one in its own plastic evidence bag. The melted water pistol. The spinning top, perforated with jagged holes. And finally, the photo of a young boy.

Ronnie sank into his chair. "So, what, we're dealing with a gang who's brought their kids along for the ride?"

"The guys who took out our team were well-equipped," Drake said, quietly. "Having kids around? Amateur hour. These guys knew what they were doing. And these aren't the kind of toys you give kids to play with." His eyes locked on the pile, the face of young William flashing across his mind. It was cruel, criminal, that kids were being drawn into madness like this.

"Then they're screwing with us. Leaving random junk at the scene to distract us. What else did you find?"

"Nothing but fuel stains all over the concrete. Smelt like the fuel oil from a furnace."

"From the trucks, I'd guess," Ronnie said. "I can get these analysed for prints, drug traces, but it'll take a while to get it done discreetly."

Drake nodded, fighting back a yawn.

"Well, while you were toy shopping, I did a phone trace of all the police who were on shift on Tuesday and who might have found out about the boat." Ronnie slapped a thin sheaf of papers on the desk.

Drake opened it, scanning his finger down the list of phone numbers and suburbs. It showed distances from cell towers during that day and approximate locations. On the second page, he stopped, tapping a suburb name.

"This is where I just was."

"Big suburb," Ronnie said, rubbing his chin.

Drake nodded, grabbing the papers and striding over to a map of the city on the wall. He glanced at the list. "Five hundred metres from this tower." He drew a small circle around a point on the map. "Fourteen hundred metres from this one." He drew a second, much larger circle around a different point. "And three thousand metres from this tower." He draw a final, larger circle around a third point, then stepped back.

Ronnie reached from behind Drake's shoulder, tapping the point on the map where the three circles intersected. "Looks familiar."

"Yes it does," Drake said, grimly. Ronnie's finger was placed squarely on the warehouse.

"Let me check whose phone that is," Ronnie said, taking the list back from Drake. He tapped at the keyboard of his computer.

"Riley," he said, glancing back up at Drake.

Drake's blood turned cold. "He signed off on Jeffrey's accident report. Where is he now?"

Ronnie clicked and tapped and peered at the screen. "Off shift until Friday." He dragged the phone closer, and punched the keypad.

Drake waited. After a moment Ronnie hung up.

"Phone's off," he said, his face darkening.

"So we've got an officer involved in both the analyst's accident investigation, and located at the scene where all this was left," Drake said, gesturing to the pile between them. "And no idea where he is now."

Ronnie nodded. "We don't know for sure that he's involved. Or who else might be, if he is. I can't ask the intelligence guys to track one of our own. It'll spread like wildfire. But I've got a PI that I use sometimes. He might be able to."

Drake clenched his fists. "And in the meantime? Just sit on our arses?"

Ronnie was silent for a moment. "There's someone else we can talk to. The only others who might know who killed your team." He met Drake's gaze. "The refugees. They were brought into Brisbane for treatment. If there were drugs on that boat, maybe they saw or know something."

Drake pushed himself to his feet, grim determination flooding through him. He rolled his shoulders,. "Where?"

"Royal Brisbane Hospital."

"Traffic's going to be fun," Drake muttered. He smothered a yawn that threatened to crack his jaw in two. "Hey, the Royal has a helipad. Don't suppose I can take the chopper?"

"Have a good drive, Drake," Ronnie said, a wry half-smile twitching his cheeks.

*

The main hospital in Brisbane was a mismatched collection of new and old buildings crammed together near the city showgrounds, about three kilometres from the CBD. Drake screwed up his nose as he strode towards the reception. Everything smelled of cleaning fluid.

"I'm here to interview the refugees," he said, flashing his badge at the nurse sitting at the front desk.

The nurse looked up. "They're in a bad way. Throwing up as they took them out of the ambulances. They've locked down an entire wing of the hospital, kicked the other patients out."

"Where?"

"Eighth floor. Chemotherapy ward."

The lift moved at a glacial pace. On the eighth floor, a security guard stood in front of an airlock door. Drake stepped inside after flashing his badge again. His ears popped as the airlock flushed, the change in pressure a strange sensation outside of a plane.

On the other side, there was a normal-looking ward, filled with equipment and beds. As he entered, a woman dressed in scrubs and a suited man emerged from a bed shrouded by curtains.

The woman strode towards him. "I'm Dr Rebecca Robinson," she said. "Sergeant Wessley, I presume?"

Drake nodded. "I'm here to talk with the refugees."

"I'm afraid I cannot disclose any information about my patient without the approval of his legally-appointed guardian. Or a warrant. Which it didn't sound like you had, from what your boss said on the phone." Her voice turned stony, and she glanced at the man standing beside her.

"Patient? I'll need to speak with *all* of them."

"Look around, officer," Rebecca said, gesturing to the room. "There is only one patient."

Drake glanced around. All but one bed was empty. "Where are they?"

"Ten floors down," Rebecca said. "In the

morgue."

Drake's throat went dry. What sickness had killed *all but one* of the refugees? He swallowed hard. "I still need to speak to whoever's left."

"And you can, if you meet our terms," said the suited man. With a glance at Rebecca, he placed a hand on Drake's arm, leading him towards the bed.

"Jerry Norman," he said, extending his hand to shake. "I'm Namir's legal guardian." He inclined his head towards the bed, and Rebecca, her lips pursed, twitched back the curtain.

A teenage boy lay on the bed, his eyes closed. His head was completely bald, his arms emaciated. Every exposed area of skin was red and swollen, as if horrifically sunburnt. For a moment Drake thought the boy, too, was dead, but then he saw the slight movement of his chest. Drake clenched his fists. Yet more children involved in... whatever this was. A sinking dread welled in his stomach. What *was* this madness?

"Namir may never be able to speak for himself again," Jerry said, guiding Drake away, as Rebecca drew the curtain again.

Frustration rippled through Drake. "Then I need you to tell me everything Namir has said about the boat."

Jerry held up a hand. "Before Namir lost consciousness, he gave me specific instructions. I can reveal what he knows only if appropriate arrangements can be made."

"What arrangements?" Drake ground out.

"One hundred thousand dollars in an offshore bank account of our choosing."

"You've got to be kidding," said Drake, his voice rising. "I'm trying to conduct a police investigation, and you're fishing for money?"

"Then you are welcome to return when you have obtained a warrant," Jerry said, his voice hardening.

"I'm trying to help people here," Drake snapped. "Including Namir, and the rest of the refugees who died. And you're trying to flip some easy cash?"

Jerry glared. "Don't presume you're the only one trying to *help people*," he said. "Namir will soon be dead. His two oldest brothers, also on the boat, are dead. Namir's father was murdered by extremists in his country. His oldest sister was shot dead when she spoke to a journalist about her father's murder."

Jerry stabbed Drake in the chest with his finger. "His mother, and his two younger sisters are all he has left. With his brother and himself dead, there will be no money to buy food. They will be forced out of their home – sorry, *hovel* – into the streets. There they will beg for enough food to survive. Or worse. Last year half of girls under the age of..."

"Okay, enough," Drake said, but Jerry wasn't done.

"That money will enable us to safely evacuate Namir's remaining family – not like the way he came out – and ensure that his and his brothers' deaths were not in vain. So how about you think twice before you accuse others of *not helping*?"

Drake gritted his teeth together. "Okay. I apologise. I've had a rough few days."

Jerry raised an eyebrow, but said nothing.

"I've got to call my boss," Drake said, sighing.

Ronnie answered on the second ring. "What did you get?"

"A guarantee of valuable information," Drake said. "For cash."

"How much?"

"A hundred grand."

Ronnie laughed. "You're kidding me."

Drake glanced at Jerry, then stepped away, lowering his voice. "Can't we access the informant fund?"

"Too risky," said Ronnie. "Narcotics runs the fund and that's Riley's unit. We've got no idea who else is involved. You're going to have to find another way. Intimidate. Threaten to lock 'em up. Whatever it takes."

Drake glanced at Namir's bed. A bandaged hand protruded from the neat, white blanket.

"Not going to work here," he said.

Ronnie cursed. "Then we'll just have to wait for another lead. One that doesn't cost so much."

Drake grunted, and hung up, glancing back at the comatose boy. The boat, the trucks, the warehouse, the shots ripping through his fellow team members, flickered across his memory. He needed Namir's information. But a hundred grand: where was he going to get that? He might as well buy a lotto ticket. Or take his life savings down to the race track.

He froze, his mind ticking over.

"What did your boss say?" Jerry said, his eyes narrowed.

Drake swallowed, guilt welling. This was the way, he knew it. But getting the poor kid in even deeper? It wasn't fair. But what choice did he have?

"He said we can get your money," Drake said, striding towards the airlock. He glanced at his watch. 7:00 PM. "Give me twelve hours."

Chapter 12.

47 hours and 42 minutes left

Will sat at the table, staring into space, the low hum of Eliza and Abby cleaning up after dinner a blur in the background.

Dimly, he registered a knock at the door.

"Officer." Abby's voice, slightly surprised, drifted back into the kitchen. Eliza looked at Will quickly, and he frowned, standing to follow her into the front entry.

"He's here, obviously, but can't this wait until tomorrow? You know the day he's had," Abby was blocking the door with her body, but beyond her, Will could see Drake's bulky form.

"Afraid not," Drake said, and reluctantly, Abby stepped back to let him enter.

"William," Drake said, nodding his head. "Eliza."

"What's this about?" Abby said before Will could answer, crossing her arms.

Drake glanced at her. His eyes were red, his shoulders slumped.

"He's exhausted," Eliza whispered, at Will's elbow. Will nodded.

"In my investigations, certain… past events concerning William have come to light."

Will felt cold flow over him like he'd just been doused. Abby glanced at him quickly, then back at Drake.

"Will, Eliza, meet us in the living room," she snapped, her eyes flashing.

Eliza grabbed Will's arm, dragging him back. Abby started speaking fast, in a low, angry tone, softer than he could hear.

"Is he talking about the bots?" Eliza breathed through her teeth as she got him into the living room.

"I don't know," Will said. "Jeff said he made it all go away."

"What's it got to do with anything *now*, anyway?" Eliza said. Her face was a little pale.

"I don't know," Will repeated.

"Mum doesn't know I was involved," she said. She sounded scared. "Jeff didn't know, right?"

Will shook his head, and squeezed her arm. "It'll be fine."

She nodded, but didn't look convinced.

"Officer Wessley has some questions for you, Will, that apparently can't wait." As Abby led Drake into the living room, Will felt Eliza tense beside him.

Abby turned on Drake. "Go ahead. Ask."

Drake glanced between Will and Eliza. "Eliza – "

"Mum, maybe it's best if we let Will talk to Drake

alone," Eliza burst out suddenly.

Abby turned to her daughter, her eyebrows raised.

"You don't need us here for this, right?" Eliza said, glancing fast between Drake and Will. Drake's eyes narrowed, but he said nothing. Will shook his head.

"I'll be fine," he said, meeting Eliza's pleading gaze. She breathed out, and nodded. He knew she liked doing... what they did together. But he also knew how important it was to her that her good girl persona stayed, well, intact.

"Are you sure?" Abby said, her brow creased. Will nodded. She strode towards him, and wrapped her arms around him, fierce.

"We'll be right next door, okay?" she said.

Will nodded, blinking back tears. Abby's arms around him took him back, too quick, to when he was tiny. Alone in the world then, too.

She glared at Drake, a warning unspoken in her face, then let Eliza half-drag her from the room.

There was a beat of silence, as Will and Drake stared at each other.

"Certain financial... irregularities have popped up today, William," Drake started, his brow furrowed. "With your name attached."

Will folded his arms. "Why would you bring this up now, of all times?"

"Your uncle did a good job of sweeping it under the rug."

"I thought you were trying to *help* me," Will

snapped. "That reporter was right."

Drake froze. "Reporter?"

"Melissa Green. Channel Eleven – "

"She *came* here?" Drake exploded. "What did she tell you?"

"That you walked out of a gunfight unscratched after your team was wiped out," Will said. He felt hot all over. "And that there's a traitor in your department."

Drake's face reddened. "I should have her arrested – "

"Is it true?" Will interrupted. "Is anything true that you've told me?"

Drake fell silent for a long moment. Then, he sighed. "My team was wiped out," he said. "Last night, at the port. We were ambushed, massacred. And I think the people who murdered my team may have something to do with your uncle's death."

He sank down onto the couch. "Your uncle is involved. We were sent to inspect a refugee boat suspected to be carrying drugs – a boat your uncle had helped get into Australian waters in an undercover operation."

Will blinked. "Jeff was in an undercover operation?"

Drake nodded. "He helped the drug runners avoid patrols. They'd got close, real close, before our navy picked them up. But when they found the boat, the refugees on board were all dead or severely sick. They took the boat under tow into Brisbane."

"Why would you *help* drug runners get a shipment into Australia?"

"To convince them that this is their big chance," Drake said. "So they send their biggest load, then by seizing the drugs we do enough financial damage to ruin the operation for good." He sighed again. "But it didn't work. They got the jump on us. They cleared the shipment right under our noses and beat us to a pulp in the process."

"So they killed Jeff *why*, exactly?"

"I don't know, yet. Maybe they thought he was a liability."

"Or he found out something he wasn't supposed to know," Will said quietly.

Drake glanced at his watch. "Maybe. That's why I'm here. There's one way we can find out."

"Then go find out. Why come here, exactly?"

Drake looked after Abby and Eliza, then back at Will. "It's not quite legal. I need…" He paused, and Will saw him swallow. "I need you to help me get some money to pay an informant. By tomorrow morning."

Will's heart thudded. "*What*? Don't you guys have money for this sort of thing? A slush fund, or whatever?"

Drake sighed. "The reporter was right about that too. We… may have a leak. If I request informant money, they'll spook. We'll lose any advantage we've got."

"She also said I shouldn't trust you," Will's eyes

narrowed. "For all I know, you're trying to set me up."

"I have enough evidence already to bust you up to juvenile court for online racketeering." Drake's voice hardened. "And I'm choosing not to do that. For now, at least." His voice took on an ominous tone.

"You don't have anything," Will said, his blood running cold.

"Actually, I do," Drake said softly. "IP logs, financial records, the whole shebang. Jeffrey's intervention is the only reason you don't have a criminal record. He risked his career to make sure you had a *future*, William. And I need you to help me now, to show that wasn't all in vain."

Will said nothing. Everything inside him jangled, rearranging.

Drake's face changed suddenly, softening. "Look," he said. "I know this is unorthodox. Believe me, I know. But I'm getting the horrible feeling that this is big. And this informant – he's got a whole lot of no time left on the clock. There's no other way. I don't like having to ask for your help like this. But you've got to trust me. It's this, or you never know whether someone killed your uncle in cold blood."

Will hesitated. Is this really what Jeff would want? For him to do this? He glanced at the coffee table, where Abby had put out a photo of Jeff next to a spluttering pink-orange candle. His uncle's face flickered in the candlelight.

He had to know. Whatever the truth was, he had

to know.

"Okay," he said. "What do you need me to do?"

*

Melissa tapped her fingers against the steering wheel of her blue sedan, her eyes fixed on the door that Drake had bullied his way into. Her gel nails made a rhythmic click against the leather.

Suddenly, Drake emerged. Beyond him, she could see Will's new temporary legal guardian closing the door behind him. Her eyes narrowed. She'd give anything to know what he'd come here for.

Drake's squad car pulled out, and she slumped down in her seat, waiting until he'd turned the corner. Then she gunned her car, and spun the wheel after him.

Around the corner, she slammed on the brakes. The squad car was parked, by the side of the road, interior dark. What now? Was he setting up surveillance on the house?

She pulled up, her eyes on the motionless car.

There was a sudden banging on her window. "Get out of the vehicle!"

She jumped, her heart leaping into her throat. She peered into the blackness, thoughts skittering.

Her door was wrenched open, and she blinked as the interior light flashed on, dazzling her. Then she felt large, rough hands on her arm, and she was being dragged from the car.

"Do you think this is some big game?" Drake's voice barked from the other end of the hands. She blinked, desperately trying to get her night vision back. "Just some chance for a shiny promotion?"

Anger flooded through her. He had no idea what this meant. How big this was. She yanked her arm from his grasp.

"You're one to talk about playing games," she said, her voice harsh, breathless. "What are you doing here, talking to that kid, completely off the books? I talked to my source at your station. Whatever you're doing: no one else has any idea about your little *private investigation.*"

He goggled at her, his face turning red. "Do you ever stop to think about the consequences of all your digging, beyond getting yourself a nice corner office with a great view of the river?"

She flushed hot.

"You need to back off," he continued. "You've got no idea what's going on here – "

"Or else what?" she said. "You'll arrest me?"

Drake's face was stony. "I won't hesitate for a second." He turned to go, but before he could move, she grabbed his arm.

"Stop. Look, I can help you. Jeff was one of my many sources," she said, her heart thudding hard in her chest. "With my access to the others, I can help you find out who wiped out your team."

He paused, his eyes on her face. "Why? What do you get out of this?"

She held back the torrent of words that threatened to spill over. That she had to know what had happened to Jeff, *really*. She had to, for everything he'd been to her, for everything *they'd* been. That this whole mess was bigger than Drake understood – bigger than she, really, understood. That things might go bad, really, really bad, if Drake didn't know what she knew. But she bit back those words, and chose carefully. Chose the ones that she knew he was expecting to hear, because that was what he thought she was.

She deliberately steadied her voice. "Exclusive first rights to the story," she said. "You promise me that, and I'll help you."

Drake sighed, rolling his eyes. She quashed the emotions roiling inside her, steeling herself. It didn't matter what he thought of her. None of that mattered now.

Drake rubbed his hand across his forehead, then moved in close until his face was right against hers. "If you go public even one second before I say so, then the deal's off," he said. "If you hold back any information, the deal's off. If you get in the way or slow me down, the deal's off. I will arrest you and dump you all alone in a safe-house without a second thought. There's your deal."

Melissa nodded, relief washing through her. She could work with that.

"Right," Drake said, stepping back. His eyes narrowed. "I have to go pick something up, and you're going to come with me and tell me everything you know. You can start by telling me how you knew

Jeffrey."

She swallowed hard. No information held back. Jeff was dead. His undercover status didn't matter anymore. "Fine," she said.

Chapter 13.

46 hours and 28 minutes left

Drake dropped Will's computer onto Eliza's desk, next to her tower machine. Will's tower teetered, before Will launched forwards to grab it.

"Whoops," Drake said.

"Be careful," Will snapped. "You break it, it's your money I'm not getting."

Drake had just returned from picking up the computer from Jeff's. He'd asked Will if he wanted to come before leaving forty-five minutes ago, but Will had made an excuse. The thought of the house, dark, empty, silent, was too much. Not tonight.

Will studied the computer, tilting it this way and that, irritation coursing through him. Had Drake been as rough with it on the way over as he had been dumping it here?

"You need anything else from me?" Will heard Drake say from behind him.

Eliza answered from the armchair in the corner of her room, where she was curled, her laptop on her knees. "Cash. Whatever you can transfer to us, right now." She spoke quietly, but confidently. Abby was downstairs, had returned to her TV show after letting Drake in.

Drake frowned. "Why do you need cash? You're hacking some gambling website to get the money."

"I'm not *hacking* anything," Will said.

"That's what it says on your rap sheet," Drake said. "Or at least what should have been on it, if your uncle hadn't intervened."

Will raised his eyebrows. "Great IT department you guys have. There was no hacking. In fact, what I did wasn't, strictly speaking, illegal at all."

"Oh really," Drake said flatly, his eyebrows rising.

"Bots," Eliza added. "Not hacking."

Drake said nothing, but Will could see his jaw working, the muscles popping.

"It's a computer program that gambles automatically," Will said, as if Drake was a very small child who didn't understand something very obvious. "It works by – "

"Can you get me the hundred grand or not?" Drake cut him off.

"If I have a big enough starting bankroll," Will snapped. "My program is good. Really good. But it's not infallible. Long runs of bad variation – or bad luck, if you want to call it that – will still bankrupt me. I need cash up-front, as much as you've got, to make sure that doesn't happen."

Drake sighed, and pinched the bridge of his nose.

"Right. Okay. Whatever. I can get you three grand right now."

Will's eyes narrowed. That wasn't going to be enough. Not for the payoff Drake wanted. "Not good enough."

Drake paused, his eyes searching Will's face. "I *might* be able to get you another few grand in the next half-hour. But that's it," he said, finally.

"Fine." Will shook his head and lifted his eyebrows. It'd have to do. He grabbed a pen and scribbled on a piece of paper then handed it over. "Make the transfer into this account, and message me when you're done."

*

"Damn it." Will grunted as he struggled with the screwdriver.

"Here, let me do it," Eliza said, her voice a mix of amusement and exasperation. "You're just going to break something." She took the screwdriver from him, bending over the computer case, her hair falling in a veil around her face.

There was a metallic clang as the case popped off. Eliza coughed, as a cloud of dust spewed out.

"Wow, you treat this poor thing well, don't you."

"Just pull out the hard drive," Will said. Using his computer was too risky. If Drake was telling the truth, then there were already police tracers on his computer.

"Which one?"

"There's only one drive," Will said, craning his

head around Eliza's curtain of hair.

Eliza leaned back, raising an eyebrow, and Will saw it.

"That's not mine," he said, his voice going quiet.

"Then whose is it?"

"I don't know." Will frowned. "Can you get it out?"

Eliza fiddled for a moment, then shimmied both drives from their bays, one after the other.

"Are we putting both in mine?" she said, working the clips on the side of her own computer tower.

"Wait," Will said, touching her hand to stop her before she could open the case. "Eliza – what I said to Drake, you know that's not entirely accurate. If the police detect us on your computer, it won't be good. For you, and maybe even for Abby and Amir. We need to operate on another network. On another computer, preferably, one that's nothing to do with either of us."

Eliza stilled. "Will, Drake needs the money by morning. We don't have time for that."

"This is dangerous, though. If you get caught, there won't be anyone to sweep it under the rug – "

"This is the only way to find out what happened to Jeff, right?" she interrupted. Slowly, Will nodded. "Then we're doing it. My computer's the one we've got. We've got limited time. So we do it here." Her voice was firm. Determined.

"I can put a bunch of stuff in place to try and stop them tracking us, especially now that I know that they *were*, but Eliza, it's not going to be foolproof. There's still a chance – "

"I get it, Will," she said. She reached over, took his hand and squeezed. "If I take the hit for it, I take the hit for it. We're a team. We're in this together, right?"

He hesitated, his eyes searching her face.

"Besides," she added. "I think you underestimate the powers of my reputation. People believe a lot of what they want to see. And I've put in a hell of a lot of groundwork. May as well use it, right?"

He forced a smile. "I guess. I hope you're right."

She scoffed, and shoved his chest with her palm. "Will. Please. I'm always right."

When the drives were installed and the computer booted up, Eliza held out a hand. "All yours."

Will pursed his lips into a tight smile, and sat down in her swivel chair. He started to click and type. Windows popped open and filled the screen as he arranged them in a grid-like pattern.

He glanced at Eliza, now back in the armchair with her laptop.

"Money's in," she said, without looking up. "He's put in six thousand. Is that going to be enough?"

Will jittered his fingers against the edge of the desk. "With one night to turn that into a hundred grand? I'm going to have to set the bots to a really high risk strategy."

"Which means a good chance you'll go bust," Eliza said, meeting his gaze.

He nodded. "No choice though, I guess."

"On the plus side, not our money," Eliza added, and forced a smile.

"Yeah," Will said. He reached forwards, paused, and then with a sharp jab, hit the enter key. Numbers started to scroll in each window. He looked at Eliza, the corner of his mouth quirking up. "Here goes nothing."

*

Eliza rubbed her eyes, the screen glimmering through her squinted lashes. On her laptop, tiny figures hit a ball back and forth across a tennis net.

"You do know actually watching the matches doesn't affect the odds," Will said, his voice tired. One finger hovered over the enter key, and he hit it periodically, at seemingly random intervals.

"You do know that most humans find it incredibly boring to watch numbers go up and down," she said, glancing at the scrolling digits on his screen.

"Eh. I'm a unique thinker."

Eliza yawned. She checked the clock. "Are we on track, at least?"

"You mean you can't tell from the match scores?" Will said sarcastically.

"Shut up," she said, and snapped her laptop closed with a swift flick of her wrist. "We can't all be hardened money grubbers like you."

"Hey, I'm just looking out for myself."

Eliza tensed. He said it casually enough, but there was too much underneath what he said. He had to take care of himself. Because no one else could. She leaned over Will's shoulder, peering at his screen. She deliberately lightened her voice. He needed to focus back on the problem at hand. "Just tell me how we're going."

Will pointed at one of his open windows.

	Current Back	Backed at	Back at	Bail at
Sergei Youzhny	4.5	5.27 / $210	NA	
Mikhail Stakhovsky	1.27	NA	1.4 / $790	1.2 / $814

"The bot just placed a $210 bet on Sergei at the start of the match. His odds were at 5.27 then."

"It bet on the underdog? What does it know that we don't?"

"The historical data of both players," Will said. "Right now it thinks that Mikhail has a good chance of writing himself off, because he's got a statistically significant higher than average historical injury risk."

"So it's hoping Mikhail injures himself, Sergei gets the win, and we get the payout?"

"It doesn't actually care who wins. It's just waiting for the first hint of an injury from Mikhail. Then the odds will swing in Sergei's favour, and the program will place a bet on Mikhail to win."

"When he's *less* likely to win? Why?"

"If Mikhail looks like he's gone, then his odds will lengthen. The bot's waiting for them to get to 1.4 – at which stage it's going to…" Will clicked on another window to bring it to the front of the screen. "Bet $790 on Mikhail to win."

"Ergh. Too late. I need paper. I can't do this crap in my head." Eliza grabbed a calculator and flipped open a school book jumbled in a pile beside the computer.

Total outlay: $210 + $790 = $1000

If the $210 bet won, return is $210 × 5.27 = $1106.

If the $790 bet won, return is $790 × 1.4 = $1106.

"So you make a profit of $106, whoever wins. Unless the odds don't change the way you need them to." She dropped the open book with her calculations beside the keyboard.

"That's covered by the *bail at* number," Will said, pointing to the table on the screen again. "If Mikhail firms even more as the favourite, and the odds for him drop to 1.2, the program will place a $814 bet on him. In that case, we'd lose money. That's where the injury databases come in handy – the program's trying to tilt the odds in our favour."

"Sweet," Eliza said, throwing herself onto her stomach on her bed and yawning as she flipped her laptop screen open again. The tennis match was almost as monotonous as the numbers, but at least Mikhail was vaguely attractive.

There was a long silence interrupted only by Will's occasional clicks and the tinny noise of the match, turned way down, from Eliza's speakers.

"What do you think of Drake?" Eliza said, after a while. "Can we trust him?"

Will glanced at her. "I don't think we have a choice."

"Nice that we have proof he bankrolled this, at least," Eliza said. She'd screenshotted the deposit confirmation and uploaded it to her cloud storage the minute the funds had hit the account.

Will nodded. "And he's the only connection to what happened to Jeff. I mean – I had no idea he was undercover. Not, like, in the field. Actually doing stuff. He always made out he was just data crunching. I thought his specialty was coding phone transcripts or something.

"It's just mental," Eliza said. "You were just this boring person who follows me around until twelve hours ago. Now you're the nephew of an undercover agent?"

"Thanks," Will said, his voice wry. "I'm glad I know how you really feel."

She shot him a grin. "And now you're illegally gambling police money to pay informants for information."

"This isn't so different to last time," Will said. But his voice dipped as he said it.

She knew what he was thinking. Because it *was* different to last time. Last time, it hadn't been to make a hundred thousand dollars in one night. Last time, it had been more of a game, to see what Will's program could do, bankrolled half-and-half by her savings and Will's… alternative sources of income. She remembered the elation, the excitement, as it had worked. The gleeful *cheers* as they'd smashed their energy drink cans together and admired their takings.

"The reporter too," Will said after a while. "She's odd too. Intense. What's her interest in this?"

"The story?" Eliza said, but even as she did, doubt rippled through her. "That could be it, but... I don't know. She was desperate to talk to you. And she wasn't after a statement, or whatever. I mean, Jeff dying in a crash – " Her voice cracked, and she swallowed hard before going on. The words still felt wrong, too hard, to say. "Jeff dying, if it was an accident, then that's not, I mean, news, right?"

Will looked over at her sharply.

"I don't mean it like that," she said quickly. "Not like it shouldn't be news, or it's not important..." She trailed off, but she could see Will's eyes soften.

"I get what you mean," he said. "People die all the time. It's not news – "

"Unless it's *news*," Eliza finished. "And she seemed to think it was."

"And Drake thinks so too, maybe."

Eliza nodded. "I think there's more to her than we're seeing," she said. She paused, squinting at her screen. "Will. Action on court seven."

Will turned to see lines of scrolling numbers. An injury time-out had been called for Mikhail. In another window, Mikhail's odds steadily increased, going past 1.35, then 1.5, and steadying at 1.67.

"The punters are abandoning the favourite and betting on Sergei," said Will. He tapped on the keyboard. "The bot missed the 1.4 point, but got the bet in at 1.5."

Eliza smiled, and closed the laptop lid again. "So now it doesn't matter who wins. How much are we

111

up?

"Thirty-eight grand so far, including the original six," Will said. There was a chime, and Eliza glimpsed a notification in the corner of his screen.

"What's that?"

"The betting exchange checking if the thing laying the bets is a human or a program. Hence why I have to stay awake."

She closed her eyes, her lids fighting her. "Hmm. Why *you* have to stay awake."

She started as something landed on her stomach. "Hey! Don't be rude." She opened one eye. It was the notebook she'd scribbled the numbers in.

"Here. Make yourself useful while I do this," Will said, and tossed a USB drive on top of the notebook.

She groaned. It was lucky that Abby had organised for both of them to have the rest of the week off school, that was for sure. "What is it?"

"Everything off the random hard drive."

That chased some of the sleepiness away. "So you're *sure* you didn't put that drive in there when you built the machine and, like, forgot about it?" She sat up, flipping her laptop back open.

Will looked at her. "I'm sure," he said, flatly, as if she were an idiot for suggesting it.

She inserted the USB and opened the folder. "You encrypted it before you copied it."

"No I didn't."

"Well, it's encrypted."

Will opened the drive folder on his machine. "It's

encrypted here too."

"Why would there be an encrypted, unconnected drive in your computer?" Eliza started clicking, pulling up crack programs already on her machine.

"Why indeed," Will said grimly. "Because someone who lives... *lived*... in my house was paranoid about something he knows?"

The reporter's words flashed back through Eliza's mind, and she met Will's gaze. "Yeah. Why indeed."

"Can you crack it? You've still got the program you cracked the school network administrator account with, right?"

"Yeah, but the system admin at school is... not so bright."

"I still say you should have let me download all our future exams off the teachers' drives."

She ignored him. "His password was numeric-only. It cracked it in under a day. If this is Jeff's drive, he'd have been smarter than that." She clicked and typed for a few moments. "And this is 256-bit encryption. *No* chance."

"But you're so *good* at that stuff," Will said sycophantically, his eyes back on his screen. "You've been doing it for years, sneaking in the back doors and giving yourself the grades you want on your report card."

"That you think I would stoop to such levels makes you a boor and a cad, sir," she said, sniffing and lifting her nose. "I earn my grades. Unlike some."

"I earn my grades too," Will said. "I slack off for

every inch of those Ds and Cs."

"The Ds, sure. But next time you accuse me of grade-fixing, think about how many times you've *not* had your enrolment cancelled this year so far."

He looked at her sharply, and she raised her eyebrows challengingly.

"All right, then, I will," he said, smiling slowly.

She grinned back, and turned back to her program. It was good to see him smile again. Relax a little.

"Well, going back to the drive, Jeff used numeric passwords all the time," Will said after a moment. "Like the door code to the house. And you know what his phone password was?"

Eliza looked nonplussed. "Why would I?"

"It was 3263827."

"Is that meant to mean something?"

"It's the number for the garbage compactor in Star Wars Episode IV. Everything in Jeff's life had some kind of geeky connection. Usually Star Wars."

Eliza pursed her lips. "I can try a brute force attack then, using Star Wars terms and variations, and see how that goes. It'll take a while, though."

Will turned back to his screen. "Settle in. Not like we're going anywhere."

Chapter 14.

34 hours and 41 minutes left

The crackly theme music of *Garth Marenghi's Dark Place* seeped in through Eliza's half-sleeping ears. Slowly, she came back to the world.

She was curled in her armchair, her laptop half-open on the floor beside her, her black-rimmed glasses askew on her face.

"Urgh," she groaned. Her eyes stung, her back hurt, and her legs were completely asleep. She reached down and closed the laptop's lid, shutting off the show that had been playing on repeat while she'd worked on the encrypted file.

Will was splayed across her still-made bed, one arm over his face.

Eliza forced herself up. What time was it? She staggered to her feet and glanced at the computer screen on her desk.

And froze as she saw the total in the bank account.

"Will," she whispered, then grabbed his leg and

shook him, hard. "Will!"

"Wha – "

"You did it." She turned as he struggled to sit up. "You did it!"

Will looked, and then a lopsided grin split over his face. "Wow. A hundred grand and change. High risk, high reward, I guess. We got lucky."

She grinned. "I'll text Drake."

She threw herself back into the armchair and moments later her phone pinged. "He'll be here in ten," she said. "Naturally, no congratulations or commendations."

Will raised an eyebrow. "I don't think he knows the meaning of appreciation." He stood and stretched, then tugged off his shirt, rummaging for another in his backpack. "How'd you go with the file?"

Eliza grabbed the laptop and opened it. "Oh. Sweet. It cracked it," she said, her voice rising. The warmth of success flooded her and she quickly scrolled through the log file. "Looks like Star Wars was the answer."

She glanced at her watch, then thrust the laptop at Will. "Here. Copy it to your tablet. I'm going to get dressed."

Seven minutes later, she re-emerged from the bathroom, her hair damp and wrangled into a side plait. Will was flicking quickly across his tablet screen.

"What was the file?"

"A PDF of some kind," Will said, slipping the tablet back into its case. "Drake's here. We can read it in the car."

Eliza nodded. She detoured past her mother's room – who was getting dressed for work – to tell her they were going with Drake. By the time she got to the car, Will was already in the back seat and Drake's fingers were rapping impatiently on the steering wheel.

"Sorry," Eliza said, as she slipped into the backseat beside Will. Will glanced up, his face taught. And then she noticed who was sitting in the front seat beside Drake.

The reporter.

"What are you doing here?" Eliza said.

"Melissa and I have come to an agreement to share resources on this case," Drake answered, as Melissa turned in her seat and smiled tightly at Eliza and Will.

"Despite what you said about him?" Will said, his voice snappy.

"And despite what you said about her?" Eliza followed.

Melissa's eyes snapped to Drake. Eliza could see Drake's jaw working.

There was a long pause.

"Yes." Both spoke in unison.

Eliza looked at Will, raising her eyebrows.

"Great," Will said flatly.

"Drake tells me you've been successful with your hacking," Melissa said, twisting back around again.

"I would have thought that you'd be downplaying

what you had us do," Will said sharply to Drake. Eliza saw Melissa flinch. She frowned. There was something strange in the way that Melissa looked at Will. Like she was hiding some kind of pained emotion. Like her polite disconnection was carefully constructed over… something else.

"She needed to know," Drake said. "And in fact, she contributed to the starting fund." His hand jerked forwards and he spun the knob on the car radio. The dB number on the display jumped up and the car filled with the sound of country music. The conversation was over.

In the privacy of the noise, Eliza pulled out Will's tablet from the case between them and clicked it on. The irritated look faded from Will's face, and he leaned towards her, the tablet perched between them. Eliza hit the icon for the PDF.

It was a single page, and it consisted of a satellite photo. Eliza's eyes flicked over it, quickly picking up the patterns, though it was oriented differently to the familiar view of Google maps.

"Where is this?" Will said quietly.

"Brisbane," Eliza said. She pointed, touching the straight lines bridging the river that wound between urban sprawl. "See? Victoria bridge, and the Goodwill bridge…"

Will frowned, then spun the screen around. "Oh. Okay. I see it. What are the circles, though?"

Eliza squinted, pinching the screen to zoom in on one of the small yellow circles dotted throughout the map. "Drug deal locations? There's numbers next to them. Maybe… ten dealers in the area?" She touched one with *10* marked next to it. "Seems high. Maybe ten drug *deals* in the area?"

Will swept a finger across the screen and it moved to another circle. "This one is a little bigger and says twenty. Bigger circle, bigger number?"

"Except that one says fifteen, and it's the biggest of the lot." Eliza zoomed out to show a circle that covered most of the photo.

"So not drug deals, then," Will said. "Fifteen over the whole city but more than that in an area *within* the city. That makes no sense."

Eliza zoomed out until the whole map was showing. She frowned. The picture looked somehow familiar but wrong at the same time. Like an earthquake epicentre diagram, only not.

"Maybe he knows," she said after a pause, nodding her head towards Drake.

Will glanced up, where Drake and Melissa were silently ignoring each other, their faces rigidly forwards. "Let's keep this to ourselves, for now," Will murmured.

Eliza nodded. Whatever game these two were playing: it wasn't clear yet who was on the right side.

The music cut out abruptly.

"We're here," Drake said.

*

Will followed Drake through the airlock, Eliza at his side. The room hissed, and then they were in a boring-looking, silent ward.

Drake led the way in. Will heard a sharp intake of breath as they entered the ward. He followed Drake's eyes to see a thin, emaciated and very sick-looking boy propped up in a bed.

"He's recovered," Drake murmured.

"Drake."

A voice from behind made them turn. It was a man in a suit, his face stern and serious.

"A word," he said, gesturing to Drake, his eyes flicking over Will, Eliza and Melissa.

Drake frowned, but followed.

"I thought he wasn't likely to recover – " Drake started, but the man waved a hand and cut him off.

"Do you have the money?"

"It's being held in escrow by the third party you requested. You'll get it as soon as Namir tells us everything he knows."

The suit shook his head. "Before. Make the transfer now."

Drake paused. "What guarantee do I have that his information will be useful?"

The man tilted his head. "What guarantee do *I* have that you have the money?" He held out a phone. Will glimpsed a number written on the screen. "Make the transfer into this account, please. I will confirm the transaction independently."

Again Drake hesitated, and after a second, the

man went to draw back the phone.

"May I remind you, that you have no warrant," he said, his voice dropping low. "Are you really in any position to be choosey?"

Drake's hand flew out and snagged the phone. "Fine."

Moments later, the man finished his own calls, and smiled at Drake. "Nice doing business with you."

"I hope I can share those sentiments, Jerry," Drake said pointedly, jerking his head towards the boy in the bed.

The man – Jerry – nodded. He continued talking quietly to Drake, but Will was barely listening anymore. Names of people and places Will didn't know floated over his head. His eyes were fixed on the boy in the bed.

He was so young. How could someone so young be here, like this, so sick?

After a moment, Jerry and Drake fell silent, and Will dragged his attention back. Jerry was waving a hand at him, and at Eliza and Melissa.

"Whoever your friends are – they can wait in the hall. Our deal was for *you* to speak to Namir."

"Wait a minute – " Will snapped. After all he'd done to get Drake the money and he wasn't going to get to even hear what this informant had to say?

Drake jerked his hand at Will. "These people are all critically involved in this incident," he said. His voice was rough. "They hear what I hear."

Will frowned. He and Eliza deserved to be here,

but Melissa? How was *she* involved?

Jerry raised his eyebrows, but after a moment, he gestured towards the bed. "As you wish, then."

Drake strode forwards, pushing past Jerry, and Will followed, Eliza and Melissa behind him.

At the bed, the boy looked up, meeting Will's gaze with reddened eyes. Will swallowed. Under the bandaged and pink, puffy skin, he looked like they could be in school together.

"I look a sight, do I not," the boy said, smiling. His gums were bloody. His eyes were piercing, locked on Will's. Perhaps because they were the same age.

Drake cleared his throat. "I am investigating what happened to you and your fellow refugees, Namir," he said. "You're getting better?"

"So it would seem," Namir said, shrugging. "I feel a lot better, but still very tired."

"You speak very good English, for a refugee," Melissa interjected, her voice soft. "How did you learn?"

Namir smiled bloodily again. "My brothers and I went to a good school before it was destroyed in the unrest. We learnt English and watched Hollywood movies."

"This unrest drove you out of your country?" Drake said.

"At first, we had enough money to survive," Namir said. "But then they stopped all the men in my family from working, because of the tribe we came from. We tried to get other jobs but they would not let us. Then one day they came for my father. They shot him. And then they shot my sister when she tried to tell a journalist. That was when we decided to leave."

Will swallowed, his throat dry.

"How did you get here?" Drake said. "With no money, I mean."

Namir frowned. "My brothers and I made our way to the coast and waited every day for a boat, but the cost was always too high. Then, one day, a boat appeared, and there was no cost."

"You didn't find that strange, suspicious?" Melissa said.

"My father and oldest sister had been murdered and we had no money to eat. We did not have the luxury of suspicion."

"This boat," said Drake, glancing askance at Melissa. "Can you describe it? Who was on it? Did it have any cargo? What was the trip like?"

"The first few weeks were as normal as such a journey could be," Namir said. "We had enough food and water, and the crew ignored us, but did not abuse us. Then, we started to get sick. Not just one or two, but dozens. Vomiting, diarrhoea at first. Then bleeding, bleeding from everywhere, and red swollen skin. The sickest were under the deck. Then, just before your naval boat found us, everyone's hair started to fall out."

Namir rubbed his bandaged hand along his head. "I thought I would be sad that we had not made it to freedom. But by then, I did not care. Both my brothers were dead. I knew I would never have family again…" He trailed off, his voice rasping, and his eyes closed.

Will's throat felt tight. The things this boy had been through. He'd lost everyone. His brothers and sisters too. He was truly alone. He glanced at Eliza, saw the paleness in her face. A pained thrill of fear rippled through him. What state would he be in, if he lost her, too? How could anything matter then?

"Is there anything else you can tell us?" Drake said, his voice getting insistent. "Any detail, anything else you remember?"

Namir didn't move for a long time. Will watched his motionless face. Had he slipped back under the veil of the sickness that had claimed everyone else?

Then, finally, he opened his eyes. "The sickest people were nearest to the boat's hold," he whispered. "That's where they threw the first bodies overboard. I was at the other end of the ship. And I was the last to get sick."

His eyes slipped shut again.

"He needs to rest." A woman's voice made Will turn. A doctor stood behind them, her face tense. *Doctor Rebecca Robinson* was stamped on a nametag attached to her coat. She ushered them away from the bed. Drake kept glancing back at the bed, but he followed. Jerry, too, followed.

Emotions churned through Will. As they reached the other side of the airlock, he turned on the suited

Jerry.

"Are you going to use the money to help him?" he asked, his heart thudding hard. He had to know that some good could come out of this tragedy.

Jerry glanced at Doctor Robinson, then back at Will. "It'll be used to migrate his remaining family to Australia. His mother, and sisters."

Will breathed out. "So he won't be alone for long, then."

Jerry didn't speak. He looked at the doctor again.

"I'm afraid that reunion will never happen," she said. She held up a chart. At the bottom, below paragraphs of scrawl, there was one larger line of text: *Best Estimate Exposure: 45 Gy.*

"Gy stands for Gray, a unit of radiation absorbed by a human," she said. "We estimate Namir was exposed to forty-five units."

Drake scowled. "I thought the refugees were just, well, sick?

The doctor nodded. "Yes, but not from a virus or bacteria. Namir is dying from radiation poisoning."

"But he's talking," Eliza protested. Her voice sounded thick. "Smiling."

Doctor Robinson shook her head. "Namir is what we call a walking ghost. Forty-five Gray will kill most humans within a couple of days. The exposure has destroyed his bone marrow and killed a lot of his cells, but the effects of that aren't showing yet. They will. Soon."

Will sucked in a breath.

"We'll medicate to make the end as painless as possible," the doctor continued. "And he will die at least knowing that his remaining family will have a better life." She glanced at Jerry, and he nodded.

"This exposure killed the other refugees too?" Melissa said.

"They scanned clean for all other biological agents or chemicals. Sometime in the last week, they were exposed to an extremely potent radiation source for an extended period of time. It's the only way they could have got that dosage."

"Exposed how?" Drake said. "They ate or drank radioactive material?"

The doctor shook her head. "Our analysis indicates that they didn't ingest any radioactive material. Our best guess at this stage is that they were all exposed to a large quantity of Cobalt-60, a highly radioactive isotope. We use it in radiotherapy here at the hospital, but only in tiny, tiny amounts. And unless they washed with it, we're talking possibly tonnes of the stuff."

A chill rippled down Will's spine, and he looked at Eliza, seeing the same horror mirrored on her face. Radioactive material. *Tonnes* of radioactive material. What *was* this?

"What would happen if that amount was dispersed over a crowd of people?" Drake said, slowly, his voice dropping low.

"In small particles, without protective gear, people would breathe it in." She waved at Namir's ward. "We don't have any ability to deal with large radiation incidents – the refugees already overloaded the hospital. We can't treat a crowd. And even if we had the facilities, there'd be very little we could do for them after exposure."

Her eyes locked onto Drake's. "There would be widespread fatalities," she said grimly.

Drake shook his head. "I've got to talk to my boss. As soon as possible." He paused, then glanced between the doctor and Jerry. "How long can you keep a lid on this?"

The doctor glanced at the airlock door and frowned. "A week, maybe. The autopsies won't all be…finished until then."

Drake nodded. "I'll be in touch. Please, understand how sensitive this information is."

She nodded, her face serious. Drake thanked her, then headed for the elevator. Will followed, his heart thumping. This was no drug cartel. This was death, and people bent on destruction. He felt unmoored, and the world spun as the lift descended, leaving the dead and the dying behind.

Chapter 15.

32 hours and 32 minutes left

The container truck rumbled off the street and through the entrance to the university. Danial sat in the passenger seat, staring at the leafy trees lining the avenue. Soon all this would be decimated. Just like his home. Just as they deserved.

He, and the driver beside him, were dressed in fluorescent yellow vests. Hard hats hung on the cab wall behind their heads.

"There," Danial said, pointing across the deserted campus. Sturdy metal temporary fencing ringed a vast site encompassing a collection of partially-unpacked trucks, trailer buildings, skip bins and portable toilet cubicles.

The truck pulled up to the security hut outside the fencing. Danial looked at the newspaper covering the gun in his lap. His fingers clenched and unfurled around the handle.

"Hey fellas, what have you got?" A guard, his once-white uniform stained with sauce, leaned out of the hut, peering down at a clipboard. "Not expecting anyone else today for the festival bump-in." He gestured to the activity beyond the fencing.

Danial leaned across the driver. "G'day mate," he said, in a broad Australian accent. "It's not for the festival. Bloody council's spec'ed the wrong containers for the construction site at the bridge. Damn things are rusting out. We've got to swap 'em over, quick as possible. Didn't head office tell you we were coming?"

The guard shook his head.

"Right," Danial said with a long-suffering sigh. "Well, let's get 'em on the phone now, they'll confirm the job."

"Can't mate. Comms dropped out about an hour ago," the guard said. His eyes slid over the container on the back of the truck. "What about the investigation? I thought works at the bridge site were shut down for the week. Or at least until this menagerie is over." Again his gaze flicked to the brightly-coloured rides and food trucks being set up.

Danial tightened his fingers on the gun. He shrugged, keeping his voice casual. "I dunno anything about it. All I know is I was told to get down here with these containers."

There was a beat of silence. Danial took a long, slow breath. There was a wide expanse of green grass between the hut and the first of the festival workers. And he had a silencer. It wasn't ideal, but it would be over in moments.

But then the guard shrugged.

"Just come on through," he said.

"Thanks, mate. Four more trucks coming through after us, too." Danial relaxed his grip on the gun. The man didn't know it, but he'd just saved his own life.

The guard nodded, already disinterested. The boom gate jerked open, and Danial shot a tight smile at his driver, Ayman.

Ayman was frowning. "We should have killed him," he hissed, as the truck trundled into the festival site. Danial looked away from Ayman, dismissive.

"He will have forgotten about us in an hour's time," he said, his voice calm. To the right of the road was the river. So peaceful now, but not for long.

"He could tell his boss about us," Ayman said.

Danial's head snapped around. "And then what? These people do not know the meaning of fear. Even if he tells his boss, it means nothing to us."

"I wasted an hour on those comms. He deserves to die; they all do for what they've done."

"Do you want vengeance," Danial said, his voice becoming dangerously low. "Or do you want failure, because of a stupid decision to kill a guard?"

Ayman seemed to catch the tone in Danial's voice, and he fell silent, his face paling slightly.

"They do deserve death," Danial continued. "But patience, Ayman. You cannot be distracted when our goal is so close. Do you understand?" He clamped a hand on Ayman's shoulder, the gesture starting gentle, almost comradely, but as he spoke, he tightened his grip. Ayman was a good man, but he was too hot-tempered. And that would not be tolerated.

Ayman audibly swallowed, and then nodded.

"Good," Danial said, and turned his eyes back to the road ahead. Ayman was slowing as they reached a wide area cordoned off by another, more industrial boundary of temporary fencing and tape marked *Danger*. The fence encompassed a number of buildings as well as the pylons for an arched white bridge that reached across the river to South Bank.

A man emerged from a silent site office beside the barrier, raising a hand to the truck. Danial nodded in greeting. Jogging forwards, the man opened the wide gate leading into the barricaded area, the sound of metal screeching on metal filling the air. Beyond the gate, a bulldozer was parked, its shovel embedded in a concrete pylon. More *Danger* tape was pegged in a wildly-coloured weave around the dozer.

Danial smiled. It had been easy to engineer the accident. Now they had the construction site to themselves, while the authorities tried to work out what happened.

Ayman parked the truck, and they both jumped down from the cab. Danial followed as Ayman walked the length of the truck, and waited as he clambered up behind the shipping container. He heaved at the bolt until it screeched open.

Two men, both in construction worker outfits, emerged blinking into the sunlight. Behind them, the sunlight silhouetted row after row of barrels.

131

Danial glanced up as a rumbling announced the arrival of the second truck. He clapped Ayman on the shoulder and left him talking to the two men who'd been in the container. They were perfectly on schedule. Within half an hour they'd have twenty men and all five containers on site.

"Danial, we're ready to start unloading," Ayman called, his voice tight with impatience.

"After the last truck is in," Danial said over his shoulder. "Then we will shut the gate and start work without being seen." He cupped his hand over his eyes and looked towards the sun, still low in the sky, then glanced back at his companion. "We have almost two days, Ayman. We will be ready."

Chapter 16.

32 hours and 24 minutes left

"This is… horrific," Melissa murmured, ridged in the front seat. "Radiation poisoning – we're talking a full on terrorist attack, aren't we?"

The car was silent. All Will could picture was the bloodied teeth of Namir. Smiling. Smiling even as death stood waiting.

Then suddenly, Drake yanked the steering wheel across the lanes of traffic. Will grabbed at the door handle, Eliza slamming into him with a soft yelp.

"What are you – " Melissa exclaimed, as Drake wrenched the car to a stop in an emergency bay.

Drake turned and looked at her. "Melissa," he said, his voice very low. Dangerous. "When I spoke to you yesterday, you asked whether we found drugs at the port." He stopped, and looked at her. She was very still, and very pale. "Did you know that there weren't any drugs?"

Beside him, Eliza sucked in a breath. Will caught up a second later. Melissa… *knew?*

There was a long silence, broken only by the click, click, click of the car's indicator.

"Melissa!" Drake suddenly exploded. "Did you *know* about this?"

"I – I didn't!" she exclaimed. Her hands were clenched before her, pressed so hard her skin was rumpled. "Not – not for sure."

Will's heart rocketed. "Then you knew something? You knew *some* of this and did nothing?"

She twisted in her seat, her face blotched red and white. She looked close to tears. "It was rumours. Just rumours. I had no idea it would be confirmed. I *dreaded* it being confirmed. How could it? Here, of all places?"

"Who?" Drake barked. "Who told you about this rumour?"

She fell silent again, her eyes darting between Will and Drake.

"Melissa, I swear – " Drake started.

"Jeff," she blurted, everything about her oozing misery. "It was Jeff."

"Jeff?" Will breathed. Jeff knew about this? He glanced at Eliza, saw the shock mirrored on her face. "But – but why would he – why didn't he tell anyone? Warn them?"

"He was collecting evidence," Melissa said. Her eyes glistened, and she blinked quickly. "He was afraid that there were traitors working on the inside, within the force. He was gathering information."

"And he told you this?" Drake said. "When?"

"I've known for…" She glanced quickly at Will and then down at her lap. "Several weeks." She looked back up at Drake. "I was going to help him. Bring the story to the world. But not before we were certain that the whole lot of them, the insiders, the terrorists, everyone, would be brought down."

She paused again. When she spoke, Will could hear her warring for control over her voice. "He'd… I believe that he'd finally gotten the evidence he needed, when he made plans to meet me on Tuesday night. But then… he didn't show up." She looked down at her lap again.

Because by then, he was dead. It was like someone had punched Will in the stomach. Jeff knew something. And he died before he could tell anyone else.

"Did anyone else know of your involvement?" Drake said, his voice urgent.

Melissa shook her head. "I don't think so." Again she glanced at Will.

"Then you may – and I stress *may* – not be in danger. Yet," Drake said grimly.

"So what do we do now?" Eliza said. Her arms were wrapped around her chest, and her face was pale.

"I have some possible leads," Melissa said, her voice shaking. She cleared her throat. "I developed a shortlist of potential candidates by running a background search on plausible threats to Australia." She tugged a tablet from her bag, and in a few seconds had a list of countries on the screen. Will and

135

Eliza leaned forwards to see.

"Not a very short shortlist," Drake said, his finger flicking across the screen.

"Wait," Will said. Something Drake and Jerry had discussed before they'd talked to Namir came back to him. "Isn't that where Namir got on the boat?" He stabbed at a name halfway down the page.

Drake squinted. Then he nodded, slowly. "It is."

"Here," Melissa grabbed the tablet and opened another file, her fingers moving in a blur. After a moment she paused. "They have an embassy here."

"Please tell me you have a contact," Drake said.

Melissa glanced up at him, a tight smile on her lips. "I've got an intelligence source there, yes."

"Good luck at last," Drake said. "Right. We're shorthanded, so we're going to have to work with what we've got. Melissa – you're going to the embassy. I'm going to need to talk to someone else."

Will glanced at Eliza. He saw the determination spill quickly over her face. They weren't going to be cut out now.

"I'll go with Melissa," Eliza said quickly.

"I'll go with you, Drake," Will added.

Drake nodded. "We'll meet back at Jeffrey's house."

Will sank back into his chair as Drake swung back into traffic. He quashed the roiling tremors of anger and fear in his belly. They had a plan. This was a puzzle, and he could do puzzles. And he was not going to give up until he cracked it.

136

Chapter 17.

31 hours and 47 minutes left

"You can wait here," the receptionist said, her eyes drifting lazily over Eliza and Melissa. Everything about her read *bored* in giant neon letters.

"Thanks," Melissa said, sitting in an architectural-looking black resin chair and smoothing her skirt. Eliza sat beside her. The chair was surprisingly comfy. The receptionist wandered back the way they'd come, to her desk in the front entryway of the embassy.

Melissa's fingers tapped on the plastic, her nails filling the small antechamber with a rapid clicking.

Eliza studied her out of the corner of her eye. The woman was clearly agitated. Upset. Eliza's eyes narrowed. She didn't think it was simply the confirmation of terrorist rumours that was getting under Melissa's skin.

"How do you know Jeff and Will?" she asked. Melissa glanced at her quickly.

"As I said. Jeff and I were working on – "

"Yes, but you must have met him before that,"

Eliza interrupted.

"We met a long time ago, when I was working on a story about intelligence officers."

"So you're friends?" Eliza pressed.

Melissa stared at the floor. "More like colleagues."

"But you know Will," Eliza stated.

Melissa looked at her quickly and then back at the floor. "No. No, I've never met Will."

"You called him Will," Eliza said. "When you first came to my house. He only lets some people call him Will."

"Oh," Melissa said. She was still looking straight ahead but Eliza saw her cheeks colour beneath her makeup. "I guess because Jeff has always talked about him as Will. I didn't realise."

Okay. She was definitely hiding something. Eliza fell silent, sitting back in her chair. Colleagues, but close enough that Jeff has *always talked* about his nephew-slash-adopted-son to her?

Melissa's nails rapped out a staccato beat.

"So you *were* friends then," Eliza said, after a pause. "If you were talking lots about Will."

Melissa swallowed. She kept staring down, and now her fingers were winding together in her lap. The silence was almost as loud as the rapping.

With shock, Eliza heard Melissa's breath catch. In a... a *sob*?

Frowning, she leaned closer, put her hand on Melissa's arm. "Hey. It's okay. I don't care if you were friends."

Melissa looked up, her eyes red. "Oh, Eliza," she said, her voice thick. Another sob hiccupped, strangled, from her throat. "I guess there's no point anymore."

"No point of what?"

Melissa hiccupped again. "Of hiding it." She dashed a hand across her eyes. "Jeff and I... we were... together."

"Together... like, a couple?"

Melissa nodded, sucking in an unsteady breath.

Eliza held still, her hand pressed on Melissa's arm. Jeff – with a girlfriend? The concept was as foreign as frogs on Mars. She'd never known Jeff to even *interact* with other adults, let alone *date* one.

"How long?" she said.

"Almost a year," Melissa said.

"Why didn't Jeff tell Will?" There was no doubt in Eliza's mind that Will didn't know. There's no way this would have escaped her attention, no matter how engrossed in her school work she might have been when he told her.

"At first it was because of Jeff's work," Melissa said. Her voice was steadying, though it remained thick with repressed tears. "And... Jeff felt a great sense of duty to Will. I was the first person he ever... really let *into* his life." She glanced up at Eliza, and barked a short laugh. "And didn't it take forever! He's lucky I like a challenge."

Eliza smiled, but her chest panged. When Melissa spoke she could see some echo in her face of what had been there.

"He felt guilty, always guilty, over what happened to Will's parents," Melissa continued. "It made it... hard for him, to have a relationship with anyone, I think."

"You could tell Will now," Eliza said.

"I thought about it," Melissa said, staring blankly into space again. "But I wondered: what would be the point? Would it hurt Will more, to know now that Jeff kept our relationship secret? Would that be worse than anything *good* to be gained in telling him?"

Eliza's brow creased. Melissa looked so sad. What a horrible thing to be grieving, and have no one to share it with. The only person who would understand what she was going through didn't even know she existed – at least, not in the way that she had, in Jeff's life.

"You should tell him," she said, her voice soft. "I think... I think it'd be better if he knew."

Melissa looked at her, her face torn. "I don't know."

Someone cleared their throat. Eliza glanced up, saw a young, spectacled man standing a few metres away in a doorway.

"Melissa," he said.

Eliza swallowed. He did not sound happy to see them.

Hurriedly, Melissa wiped her eyes, and stood, tugging her dress suit straight. "Steve," she said, and immediately, her voice slipped into the smooth, trained tone that Eliza recognised off the television. She gestured for Eliza to follow, and Steve held out his hand to usher them into his office.

"I told you not to come here," he snapped, as soon as the door closed behind them. "We are not supposed to meet at work."

"Steve," Melissa said, holding her palms out before her, placating. "I tried to call you, but if you're going to screen my calls, then – "

"I'm going to lose my *job* if they know you're here!" Steve half-whispered, half-yelled, planting his hands on the desk between him and Melissa.

Melissa crossed her arms, and Eliza saw her jaw clench before she spoke. "I pay you too much god-damn money to have you decide to cut me off," she said bluntly. "We've always had a good relationship, you and I. But don't think for a second that I won't tip your boss off *myself* if you don't start being more forthcoming."

"You ruthless parasite," he spat.

Melissa didn't even flinch. "However you want to put it: just don't forget it," she said. Her voice was steely. Underneath it, Eliza sensed the blunt desperation in the tiny, almost-invisible fidgets of her fingertips on her folded arms. "You work for *me*, Steve, not the other way around."

Steve goggled at her, his face reddening. There was a long, fraught silence.

"So, we going to talk?" Melissa said. She stepped forwards, calmly drawing out a chair from before his

141

desk, and sitting down. With one elegant swipe of her hand, she gestured Eliza forwards into the other chair.

"Who is this?" Steve huffed, still standing on the other side of the desk.

"My intern," Melissa said smoothly. "Eliza. She's helping with this story. Speaking of which…" She held her palms out. "What have you got for me?"

Steve finally sank into his chair. "The situation is being controlled. That's all I can tell you."

Melissa leaned forwards. "What situation would this be?"

Steve stared at her for a long time, glanced at the closed door, and then sighed. "This is the last time. I tell you this now, and you promise not to contact me again. And I get you assurance that there's no way the information can be traced back to me. Right?"

Melissa nodded. "Of course. Whatever you want."

Jerkily, he tugged a filing cabinet open, and pulled out a folder, slapping it onto the desk.

"As you know, our country is in a state of unrest," Steve said, flipping it open. "Like many other countries, there are… issues with uncontrolled groups operating out of rural areas."

"Terrorists," Melissa said.

"Freedom fighters to some," Steve said. "They receive support from the local population, which is why attempts to weed them out have been largely unsuccessful. Even those by you and your powerful allies."

Steve pulled out a sheet of paper and slid it over

the desk. "Since we cannot fix the problem, we monitor it instead. We've identified at least three major organisations with training camps in the mountains."

Eliza leaned forwards. The sheet was covered in squiggly graphs.

"What is this?" Melissa said.

"Seismograph readings," Eliza blurted, as Steve opened his mouth. He nodded.

"In English?"

"Earthquakes," Eliza said, her eyes still on the page.

"From a seismic monitoring station in the mountains," Steve said.

Melissa frowned and shook her head. "Point being?"

"This particular station picked up some anomalies after a large quake," Steve said. He ran his fingers along the squiggly line on the page. "These two big spikes were two large quakes hitting around 6.0 on the Richter scale. That's strong enough to knock buildings down in a city." His finger traced along the line to some smaller spikes. "These later ones are the aftershocks."

"Aftershocks occur at a rate inversely proportional to time," Eliza added quickly. "So if there were twelve aftershocks the first day after the earthquake, there should be eight the second day, four the third day and so on. They get smaller and more spaced-out."

Melissa was looking at her oddly.

"I had an earthquake phase as a kid. Instead of dinosaurs," Eliza said, scanning along the graph. "Wait." She read the time axis. "There's three spikes on day twelve."

"Right," Steve said. "And that's the point. There should have been one." He pointed at the two smaller spikes. "These two are relatively small, around 2.8 on the Richter scale." His finger shifted right to the largest spike. "This one was bigger, around a 5.3. The geologists were suspicious, so they passed it on to us."

He looked up at Melissa. "And because earthquakes aren't the only things that can cause ground tremors…"

Melissa sucked in a breath. "Then these could be something else."

"Exactly," Steve said. "A source stated that the group were testing a bomb that day, around fifty tonnes of explosive. Based on the distance between their camp and the monitoring station and our intel, our analysts tied it to one of the 2.8 tremors."

"So you've got terrorists running around your country testing massive bombs," Melissa said, her voice low.

Steve looked uncomfortable. "Well, that's the problem. We actually don't. The site was raided the day after this analysis was finalised. They'd all disappeared. All we found was some tents and a heap of collapsed tunnel shafts."

"So they went somewhere. Bombed a city, or something?" Melissa said.

"There's been the usual bombings, but nothing big," Steve said. He hesitated, his face tense. "The analysts believe… well, I guess, for lack of a better explanation, that they're no longer in the country."

"And that's the situation you're trying to control," Melissa breathed.

Steve nodded miserably. "You have no idea what would happen to our country if this got out. We are on the brink of complete collapse already. Millions could die if another civil war breaks out."

Eliza looked up from the page. Melissa's face was pale. She glanced at Steve. "What's this other spike?" she said, tapping the page.

Steve blinked, then squinted at the page. "That's believed to be a legitimate aftershock," he said.

"But if not," Eliza said slowly. "Double the reading means double the bomb size, right? A hundred tonne bomb."

Melissa looked sharply at Eliza, and then back at Steve. "What would that do in an urban environment?"

Steve paused. "The Oklahoma bomb was two tonnes, and it destroyed a huge building and killed hundreds," he said quietly. "I can't even imagine what a hundred tonnes would do."

Chapter 18.

31 hours and 18 minutes left

"This way you kill a lot more people," said the man, gesturing at a whiteboard covered in equations and diagrams. "Irradiates the entire area and everyone in it." He paused, and glanced at Drake, where he stood beside Will in a tiny area of free floor space in an office otherwise filled with books and papers. "Really, ahem, screw things up, if you like."

"Professor Harris," Drake said, "we understand that, but how would you deliver the radioactive material? How would you get it on or inside all those people?"

"Explosives, of course," the Professor said. "A classic dirty bomb. Cram all the radioactive material into the biggest bomb you can build, detonate it and voila. Chaos. Destruction. Death."

"How much death?" said Drake. "Are we talking Hiroshima?"

Chills rippled through Will's spine. He vaguely remembered studying Hiroshima in school. Though he didn't remember the details, the pictures of the immense mushroom cloud were branded into his mind.

"No, no, no," Harris said. "A dirty bomb is a completely different beast to a nuke. Hiroshima was a nuke detonated six hundred metres above the city. With that kind of bomb, you're talking hundreds of thousands of casualties. Dirty bomb, just a few thousand."

"*Just* a few thousand?" Drake said, his brows rising.

The Professor turned from the whiteboard and studied Drake. "Right, now that I've answered your question, how about a bit of context? What's your sudden interest in dirty bombs?"

Drake sighed. He sank down onto one of the chair-height piles of books. "I'm investigating a possible terrorist threat to our city. A potential bombing."

Harris went very still. "And you think radioactive because…"

"Because we have credible evidence that a large quantity of highly radioactive material was recently brought into Brisbane. Tonnes of the stuff."

"You said you'd need a bomb to deliver it," Will interrupted, and Harris glanced at him as if he'd forgotten he was even there. "How big a bomb?"

Harris glanced at the board and then back at Will. "The bigger the better, up to a limit. There's no point making a ridiculously large bomb, because the blast radius scales in an inverse cube manner. You have to make the bomb eight times as powerful to double the blast radius. Not very efficient." He pushed aside a pile of papers and opened a cupboard door, and pulled out a bucket of white powder. "Here. Let me show you."

He wove through the room to a set of French doors half-hidden by bizarre-looking apparatus and yet more piled books. Beyond the doors, there was a tiny paved courtyard, surrounded on all sides by ivy-tangled walls.

He plopped the bucket onto the ground and scooped out a handful of the power. "With a small bomb, you'd get this," he said, snapping his fingers open. A cloud of powder spread out from his hand, before settling on the moss-covered pavers. "A dense distribution of radioactive material, but only in a small area. Good for small dense crowds."

He reached back into the bucket.

"Bigger bomb," he said, throwing his arm up into the air and opening his hand. Powder filled the courtyard in a white haze, before it again settled down, covering everything in a much thinner layer of white. "Less dense, but a much bigger area, especially from a height. If you double the diameter of the blast circle, you need four times as much radioactive material to achieve the same lethality. Good for large gatherings, but only effective if the material particularly radioactive."

He brushed off his hands, scattering powder all

over his clothes. "Do you know what it is?"

"Probably Cobalt-60," Drake said.

Harris crossed his arms. "Well. That is serious indeed. It's so potent you could spread it out a lot and it would still be lethal. If you inhaled even a small particle..." He rolled a dot of the flour between his thumb and index finger. "You'd likely die. If I wanted to kill a lot of people and I had a large quantity of Cobalt-60, I'd build the biggest bomb I could practically deliver to my target, and surround it with radioactive material. You can fit a tonne of explosive in a car, and that's enough to take down a large building. Five tonnes in a small truck. Ten or more in a larger one, or a train, or a boat. No-one thinks twice about seeing a semi-trailer rolling around on the roads, do they?"

He picked up the bucket and ushered them back inside. "You see, there hasn't been a dirty bomb attack yet. It's all about getting your hands on enough radioactive material. The explosive's easy – with enough time and patience, you can make as big a bomb as you want. Of course, the bigger it is, the higher up it needs to go, otherwise you waste the blast digging up dirt."

Drake nodded, his face drawn.

"Of course, there's one good thing about a great big dirty bomb," Harris said, shoving the bucket away and sitting on a stack of books.

"Good?" Drake said.

"Well, relatively speaking. A genuine nuke is hard

149

to detect. They're usually not very radioactive, often quite small. But a dirty bomb the size you're describing – that's a whole other matter. It'll have a massive radiation signature, something you can track with the right gear. And anyone who's been around it for any period of time will get sick, really sick. It'd be obvious physically."

"The right gear?" Will said.

Harris looked to Drake. "You have contacts in the federal police?"

Drake nodded.

"You should have access to the units in Sydney or Melbourne. Put in a call, get them to send you some help."

"What if we needed something right now?" Drake said.

The Professor's eyebrows rose, but he said nothing, turning to another cupboard. "Well. I've got some old counters I used to use in teaching."

He pulled out several small boxes, then passed one to Drake. "Here. Consider it a loan."

Drake nodded, turning the box over in his hands.

"And," Harris suddenly held up a hand, one finger pointing to the ceiling. "I have something else that might help." He manoeuvred through the piles and began rummaging in a box on the floor. After a few moments he stood up with two vials in his hand, one dark blue, the other light blue.

"If you are so unfortunate to be nearby when a dirty bomb goes off, you'll want to take this." He handed the vials to Drake.

"What is it?" Will said.

"Prussian Blue – you drink it to help counter ingesting radioactive material. I got this from a foreign aid worker who did radiation cases. It's only stable at certain concentrations though. You'll have to mix it to the right proportions just before you take it."

"Drinking this will protect us from radiation?" Drake said, peering at the vials with narrowed eyes.

"Up to a certain dosage, yes."

"And if we're close to the bomb and get a really strong dose?" Drake said.

"Well, it won't really matter then, will it," said Harris. "You'll already be dead."

Chapter 19.

27 hours and 10 minutes left

Danial wiped his forehead and looked around the interior of the shipping container. It was tightly packed with fifty-five gallon drums, most topped by a small metal crate. Two men were currently clambering over the tops, dragging another crate towards one of the uncovered drums.

"Keep going," Danial said. He jumped down to the ground and surveyed the construction site. The trucks were gone. Each of the containers had been unloaded and were now elevated half a metre above the ground by four black cylinders about a foot in diameter, one at each corner. Four of them were finished. And in minutes, the one he stood outside would be too.

Footsteps crunched on the gravel behind him.

"That detective is here," Ayman said, spitting into the dirt. "I tried to turn him away but he insists on speaking to you. He is becoming... inconvenient."

"Get them out and shut the door," Danial said

coldly, jerking his head in the direction of the men inside the container. "I will deal with him."

Ayman didn't move. "We do not need him anymore," he said. "Our plans are finalised."

Danial paused, meeting Ayman's gaze steadily. "I will deal with him," he repeated, and reluctantly, Ayman nodded.

Danial strode towards the gate, nodding to his men there. They stepped aside, and Detective Riley pushed past, his eyes darting from side to side as he looked around the site.

"I did not expect to see you again so soon, friend," Danial said, stepping to block Riley's path.

"You've got a big problem, *friend*," Riley snapped. His eyes flicked between the men dressed in their bright construction vests. "That detective and a journalist – Melissa Green, from Channel Eleven – came into the station and pulled the rest of the files on Jeffrey Roberts. And he had the kid in there too – Jeffrey's kid, his adopted kid or whatever, and some other little ankle-biter. They're digging, and who knows what they're about to find."

Danial crossed his arms. "You assured me that you had covered our tracks," he said.

"From casual inspection, yes," Riley said. Danial saw a vein bulging on the side of his neck. The man was sweating, too. Pathetic. "Not from someone specifically *digging*."

"Tell me then, what will they see?"

"If he looks properly at the crash report, he'll find

out."

"Then my understanding of this situation is that it's *your* job to make sure he doesn't look properly. Buy him off. I have paid you enough already for you to afford that."

Riley shook his head. "No, no, no. He's one of those idealistic types. Won't come within a million klicks of a bribe."

Danial stared at Riley, his eyes piercing. He waited until the other man began to squirm before he spoke again. "So he will not be silenced. What happens, then, if he sees the report?"

"Game over," Riley said, the words tumbling out. "He'll report it up the chain – no idea why he hasn't already – and everything will come crashing down."

"Then it sounds like *you* have a big problem," Danial said flatly. "One which might be solved by a nice long overseas holiday with what I have paid you."

"I can't just up and leave," Riley said, his voice pitching high in indignation. "I live here. I have a wife. I'm not moving just because your men had to go and kill some analyst."

Danial kept his face impassive. This nonsense meant nothing to him. By the time the useless officials in this forsaken country started to act, it would be far, far too late.

"And this is *your* problem," Riley spluttered. "He's not going to just stop with the crash report. He keeps going back to Jeffrey's house. Who knows what records he'll dig up there? You have to do something about this, Danial, or else – "

"Or else what, Riley?"

Riley hesitated at his tone, and Danial saw him swallow. "Or else I'll tell the boys back at the office about the little drug operation you've got going on here." His voice strengthened as he spoke, and he waved a hand around at the containers.

Danial didn't answer.

"I can't be held accountable anymore for this," Riley said, his voice rising. "You need to step up and fix this problem. And what were you thinking, moving the drugs here? In plain sight?" He stepped to the closest container, and slapped the door. A dull metallic boom rattled around the site. "What was wrong with the warehouse?"

"It no longer met our needs," Danial said smoothly. Subtly, he nodded to one of his men at the gate. The guard began dragging the gate closed.

"So, what, you're going to start hitting the cashed-up university students from inside party drug ground zero?" Riley reached up and yanked on the door handle, but it didn't budge.

Danial nodded, and a sudden smile broke over his lips. "You'd like to see the merchandise?"

"I'd like another hundred grand for my trouble," Riley snapped, turning on Danial. "You've got enough here to buy several not-very-small islands. I think you can afford to give me a pay rise for everything you've put me through."

Danial glanced at one of his men, and quietly, the

man picked up a buzz saw.

"Let's step inside and negotiate," Danial said. "Away from prying eyes." He gestured to the building windows overlooking the construction site fence. He nodded to one of his men with limbs like a rhinoceros. "Open the container."

His man nodded, his muscles bulging through his neon outfit as he yanked the door slowly open. Danial lithely leapt up, then extended his hand back to Riley.

As he hauled Riley into the container, the man with the buzz saw turned it on. Riley stumbled into the darkened space, and swiftly, Danial tugged the door shut behind them.

It closed with a clang.

"What – I can't see – " Riley's voice was high and panicky in the pitch blackness.

Danial smiled. "Let me shed some light on the situation for you," he said, and flicked a switch on the wall.

A single incandescent bulb flared to life in the middle of the container roof, casting a harsh light on the contents of the container.

Danial watched, his smile tugging higher, as Riley peered around the space. He saw the buffoon's eyes slide over the crates and the barrels beneath. Read the labels marked there in black, bold text.

Ammonium nitrate fertiliser.

Outside, dulled by the metal walls sealed around them, a loud whining noise joined the buzz saw, followed seconds later by the whirring of a drill.

"What is this?" Riley whispered. He turned slowly to face Danial. His flesh was pale and blotchy. Like a fish, dying fresh from the ocean.

"Twenty tonnes of ammonium nitrate," Danial said softly. "A hundred tonnes all told. And these – " He stepped forwards, placing a hand gently on the closest crate. " – Are full of Cobalt-60."

In that hand, was a silenced pistol.

Riley goggled at him, his mouth slack. Yes, he was a doomed fish all right. Gasping for air already. A welling of disgust and satisfaction to be finally rid of the cretin rose up inside Danial.

"Do you know what that is, detective?" Danial asked, tilting his head.

"You… you said it was drugs!" Riley spoke as if he were being strangled. "Not – not this *insanity*!"

"I like to believe that's a matter of perspective," Danial said, his voice still smooth as silk.

"When?" Riley stepped backwards, his hand fumbling at his pistol holster.

"Tomorrow night."

"Friday night?" There was a fractional pause, and then realisation dawned on Riley's face. "Oh my god."

"I'm glad you're catching up," Danial said. With a swiftness to match a snake, he raised the gun.

Riley finally got his fingers to obey him and tugged his own pistol out, his hand shaking as he held it out in front of him.

"You don't want to do that," Danial said, waving at the dozens of barrels of explosive now at his back.

Right where Riley was aiming.

Riley's eyes bugged. "You're going to kill hundreds. Thousands," he said. "Think of the children!"

Heat flushed through Danial like a tidal wave. "I am thinking of the children," he snarled.

He fired.

Riley jerked backwards, collapsing around his chest as if punched by an invisible fist. He came to a stop with his back against the door, his legs buckling beneath him.

Danial stepped forwards calmly. Riley was clutching his chest with hands stained ruby red in the harsh light. His mouth opened and closed, tiny burbling noises escaping his lips.

Danial stood in front of him and watched, as the pathetic creature spluttered. Then he raised the gun, and pointed it at Riley's head.

"Goodbye, Riley," he said.

*

Danial stepped over Riley's corpse as the door swung open, the afternoon sun flooding over the pool of blood on the floor.

Ayman was standing outside, his pockmarked cheeks twisted into a rictus of a grin. "You did the right thing, boss," he said.

Danial nodded, barely looking at him. "He was right about the detective," he said, unscrewing the silencer from his gun. "He needs to be dealt with." He looked at Ayman, his eyes piercing. "By us, this time."

Ayman nodded.

"Go to the analyst's house," Danial said. He slipped the pistol back into the holster on his chest. "Wait for them, as long as you have to. Take care of it there. The cop. The journalist. Whoever these kids are that they're dragging around. All of them."

Ayman nodded again, and gestured to some of the men, striding towards the gate.

"And Ayman," Danial said. Ayman turned. "Make sure it's done properly."

Chapter 20.

26 hours and 52 minutes left

"So we know where they come from, and we know they've got a bomb," said Drake, opening Jeff's fridge. He turned and popped the lid on a cola can. "But no idea where or when the attack will be. And who we can trust from my department. Fantastic."

Eliza cleared her throat, and Will looked at her. He frowned. Since they'd met back at Jeff's ten minutes ago, she'd been casting weird glances at him.

"Um, we might have something else," she said.

Will's heart skipped. The map. She was going to tell them. That meant something had changed. She trusted them now.

She met his gaze and gave the slightest of nods. With a sigh, he pulled out his tablet. Hopefully she knew what she was doing.

"We found a map," he said, reluctantly setting the tablet down on the kitchen bench between the four of them.

"What?" Drake spluttered, drops of drink flicking

everywhere. "You didn't think that was important enough to share?"

Will met his gaze. "You're not the only one wondering who they can trust," he said, his voice flat. Drake scowled, but said nothing, leaning on his forearms to see as Will clicked the file open.

"What did the professor say the blast radius of a hundred tonne bomb was?" Drake muttered, zooming in on one of the circles on the aerial photo. "About one hundred and fifty metres?"

Will nodded. "Just like these circles," he said.

Melissa leaned over too. She'd been quiet since the reunion, telling Drake and Will what they'd discovered in brusque, clipped sentences. "There are hundreds of them," she murmured. "No way to search them all, not without the police on board."

"Add that to the list of problems," Drake said. He crumpled the can and threw it at the bin. It missed and clattered to a halt next to the bag they'd brought back from the university.

Will grabbed the bag and hauled it to the countertop. Drake raised his eyebrows.

"You're kidding, right?" he said.

"It's the only shot we've got," Will said. He unzipped the bag and unloaded the devices onto the bench.

"What are these?" Melissa said, picking one up.

"Geiger counters," Eliza said quickly, grabbing one. She flicked a switch and the display panel glowed green. "Cool."

"Old," Drake said. "The word you're looking for is *old*."

"It measures radiation?" Melissa said.

Will nodded. "We could track the bomb with these."

Drake frowned. "They tell you how strong the radiation is where you're standing, not where it's coming from." He took the device from Eliza and pressed a button. A zero flashed on the screen. "That doesn't help us find the bomb."

"It does, if we take a bunch of readings at different locations and then triangulate the signal," Eliza said, grabbing the counter back from Drake. There was a dubious silence from Drake and Melissa. "It won't be perfect, but it's better than nothing," she finished, her voice pitching defensively.

"If she says it'll work, it'll work," Will said, looking between Drake and Melissa. "We should split up, increase our range, right?"

Eliza nodded. Then she glanced quickly between Will and Melissa. "Yeah. But – before we go, I think, um, I think Melissa has something else she needs to say. To you, Will."

Will frowned, and looked at Melissa. She had gone bone white at Eliza's words.

"I don't think now's the best time – " she started, but Eliza shook her head.

"He needs to know."

"I need to know what?"

Melissa looked down, her fingers winding around

each other. Will's heart beat faster, inexplicably. What now? He looked at Drake. He'd had gone very quiet, his arms folded across his chest, his eyes downturned. Whatever it was, he knew it too.

"Okay. You all know something that I don't. Tell me what it is," Will said, his voice turning harsh.

"I'll let you handle this," Drake said to Melissa, his eyebrows popping up. "I'll be in Jeffrey's study." He pushed past her and Eliza, and disappeared.

"Go ahead," Eliza said. She put a hand on Melissa's arm. And her voice was actually... *gentle*. Sympathetic.

There was a long silence. Will crossed his arms and waited.

"Will," Melissa said, her voice sounding kind of strangled when she finally spoke. "I, uh, have some information about your uncle. I wasn't sure whether it was a good idea to tell you, but..." She looked at Eliza, who nodded.

"So tell me," he said shortly.

"Jeff and I... we were dating." She met his eyes, and he saw they were rimmed in red. He felt like someone had just splashed cold water over him.

"No you weren't," he blurted. "Jeff didn't date – "

"We were," she said. "We've been together for almost a year."

"A *year*?" Will exploded. "No way. No way! Jeff would have told me."

"I'm sorry, Will, I know he wanted to but he wasn't sure that – "

"How could he keep that from me for a whole *year*?" Heat rushed through Will in the wake of the cold. Didn't Jeff *trust* him?

"He was waiting for the right time – he was worried about what you'd think, how you'd feel about it, because of your parents. I mean, me coming in, with you almost an adult yourself and us telling you I was going to be your new mother – "

Will held up a hand, his breath catching hard and tight in his throat. "My *mother*? I don't even *know* you!"

Melissa paled further, if it was even possible. "I didn't mean to say that," she said quickly.

"I met you less than twenty-four hours ago and the only thing I know about you is that you've been sneaking around with *my uncle* in secret without *either* of you having the decency to tell me!"

"Will, please – " Eliza interjected as his voice rose to a shout. "She's trying – "

He waved her silent. "You should leave," he said, his eyes locked, burning, on Melissa. "I don't want you here."

"Will…" Melissa's voice was little more than a whisper.

"Will, come on – " Eliza said.

"No. This is my house now, right? Now that Jeff's dead? I don't want you in my house!"

"Will, she's grieving too." Eliza raised her voice. "Try to understand where she's coming from. She's lost Jeff too."

Melissa put a hand on Eliza's arm. "It's okay. I'll

164

go." Her face was crumpled. She looked at Will for a long, fraught moment. She opened her mouth to speak.

And then the kitchen light blinked off, plunging them into silent, angry shadows.

"The power's out again," Eliza said, her voice tired.

There were rapid footsteps in the hall, and then Drake appeared. His face was tense.

"What?" Will said.

Drake held up a hand, silencing him, peering out of the kitchen.

A muffled beeping sound broke the silence.

Drake turned. "Do *exactly* as I tell you, right now."

Will's heart jumped into his throat. Drake's face... was like a thundercloud.

"Hide. Eliza – dishwasher cavity. Melissa – get in the pantry. Don't make a noise, whatever happens. William, with me. To the study."

Paling, Eliza was frozen opposite Will. And then he dove forwards, yanking the empty dishwasher cupboard open. He half-helped, half-shoved her inside. He squeezed her hand, and for a fragment of time, their eyes locked, hers wide and mirroring the fear that hammered through him. He slammed the door closed. Thank god Jeff had never, even after all Will's complaining, bought the dishwasher to fill that space.

When Will stood, Melissa had vanished, and Drake was sidling to the kitchen entrance, pulling a handgun from where it had been tucked into his jeans. He peered around the doorframe, then turned back and held a hand up to Will. "Wait!" he hissed.

BOOM!

Drake recoiled as fragments whistled past. A moment later, smoke roiled into the kitchen.

"Now," he rasped, grabbing Will by the shoulder and dragging him forwards. "Before the smoke clears."

Will struggled not to cough and focussed on following Drake's indistinct outline through the smoke. He glanced back, and caught a glimpse of daylight streaming through the ragged, flaming remains of what had been the front door.

Then they were down the corridor and into the study. Drake pushed Will behind the heavy curtain blocking the light from the single, full-length window.

"Stay here," he said, and Will saw the fury flickering like flames in Drake's eyes. "And whatever happens, don't move."

Chapter 21.

26 hours and 38 minutes left

Drake left Will behind the curtain and slipped on silent feet back towards the hallway. There were crunching sounds coming from the front of the house. He clutched his gun in both hands, and edged closer. He could feel another shoot-out coming on. The electricity in the air. The vibration of his blood that screamed *danger* at top volume.

How had this become his job?

He steeled himself, and crouched low to the floor. Closed his eyes for a second. Then propelled himself into the hallway.

Smoke.

Movement.

Masked figures in the entry.

Without thought, he fired four shots.

Two down.

Two retreating, darting sideways. No clear line of sight.

Drake yanked himself back behind the doorway,

breathing hard.

There was a muffled yelp from the kitchen. High pitched. Melissa? No. Younger.

Eliza.

Drake launched to his feet and sprinted towards the kitchen.

Then skidded to a stop, as he rounded the entryway, and saw a bearded gunman, crouched on the floor.

With Eliza in front of him. With a gun to her chin.

Eliza's eyes met his, the whites showing. Instinctively, he raised his hands, the pistol pointing to the ceiling. What was he thinking, getting these kids involved?

"Freeze."

The words came simultaneous with an explosion of pain to the back of his skull. The second assailant. The thought flickered through his mind as he collapsed to his knees, the world spinning around him.

Dimly, he registered a clunk. Felt the lack of weight in his hand. He blinked, trying to see through the fireworks clouding his vision, and saw his gun on the floor. Then saw the shape of his attacker loom in his periphery as he bent down to grab Drake's gun.

"Hello, Mr Policeman," he said, as he stood, now in front of Drake, the pistol in one hand, an assault rifle trained on Drake's chest in the other. He was leering all over his pockmarked face.

Drake raised a hand to the back of his head. His

fingers came away sticky and red. His eyes fixed on Eliza, behind Pockmark's legs. She was breathing fast, her chest heaving up and down. He tried to look reassuring.

"Where is the boy and the woman?" Pockmark said.

Drake shrugged. "Don't know what you're talking about." His voice sounded slurred, even to him.

Pockmark raised an eyebrow, then with a movement so fast Drake barely caught it, belted Drake across the jaw with the butt of the rifle.

Stars.

Pain. Pain *everywhere*.

Blood, metallic and thick, teeth jammed together.

When Drake got his eyes open again, he was lying on the floor.

"Right, well, let us search for them, then." Pockmark grabbed Drake by the jacket and hauled him up. The rifle helped Drake's motivation. He couldn't see straight, let alone work out which way was up.

"Stay here with the girl," Pockmark barked at his kneeling companion, setting the pistol on the bench beside the pantry.

The rifle between his shoulder blades, Drake shuffled from the kitchen. Pockmark jerked the barrel forwards, pushing Drake into the hallway.

There were almost-silent rustling noises coming from the study ahead. Drake blinked, trying to settle the world back into stability. William had better still be behind those curtains. Maybe the two of them could overpower Pockmark.

"Ah," Pockmark said, as they reached the study. "Come out, come out, little friend."

Drake scanned the room. No William. And no bulge behind the curtains that could be William.

But there was a small bin, smouldering, on the edge of the room. A bin containing a sleek, black laptop battery partially covered by licking, red flames.

"The cupboard," Pockmark barked, jabbing Drake forwards.

Heart racing, Drake jerked forwards and yanked the cupboard open. Had the bastard seen the bin? Or was he too focussed on finding William?

"Ugh," Drake moaned, listing forwards as the smoke filling the room started to take on an electrical twang. "My head. I don't think I can…"

He collapsed to his knees, landing inside the cupboard. He dragged the door half-shut as he fell.

"Get up! I will shoot you!"

Drake groaned louder, collapsing further until he was fully lying in the cupboard.

"GET UP!"

Pockmark jerked the rifle up, his face manic. Drake scrunched his eyes shut and curled, his hands clamping over his ears.

BOOOOOOM!

The room lit up, the flash red through Drake's closed eyes. An inhuman shrieking filled the air.

Drake booted the cupboard the rest of the way

open. Pockmark was screaming and on fire, as was the rest of the room. The bin had disintegrated.

Drake charged forwards and wrenched the rifle from his flailing hands.

"Roll," Drake ordered, stepping back, the rifle pointed at the still-dancing screaming man. "Roll!"

The second shout seemed to get through, and Pockmark collapsed to the floor, rolling back and forth until the flames were extinguished.

Drake pulled out the magazine and checked it – fully loaded – then reinserted it. "Now stay down," he barked at the burnt man. "And don't move."

*

BOOOOOOM!

Will flinched as the laptop battery exploded. He flattened himself against the wall of the spare bedroom, his heart pounding in his ears.

Then he heard Drake's voice. "And don't move."

Relief washed through him, and he darted into the hall, just as Drake emerged from the study. Drake's face slackened as he saw Will.

Will had taken one step towards him before the dark shape flew from the study behind Drake.

"Look out!" Will yelled. A blackened, charred thing in the shape of a man launched towards Drake, a knife glinting in its hand.

Drake spun, getting the rifle up as the creature hit him. There was a burst of explosive sound, a *rat-tat-tat* that punched holes in Will's ears, and then Drake and the burnt thing collapsed to the floor.

There was a beat of silence.

Then Drake shifted, groaning, underneath the now-limp monster.

Will charged forwards, shoving the man – it was a man, it was just a man – off of Drake. Bile rose in his throat. He just meant the battery to be a *distraction*. Give Drake the element of surprise to overcome the guy. But instead he'd done that. *He, Will*, had burnt that thing beyond recognition.

"Are you okay?" Drake rasped, struggling up.

Will swallowed, and nodded, hauling Drake up the rest of the way. Drake stumbled, falling heavily against Will, then righted himself.

"No!"

There was a scream from the kitchen, and Will's heart stopped. Eliza.

He took off, pushing past Drake's hands as he tried to grab him, pull him back. He careened around the corner.

And froze.

Eliza was standing. A man behind her had a pistol jammed into the underside of her jaw so hard her face was facing the ceiling. The man's heavyset arm was clamped around her torso, pinning her arms in place.

"Get back!" the man shouted, as Will appeared.

"Calm down, you're in control here." Will heard Drake say from behind his shoulder.

The men jerked, and the gun pressed harder into Eliza's throat. She made a gagging sound, and Will flinched. He had to stop him! Had to get his hands off her, before —

Drake grabbed Will, his hand a clamp on his shoulder, locking him in place.

And then something shifted, behind Eliza. Behind the man.

The pantry door exploded open, and suddenly the shadowy form of Melissa was flying towards the man. Something metallic glinted in her hand.

"Eliza, down!" Will dimly registered Drake's bellow.

The man half-twisted, as Eliza dropped her full weight and Melissa collided with him. There was a shot, and then another, louder, the sounds exploding and echoing and rattling in Will's brain.

Eliza, the man and Melissa collapsed into a tangled heap on the floor. Will yanked from Drake's grip and skidded to his knees, grabbing Eliza and pulling her towards him.

Blood. There was blood, on her, on the floor. Her eyes were glassy.

"Eliza! Eliza!" He heard his own voice, high-pitched, saying her name over and over.

She blinked. "Will," she said, and then she was crumpling into his arms, her grip locking onto him like she would never let go.

"Are you okay?" he said, his voice coming out half-strangled. She nodded, and great sobs shook her body. He held onto her, burying his face in her tangled hair. She was alive. She was okay!

"Eliza, are you hurt?" Drake's deep voice

punctured through the bubble around them.

"I'm fine," she gasped. She pulled away from Will and he let her go. "Is he – is he dead?"

Will tore his eyes from her and looked around. Melissa was sitting with her back to the cupboards in the corner of the kitchen, tears streaking her face. She held a pistol in her hand, the weapon dangling limply from shaking fingers. Beside Eliza, in a slowly spreading pool of blood, the man lay face-down. Drake was crouched between the man and Melissa, his fingers at the man's throat.

"Yes," he said grimly. He looked at Melissa, and she met his gaze, her lips trembling. Drake reached out, and took the gun from her.

"You did good," Drake said, his voice gentle. "You'll feel horrible, for a while. But you probably saved Eliza's life."

Melissa looked at Eliza and then at Will. Will felt shaken, empty and too-full all at once, and he dropped his gaze.

"Come on. We need to get out of here," Drake said, standing and extending a hand to Melissa. She took it, and he pulled her up, as Will and Eliza struggled to their feet. Will didn't let go of Eliza's hand even once he'd helped her up. He couldn't. Not yet.

"Get in Melissa's car. I'll meet you there," Drake said, his voice like iron. "Be ready to leave."

Melissa nodded, and beckoned Will and Eliza forwards, her hand still shaking. Will stepped carefully

174

around the blood as Drake bent to rifle through the dead man's pockets.

Will stepped through the blackened archway of the doorway, Eliza's hand in his. The afternoon sun was glinting off Melissa and Drake's cars, and he could hear birds chirping and singing in the bushland. His hair ruffled as a drift of breeze caught it.

He looked at Eliza. Her face was blank and stunned too, underneath the smudges of blood across her cheek.

He stopped, and reached his hand up to wipe it away. It wouldn't come off; it just smeared across her cheek in a dull red blazon.

"Come on," Melissa said.

A few moments later, Drake catapulted from the gaping doorway. "Go, go, go!" he bellowed, as he sprinted down the driveway.

Melissa jerked, slamming the car into gear as Drake yanked the passenger door open and threw himself inside.

"Drive!" he shouted.

Melissa floored it. The tyres screeched and gravel spat, and then they were flying down the road, the distance between them and Jeff's house growing. Ten metres. Twenty. Thirty. Fifty.

"Duck and cover!" Drake's voice echoed through the car.

BOOOOOOM!

A sound that turned the laptop battery explosion into a party popper shock-waved through the car. Will screamed, yanking Eliza down and shielding their heads with his arms.

A fraction of a second later, the car windows exploded.

Melissa shrieked, and Will smashed into Eliza as the car wrenched sideways. A moment later it righted, and through their tangled arms, Will saw Drake's hand on the wheel.

"Keep driving." Drake's voice was rough.

Will lifted his head. A smoky mushroom cloud was rising from where his uncle's house had been moments before. Fragments rained down on the road behind them.

"What did you do?" he shouted. Though the words tore at his throat, he barely heard them over the dully, tinny roar in his ears.

"I made a choice," Drake said, not looking back. His eyes were fixed on the road ahead.

"You blew up *Jeff's house*!"

"Which gives us some breathing room. My car's still outside, and it'll take them a while to identify the bodies. We're safe, for the time being."

He was crazy. No, scratch that: the whole *world* was crazy. "Safe? How the hell do you call *that* safe?" Will snapped.

Drake turned. "Because as far as the world's concerned," he said, his voice grim. "You, me, Melissa and Eliza: we're all dead."

Chapter 22.

23 hours and 4 minutes left

Drake checked them into a hotel, paying with cash.

"This isn't much of a hotel," Eliza said, as Drake unlocked the door to their dingy room.

Will glanced around. Stained carpet, two metal bunk beds with chipped paint and a tiny table. It wasn't exactly homey.

"If we're going to be dead, we go where they don't require ID," Drake said, a frown scored between his brows.

Slowly, as the afternoon turned to evening, the shock of what had happened began to wear off. Will found he could go longer and longer without glancing at Eliza to check that she was still alive.

"I need to tell my parents," Eliza said, as night fell and the room dimmed under the flickering light of the single uncovered bulb in the ceiling. "I can't let them think I'm dead."

Drake looked at her. "Not possible, I'm afraid."

"They'll… they'll be destroyed. I can't do that to

them."

Will hunkered against the back of his bunk, his arms slung around his knees. "She's right. We have to tell *them* the truth, at least." He felt cold at the thought of someone like Drake turning up at Eliza's house. Telling Abby that her daughter was dead. Amir wasn't even home. She'd be completely alone to take the worst possible news.

"I'm sorry, but no," Drake said. "Not until this is over. It puts your parents in danger, if they know. I really am sorry, Eliza, but until we solve this, this is the way it's got to be."

"Mum can pretend," Eliza said, her voice cracking. "She'll fake it like she thinks we're dead. They'll never suspect."

Drake shook his head. "I don't think anyone can actually understand how to fake that without... living it." He glanced at Will as he spoke, and then turned away. From her bunk, Melissa sniffed.

Eliza started to cry, and the silence was filled by her sobs for several long minutes. Will scooted off the bed, put his arm around her. But there was nothing to say. At least at the end of this, the horrible news would be undone. At least Abby and Amir would wake from this nightmare.

"Then let's damn well solve this," Eliza said, finally, her voice strengthening as she spoke. "Right now."

*

"Yes, but what does it *mean*?" Melissa said impatiently, not for the first time.

Will clenched his teeth. Between the four of them in the middle of the hotel table was a slip of paper, beside the fried chicken and sides they'd ordered for dinner. Drake had found the paper in the dead man's pocket.

Only problem was, it didn't *say* anything.

Will leaned forwards, a drumstick in his hand. His eyes scanned over the string of letters for the umpteenth time.

DROLBKFYLYWLSCVYMKDONKDDROLBS
NQONODYXKDOOKBVISPBOFOKVONAZWDR
OVSQRDCQYEZ

"If we knew that, we'd be back in business," Drake said, his tone clipped. "Run me through what we've tried already." He leaned back in his chair, his eyes closing and his fingers pinching the bridge of his nose.

Eliza flipped back through the notebook. "Backwards," she said. On the page, *ZEYQCDRQ* was written. "Every second letter, forwards and backwards." She flicked past *DOBF* and *ZYCR*. "Every third letter…" She flicked past a couple more pages then dropped the notebook on the table. "It's got to be some kind of substitution. We just need to know what the pattern is."

"That is the million dollar question," Drake said, without opening his eyes.

"Frequency," Eliza said suddenly. She stabbed the

slip of crumpled paper with one finger. "Will, find me a letter frequency table online."

With hurried strokes, she roughed out a table on the notepad, as Will tapped on his phone.

"Melissa, how many A's?" Eliza said, scribbling A to Z down the first column of her table.

Melissa ran a pen along the code text. "One," she said. Eliza wrote it down.

"And B's?"

A few minutes later, Eliza wrote two next to the letter Z.

"Right, Will: I get O, D, K and Y as the most frequent letters. What's your table say it should be?"

"So…" Will scanned over the table of English language letter frequency that he'd found. "Should be E, T, A and then O."

Eliza wrote the two sets next to each other.

ETAO

ODKY

"On this side, K is the fifth least frequently occurring letter," Will said. "But here, it's third. That doesn't make sense." His head swum, the letters all blending together.

Eliza traced her finger over what she'd written, from the E to the O and then the T to the D.

"How many letters apart are E and O?" she said.

Will counted. "O is ten letters after E."

"So maybe all the letters are shifted by a certain count," Eliza said, and Drake leaned forwards in his chair. "What about D and T?"

Will paused. "Sixteen."

Drake groaned.

"Wait. You counted forwards from E to O but backwards from T to D," Eliza said. "Go forwards."

"U. That's one," Will said. His brain hurt. "V. That's two."

Counting aloud, he kept going, but once he hit Z, he started back at A. "A is seven, B is eight, C is nine, and D is ten."

"Ten!" Eliza exclaimed. She grinned, some of the worry chased away.

Will grinned back. "And the others?"

A minute later, they'd confirmed it.

"Ten from A to K," Will said.

"And so is O to Y," Melissa added.

"Swap it in," Drake said. He was leaning forwards on the table now, the fingers of one hand tapping up and down.

Eliza transcribed the code, underlining the decoded and replaced letters.

TRELB̲A̲FO̲LO̲WLSCVO̲MATE̲N̲A̲TTRELBS
NQ̲E̲N̲E̲TO̲X̲A̲TEE̲ABVISPBE̲FE̲A̲VE̲N̲A̲ZWTR
EVSO̲RTCQ̲O̲EZ

"Need more letters," she said. "Here. Everyone get to work. Shift each letter by ten." She tore three sheets from the notepad and thrust them in front of Will, Drake and Melissa.

Minutes later, she wrote a new line of text on her page.

THEBRAVOBOMBISLOCATEDATTHEBRID

GEDETONATEEARLYIFREVEALEDQPMTHE
LIGHTSGOUP

"Chuck lines in for spaces," Will said.

THE | BRAVO | BOMB | IS | LOCATED | AT | THE | BRIDGE | DETONATE | EARLY | IF | REVEALED | QPM | THE | LIGHTS | GO | UP

All four of them sat back, staring at the page.

After a long silence, Drake spoke. "So we have a bomb at a bridge. But when? And what bridge?"

"Bravo bomb?" Eliza said. "Is that a type of bomb? And what does QPM mean?"

"Bravo as in alfa, bravo, charlie, delta – the phonetic alphabet?" Drake said. "But QPM – maybe it's a typo."

"Could be an acronym," Will said.

Eliza nodded, her own phone out already. "I've got Quality Program Manager," she said, scrolling the list. "Quality Protein Maize… Quarterly Projection Model… Queensland Premier Mines…"

Drake shook his head.

"Oh… uh-oh," Eliza stopped and looked up at Drake. "Queensland Police Museum. But a museum? Who bombs a museum?"

"Uh-oh indeed," Drake said flatly, staring into space. "The museum's on the ground floor of our police headquarters in the city. If you got a bomb in there, you could take down the whole building."

"But stations have security to stop that sort of stuff, right," Melissa said.

"It's not technically part of the station," Drake said. "It's open to the public. Any Joe Blow can just stroll on in. And... and part of it is under construction at the moment. There's crates, workmen, all sorts of stuff going on. Who knows who's been in and out. Or what they've stashed there."

"You have to warn them," Will said. "Evacuate the building, the entire area."

Drake shook his head again. "They'll be watching the building," he said. "Anything suspicious happens, they'll blow it for sure." He scratched at the stubble on his neck. "If that's the target, they've picked it well. The building's packed with police in town for the fireworks festival on Friday night."

He sighed, looking around at each of them. "I'll have to find it tonight. With the counters. If I go in stealthy, I can disarm it without them realising."

"We can help," Will said, and Eliza nodded.

Drake shook his head. Something flickered across his expression then was gone. "Not this time. If for no other reason than a couple of kids snooping around after hours makes things more suspicious."

"Then I'll come," Melissa said.

Drake smiled, lopsided, at her. "I need you to be the backup plan," he said. "If something goes wrong, as it most likely inevitably will, you need to get the word out."

She nodded, her face pale. "We've got backup emergency broadcast equipment at my office. I can set a broadcast to go out to all the TV and radio stations."

Drake nodded. "Right. I'll drop you off on the way." He stood, and Melissa followed suit. Drake shoved the two Geiger counters into his pockets and headed for the door.

"Wait," Eliza said, standing as Melissa went to follow. She put an arm on Melissa's arm. "Thank you. For what you did. Back at the house, I mean."

She pulled Melissa into a hug. Over Eliza's shoulder, Will saw surprise flicker across Melissa's face, and then she put her arms around Eliza and squeezed.

"No problem," she said, her voice husky.

Will swallowed. His eyes met hers as Eliza let go. "Yeah," he said, and he stood too. "Thank you. Really."

She nodded, her eyes glistening.

Will nodded awkwardly back. He wasn't up for hugs. Not yet. But as Melissa turned and followed Drake from the hotel room, his eyes followed her. She'd loved Jeff too. Maybe that was somehow... something that he could consider important.

Chapter 23.

A shrill electronic whining stabbed into Eliza's brain.

"Argh," she moaned, tugging the pillow over her head. "Not time to get up yet."

"Hello?"

She heard Will's bleary voice answer the phone. Then she realised that the pillow over her head wasn't hers.

Because she was in a hotel, with Will. Letting her parents think she was dead.

A horrible, sinking, dread-filled feeling pooled in her, sucking her limbs heavy to the bed.

"What do you mean, no bomb?"

She scrunched her eyes, and flicked the pillow from her face. Propping herself up on one elbow, she faced Will where he sat, half-naked and mostly tangled in sheets, on the opposite bunk. His face was twisted in a puffy-eyed scowl, the phone pressed to his ear.

"What does that mean?" Will said, his voice bleary. There was another pause, then he nodded.

185

"Okay. See you soon."

He hung up and peered at her. "There's no bomb at the museum," he said, voice flat. "And no radiation signature. Drake searched the entire station."

Her stomach flipped. "Then what does QPM mean?"

Will shook his head. "I don't know. Drake's coming to get us so we can split up and hunt."

Triangulation methods and search grids immediately flickered through Eliza's mind, followed by the circle-marked map. Maybe, with enough readings, they could cross-reference the bomb's position in the same way that earthquakes were triangulated. But where to start? There were so many circles. Did they all represent bombs?

She sighed. "It's going to be like looking for a needle in a haystack."

Will stood, tugging his rumpled shirt on. "I know. But what other choice do we have?"

*

In the front seat of Drake's police car, Eliza flicked the tablet screen, zooming in on the aerial map. "This circle is centred on the city," she said. "We should split up along this line. Will and I can take this half of the circle, and Drake the other."

Drake just grunted. If it were possible, he looked even worse than he had the day before. His eyes were ringed in bruise-like shadows.

"Did you sleep at all?" she said, flicking the tablet screen off and peering at him.

"Doesn't matter," he said, his voice gruff.

"It does if you jam the car into the river because you fell asleep at the wheel."

"I'm fine," he barked. "So we take these readings. Then what? We know where the bomb is?"

"It won't be exact," Eliza said. She quickly marked up the map with digital pen marks and sent Drake's search area to his phone. "But it might give us an idea." She sounded more confident than she felt. She glanced back at Will in the rear vision mirror. He looked back at her doubtfully, but nodded.

"Right," Drake said, pulling the car to a stop. "Meet you back here when you're done."

*

"This is the first location," Eliza said, lifting her eyes from the map.

Will nodded, and switched on the Geiger counter. As the device powered on, the screen displayed various text and numbers before beeping and displaying *Test Ready*. Will pressed the test button.

"Forty-three," Eliza read off the display. She tapped it into the tablet.

"Is that good? Bad?"

"I don't know," Eliza said. "High is bad. But all these people here – " She waved her hand around at the variety of hawkers' stalls. "They'd have been here all morning, and they don't look sick."

"Right," Will said, but he didn't sound sure.

"This way next," Eliza said, pacing ahead. After a few moments, she broke into a jog. Everything felt urgent, and she could see in Will's face that he felt the same. How much time left did they have?

She paused beside a large pit in the ground where the foundations of a new office building were being laid.

"Thirty-eight," Will said. "Similar."

Eliza nodded, keying it in. "Okay." They broke into a jog again.

"How are you feeling about... everything?" Eliza asked, panting, a few moments later. Will didn't answer for a second. His eyes were on the ground as their joggers slapped on the pavement.

"I don't know," he said finally. "I still... can't believe he didn't tell me."

"He was trying to protect you."

"But I wouldn't have cared. I would have been... well, happy for him."

"Maybe he didn't know that."

Will sighed. "Yeah. I guess not."

"She seems... like she really cared for him."

"I guess."

Eliza glanced at him. "I think she's hurting. Bad."

"So am I," Will said, his voice suddenly tense.

"I know," she said quickly. "All I mean is that she didn't tell you to hurt you. She's grieving for him too. And you've got to know Jeff wasn't keeping it from you to be mean. He just... made a call about what he thought would be the best way to protect you."

Will was silent. After a moment, Eliza signalled a stop and he took another reading.

"I do know that," he said, as they kept going, following the curved route she'd marked out through the main streets and back alleyways. "I guess I'm starting to see that he was *always* doing that. The best he could, given the circumstances."

"Yeah. Definitely."

"And not just for me, too," Will continued. "I mean – he was trying to save people. He was trying to stop… all this." He waved his hand around the city, encompassing the whole huge mess they were in. "He was trying to stop something terrible, and he was killed for it." His voice cracked at the end, and he sucked in a deep, shaking breath.

Eliza swallowed. "He gave his life trying to save Brisbane," she said softly.

They jogged in silence for some time.

"That's something, I guess," Will said, and he shot her a weak, watery smile.

"Yeah," she said, and returned the smile. "It definitely is."

*

After what felt like forever, they backtracked to their starting point. Drake was waiting on a park bench.

"Got 'em?" Drake said as he stood.

Eliza nodded. She plopped down on the bench and Drake read out his set of readings, while she added them to the map.

"One side has stronger readings than the other." Will pointed, as Eliza zoomed back out from the last data point. "So it's on that side?" He looked between

Eliza and Drake. "That's a whole lot of city to search."

"It's not just closest to that reading," Eliza said. "But also furthest from the weakest reading, over here." She pointed to the opposite side of the circle, then ran her finger in a line from the weakest to the strongest reading. A small thrill of success rippled through her. "The bomb has to be on this line."

With quick strokes, she selected a line drawing tool and marked it in.

"If the coded note's accurate, then a bridge is involved," Drake said.

"The line crosses the Goodwill bridge," Eliza said, her voice pitching high in excitement. Then her eyes traced the line further from the circle. "Oh. And the Green Bridge, on the other bend of the river. And a rail bridge, further along."

"Flip a three-sided coin?" Will said.

Eliza's brow scrunched. "Wait. Radiation levels follow an inverse-square law."

Will looked at her quickly, then at Drake. "That's right. The professor said, remember? The further away you are, the weaker the readings get."

"So we double the distance from the source, the levels drop by a factor of four. Not two," Eliza said. She scrolled back to the circle and the readings. "The strongest reading is ninety-eight and the weakest is twenty-seven. That's a factor of…"

"About 3.63," Will said, his phone out in a flash.

"We want the square root of that," Eliza said.

"1.9," Will said. "So…"

"The weakest reading is a bit less than double the distance from the radiation source compared to the strongest reading," Eliza finished.

Drake raised his eyebrows. "Which is how far?" His voice was strained with exhaustion.

"How big is the circle?" Will squinted at the map.

"About five hundred metres across," Eliza said. "So the distance from the strong reading *plus* five hundred metres is 1.9 times the distance from the strong reading. So divide five hundred by 0.9, Will."

"Five hundred and fifty-six metres," Will said.

"So the Goodwill Bridge!" Eliza said, flicking the map. She looked up at Drake and Will. Unable to help herself, a smile broke over her face.

"How certain are you?" Drake said, still impassive.

She looked down at the tablet, running through the process in her mind, checking. "It's not exact," she said. She zoomed in on the circle. "The readings on either side of our bridge line aren't symmetrical, for example. And they should be. They're higher on this side. But the sensor could be faulty."

"If you had to bet a whole lot of people's lives on one of these three bridges being the one, you'd pick Goodwill?" Drake said.

A chill rippled through Eliza. She scanned over the map again, triple-checking what they'd done. After a moment, she looked back up at Drake. "Yes. I'd pick Goodwill."

Drake nodded.

"So we call the troops in on Goodwill," Will said.

Drake shook his head. "They'll be watching. If they suspect anything, they could detonate."

"Then what?" Eliza said.

"Three presumed-dead people – we might be able to slip in under the radar. They won't be expecting us."

"How long do you think we have?" Will said, as they headed back towards the car parked on the other side of the road. "Before they plan to detonate."

"I honestly don't know," Drake said, shaking his head. "There's commuters going to and from work in the morning and afternoon, so maybe 5:00 PM when everyone's going home from work. Why else a bridge?"

Tyres squealed and a horn blared. Eliza flinched and jerked around.

Will was standing in the middle of the road behind Eliza, his face ashen white. A car, its tyres still smoking, had come to a stop centimetres from his legs.

"You bloody idiot!" The driver was leaning from the window, screeching.

"William!" Drake said, striding back and grabbing him by the shoulder, dragging him to the curb. "Are you blind? You almost got flattened!"

"Are you okay?" Eliza said, gripping Will's forearm as Drake released him. Behind them, the car drove off, the driver still yelling obscenities.

"You said 5:00 PM," Will said. "PM."

"Did the car hit you?" Drake said sharply, stepping close to Will and peering closely at his eyes.

"I'm fine," Will said, brushing him away. He met Eliza's gaze. "I know when they're going to detonate the bomb."

Chapter 24.

5 hours and 10 minutes left

"Give me the code." Will waved his hand at Eliza and she slapped the notebook on his palm.

"I'm heading for the Goodwill bridge," Drake said. He wove quickly through traffic, the car picking up speed. "Enlighten us on your brainwave."

"QPM isn't a place," Will said. "They're not going to code two locations into the same message, right?"

"And there was no bomb at QPM," Drake said.

"Exactly. So QPM is a time. As in, *PM*. As in, a time after midday."

"So the Q is a number," Eliza said. Her eyes lit, the whirring of her brain almost visible, and Will nodded.

"A single digit number."

"But *what* number?" Drake said. "It doesn't work under the substitution method that decoded the rest of the message."

"Yeah, well, we just have to work out how they've coded the time," Will said. "Eliza?" He turned to her.

Codes were her thing, always had been.

Eliza grabbed the notebook back and ran a finger along the sentence. Will could see her lips moving silently. Then suddenly, she grinned. "ASCII character codes," she said.

"Meaning?" Drake barked.

"Every letter, number and symbol has a numeric code called an ASCII code associated with it," Eliza said. "The twenty-six letters of the alphabet are represented by the codes sixty-five to ninety. But there's also codes representing *numbers themselves* – the digit zero in code is forty-eight, all the way up to nine, which is coded as fifty-seven. We only used the alphabet codes when we decoded the message."

Will nodded, the system clicking into place. "So when we decoded AZW to QPM, we counted backwards by ten in the alphabet codes."

"The character code for A is sixty-five," Eliza said. "Counting back ten from that gets us to code fifty-five, which is the digit seven. *7 PM!*"

She scribbled on the notepad then held it up to Will.

THE | BRAVO | BOMB | IS | LOCATED | AT | THE | BRIDGE | DETONATE | EARLY | IF | REVEALED | 7PM | THE | LIGHTS | GO | UP

Will's heart thudded. He glanced at his watch. "So we've got five hours to sort this out," he said.

Drake grunted something unintelligible, and pulled the car into the entrance of the university Will had visited with him the day before. It was the easiest access point to the Goodwill bridge.

"What's the fence about?" Eliza said.

Drake glanced at her. "Fireworks festival." He pulled to a stop beside the security gate.

Ice cold dread suddenly broke over Will like a waterfall.

The fireworks festival.

"Tickets can be purchased at the main gate," the guard said, without looking up.

Drake held up his badge.

"Oh," the guard said. "In that case, I suppose it's free." He peered suspiciously at Will and Eliza.

Will stared at the festival fencing that encompassed the university parklands. The festival. That was it. That had to be it.

"You on duty here tonight?" the guard said.

Drake shook his head. "Just running some checks."

"The campus is being cleared at 5:00 PM," the guard said. His voice was disdainful, like he suspected Drake was sneaking his kids into the festival without paying.

Drake nodded. He revved the car, and the guard leaned back into his hut, a scowl still on his face. The boom gate lifted.

As soon as Drake hit the pedal, Will blurted it out.

"Drake. The festival. That's what they're timing it for," Will said, leaning forwards. "They're going to set it off when the university is *packed with people for the fireworks festival."*

The car jerked as Drake slammed the brakes. He twisted in his seat. Looked at Will for a long, hard second, his face ridged. Then he looked forwards again. His knuckles were white on the steering wheel. "Not if we've got anything to do about it," he said, his voice like cold iron.

A few minutes later, they parked in an empty below-ground parking lot, just in sight of the bridge.

"We'll walk from here," Drake said, slinging the bag holding the radiation counters onto his shoulder. Will and Eliza followed him up several flights of stairs and onto an elevated walkway. At the end of the walkway, more stairs led down to a path to the bridge.

He paused, turning to scan the buildings. "There," he said, pointing at the top of a decrepit building about fifteen storeys high. "We'll have a better view from there."

He strode towards the building's automatic glass doors, but the doors didn't open. Drake stepped back and forth a few times, trying to trigger the sensor, a scowl engraved on his face.

Drake banged on the door of the building. "Hello? Anyone home?"

"Maybe we can find another – " Will started, then Eliza called out.

"There's a notice," she said, pointing to a red sign beside the door. "The building's scheduled to be demolished."

"Well, then," Drake said. He cleared his throat,

and glanced around, before looking between Will and Eliza. "Now, I don't want either of you thinking that this is appropriate, but we're pressed for time – "

With a short, sharp movement, he jerked his pistol from its holster and rapped it handle-first against the glass door. There was a crash, and the door shattered inwards.

"Whoa," Eliza said, raising her eyebrows. "That's one way to open a door."

Drake grunted, and stepped through the broken glass. He hit the lift button in the foyer.

"How does it feel, to be a badass?" Will said, as Drake punched the button again.

"It feels like every day of my life," Drake said, deadpan. Will barked a surprised laugh.

"Lifts aren't working," Eliza said, hiding a smile. "I guess that's part of the demolition criteria."

Drake swore and strode towards the door marked *EXIT*. Eight flights up, Drake stopped.

"We should be high enough," he said, and led the way through a large, open-plan office to a row of windows, smashing one again when the rusted metal mechanisms failed to let him get the window open. Glass tinkled onto a narrow concrete ledge below the window.

Below them, pedestrian paths criss-crossed a grassy area leading to the bridge.

"If there's really a hundred tonne bomb, there's only a few places it can be," Drake said. He tugged a small scope from his belt. "Look for big objects in plain sight – trucks, water tanks, crates – anything that could hold explosives."

"Could it be in the water?" Eliza said. "Attached to a bridge pylon, or something?"

Drake shook his head. "Too visible, and the tides would make it impossible to secure. And putting it underwater is a sure way to muffle the power of the bomb. It'll be on land. Keep looking."

A few minutes later, Will pointed. "What about there? Just back from the bridge." Rough, industrial-looking fencing encircled the base of the bridge.

"It's a construction site. There's some demountable offices, and a dozer. The dozer's jammed into one of the pylons," Drake said.

Will squinted. "Give me the scope for a second."

Drake handed it over.

"There's no windows," Will said. "And no air conditioning units. I don't think they are offices."

"Give me that," Drake said, snatching back the scope. Then he lowered it, his face blank. "You're right. They're not. They're containers. Shipping containers painted white to make them *look* like demountables." He looked quickly between Will and Eliza. "And there are five of them. Just like the five shipping containers I saw video of rolling out of a warehouse two days ago." He cursed. "It's them. It's got to be them."

Fear and something hot and bright like anger, only more intense, flooded through Will. "What do we do?"

There was a loud click as Drake pulled back the breech on his gun, pulling the magazine out and examining it. "We need to take out whoever's on site down there, before they get bomb-happy. *Detonate early if revealed*, remember?" He glanced at Eliza. "I need you to be lookout. Stay up here and signal us."

"How?"

Drake held up a fist. "This means *stop and stay still*." He brought his hand up to his eyes. "*I see*." Next he wrapped the fingers of one hand around his wrist. "*Enemy sighted*. Follow that by pointing at where they are, and use your fingers to indicate how many. And this is *I understand* or *Acknowledge*." He finished with his hand up, his forefinger touching his thumb to make a circle.

Eliza nodded, her face tense.

"And William – "

"Will," Will interrupted. "You can call me Will."

Drake shot him a glance, then nodded, something flickering in his eyes. "Right. Will. I need you to be decoy," he continued. "Out front. Distract them, so I can sneak in the back."

"Whoa, wait a minute," Eliza said, holding her hands up. "You can't put him out there, with who-knows-how-many armed terrorists! It's too dangerous!"

Will swallowed, looking out the window towards the containers. "I'll be fine," he said. At least Eliza would be safe, up here.

"What if you're not?" Eliza said, her voice

pitching. "You could get *killed!*"

Drake pursed his lips. "I'll have eyes on him the whole time," he said. "I won't let anything happen."

Eliza looked between Drake and Will, her face pale. "No. No, Will, you can't."

He stepped towards her, and put his hands on her shoulders. She was shaking. He cleared his throat, pushing past the terrified lump there. "I've got to," he said. "We've got to step up. You know we do. We're the best and only option for making sure thousands of people don't die tonight."

"I just don't want *you* to die tonight," she whispered.

Will blinked, his eyes stinging. "I won't."

"No one's dying tonight," Drake said. "Except them." He jerked his head towards the containers.

"We need to interrogate them," Eliza protested, shaking her head. "You can't just keep killing them all or we'll never know how big this thing is."

Drake's jaw visibly clenched. "The only times I've killed anyone has been when they've been trying to kill me, or one of you," he said. He glanced between Will and Eliza, and his jaw unclenched. "But yeah. I'll try to take them alive."

Chapter 25.

4 hours and 49 minutes left

Will crouched and retied his shoelace while watching the entrance to the construction site. Ahead, Drake disappeared out of sight down the path.

Glancing back, he could see Eliza's face at the broken window. He forced a smile, then stood and looked at his watch. *1:30, 1:29, 1:28...* he had just over a minute.

He paced towards the gate. A distraction. What was he supposed to do? Pretend he'd left something inside the site? Dance a jig?

His foot clinked against something hard. He looked down. An empty beer bottle.

He smiled. Okay. He could work with that.

A minute later, he reached the gate. There was a massive padlock on it. He glanced back at Eliza. She pointed inside the site and held up four fingers.

Will swallowed. Two on four. That wasn't terrible odds, right?

Then Eliza shifted her hand, pointing further

back. And held up two more fingers.

Will's heart skipped. Two on six. Still. Drake was a cop. He was a badass. They could do this.

He threw the bottle over the gate and hauled himself up after it, ignoring the thrumming of his blood.

He jumped down on the other side, his eyes darting. No one there. He grabbed the bottle, and walked deeper into the site, swaying and stumbling.

He passed a ute filled with construction cones and signs, then wandered around the corner of the first container.

His head jerked, as hands grabbed him from behind. There was a metallic boom, and an explosion of pain as he was thrown face-first into the container wall. Then the hands jerked him backwards and suddenly he was face down in the dirt.

He coughed, dust clogging every orifice. He struggled for breath, feeling something jagged beneath his palm. The bottle had smashed.

He struggled, but something hard slammed into his back, pushing his face back into the dirt.

"Enough," a man's voice said.

The weight disappeared, and Will, fear pulsing, rolled onto his back.

Four men in yellow and red construction jackets stood around him.

All of them held rifles.

And all of them were pointed at him.

One of the men grabbed him by the shirt and

pulled him to his feet. Will's body screamed, every fibre yelling at him to run. But he forced himself to go limp.

"You guys got any beer?" he slurred, wobbling back at forth and peering owlishly at the men as if they weren't pointing weapons at him.

The man still holding his shirt laughed, and said something unintelligible to the others.

Will pretended to see the broken bottle. "Aw, man, there was some drops left in that." He crouched as if to pick up the bottle and stumbled.

"Get rid of him." The voice came from the same man who'd told his companion to let Will up. Evidentially he was some kind of leader in the group.

Two of the others grabbed him by the shoulders and hauled him to his feet. They started to drag him towards the gate.

Relief washed through Will. He made himself heavy, and one of the lackeys grunted. They were just going to toss him out. Had he given Drake enough time to get in undetected? It would have to do.

"Idiots," the leader said. "Get *rid* of him. He's seen the guns."

Will's stomach sank like a stone. The men holding him stepped back, and he turned, wobbling.

"You guys cosplaying for the festival tonight or something?" he said, hitting the slur hard. "Good costumes. Love it, man, just love it." He reached forwards, as if to touch the gun of one of the lackeys. Maybe he could yank it from the guy's hand.

But the lackey just swatted him back and raised the gun to point at his head.

"Quietly. And away from the gate," the leader said.

The two grabbed him.

"Hey, what's going on man, I just wanted – " Will protested. Panic rose inside him. "Look, let's just talk about this – "

A backhand across his cheek stunned him into silence. When his vision cleared, the leader was standing before him, his face impassive.

Will gave up all pretence and thrashed. But the men holding him were too strong. Someone kicked his legs out from behind, and then he was in the dirt on his knees.

And the cold metal of a knife pressed against his throat.

"Hurry up," the leader said. He sounded almost bored.

Pain lanced through Will's throat. He squeezed his eyes shut. This was it. He was going to bleed out in the dirt and that was it, the bomb would go off and everyone would die, and he'd be there waiting for them on the other side –

Suddenly, there was a muffled cry from deeper in the site. Then a grunt from behind Will.

And the knife was gone.

Will rocked forwards as the man behind him crumpled to the ground, the knife falling and landing point first in the ground.

In front of him, the leader shouted in another language, raising his rifle and spinning away from Will.

Will gasped, diving to the dirt and grabbing the knife. As he moved, the leader's head snapped back, spraying blood through the air.

"Drop your weapons!"

Drake's voice boomed through the site, and hot, glad relief boiled through Will. He scrambled away from the remaining two men, as they stepped back towards the gate, rifles swinging into the air. One of them sprayed the site with bullets.

"I said drop them!"

The man just extracted the magazine and rammed home another, yelling something at the other man. Together they raised their rifles.

POP POP! POP POP!

Simultaneously, the two men crumpled, rifles empting into the air. Will dove for the ground and held his arms over his head.

There was a beat of silence.

"You okay?" Drake shouted.

Will uncurled. Drake was jogging, in a kind of lop-sided stumble, from behind a bullet-riddled crate marked with an explosive symbol.

"You're bleeding," Drake said, as he reached Will.

"I'm okay," Will said, reaching up and feeling his neck. Apparently his jugular was intact, because he wasn't gushing blood everywhere. "I think."

Drake kneeled and peered at his throat. "It's not deep."

Will nodded, feeling weak. He leaned against the container, and Drake slumped beside him.

Will sucked in a breath. Then looked over at Drake.

"Holy crap," he said. Fear reared again. "*You're* bleeding." Blood was spreading through his shirt just above his belt.

"Bastard winged me as he went down." Drake winced, fumbling with the buttons of his shirt before giving up and yanking it up instead.

"Oh crap," Will breathed. Blood was spurting out of a tiny hole in bursts.

"You got them!" Eliza's voice echoed across the site. There was a metallic rattling as she jumped from the gate.

"Give me your shirt," Drake said, and Will yanked it off, as Eliza appeared around the corner of the containers, Drake's bag bouncing against her hip.

"Oh god! What happened?" She didn't wait for an answer before skidding to her knees beside Drake, her hands helping him to clamp the wadded shirt over the wound.

"Get my belt around it," Drake said.

Working together, Will and Eliza yanked his belt from its loops and buckled it around the makeshift bandage.

"Tighter," Drake said.

Will grimaced, and pulled. Drake's head dropped and he groaned, his chest heaving. After a few seconds, he looked back up, panting softly.

"Right. We need to secure the site." He pushed himself upright then went to stand. "There could be more of them hiding."

"You need to lie still until the ambulance gets here," Eliza said, her voice shaking. She pushed him back against the container then tugged her phone out.

"No," Drake said, snatching for the phone.

"Drake, you need an ambulance!" Eliza exclaimed.

"I've been shot before," he grunted. "We don't know who's straight and who's crooked. There's a hundred tonne bomb sitting here, just waiting for one of these bastards to realise that we're onto them. We've got to disarm it before they work that out."

"You're crazy," Will said. "How long you think you're going to last without medical attention?"

"I'll still be alive in another hour," Drake said. With a ragged grunt, he got to his feet. He waved back in the direction of the waiting rides and food stalls. "We have to make sure all the people coming here are, too."

Chapter 26.

4 hours and 17 minutes left

"Oh my god," Eliza said, as the container door squeaked open. Her heart raced. Barrels packed the interior, each covered in a square metallic crate.

Will crouched. "Ammonium nitrate fertilizer. In the barrels, at least."

"What about the crates?" Eliza reached forwards and touched the closest one.

Will shook his head, his face confused.

There was a rapidly increasing beeping from behind them.

"Get out!" Drake barked.

Eliza jerked her hand back as if the crate was red hot. Spinning, she saw the Geiger counter in Drake's hand. And the flashing red light on top of it.

Her heart leapt into her throat. She grabbed Will's arm even as he spun to push her back towards the door.

They tumbled out, and Drake slammed the door shut. Eliza half-stumbled, half-ran, Will and Drake following her, away from the container.

"The crates," Drake said. He leaned against a ute parked a short distance from the containers. "They contain the Cobalt-60."

Eliza sucked in a shuddering breath. "We'll get sick if we go in there again. How are we going to find the detonators without going near the crates?" An image of the dying boy Namir in his hospital bed flashed across her mind. How much radiation had their cells already absorbed? How much more, just by standing here?

Drake frowned. "We need to dose up."

He rummaged in his bag before pulling out two different-coloured blue vials and a small card. He handed them to Will, then straightened stiffly.

Eliza saw the pained look that crossed his face. "You need to sit down," she said, grabbing his arm as he wobbled. "Or you're going to fall down."

Amazingly, he didn't argue. As she lowered him to the ground, she took a quick look at the wadded up t-shirt. Blood was spreading through it. A spike of cold fear ran down her spine. He said he'd be fine. But how long did he really have, if he didn't get medical treatment?

"The card's got the dosage concentration," Drake said.

"What is it?" Eliza peered at the bottles in Will's hand. Each bottle was marked with a series of evenly spaced lines.

"Prussian Blue," Will said, frowning at the card.

"The professor we saw here gave it to us." He glanced at Drake. "It says we need a ten percent solution. But this one's fifty percent, and this one's two percent." He held up first the dark blue bottle and then the light blue.

"What happens if we get it wrong?" Eliza said. She took the card from him.

"The professor said it becomes volatile," Drake said. "Meaning it – "

"Could blow us up," Eliza finished. She swallowed, and glanced at the containers. "Well. We need to add the dilute solution to the strong one to get it down from fifty to ten percent."

"Here," Will said, thrusting the bottles at her. "You do it. You're way better at chemistry than me."

She held the bottles gingerly. "It's all math, Will. You realise that, right?" Her heart pounded. What if she got it wrong? She glanced around. "I need something to write on."

"Here." Will scooped a stick from the dusty ground then scuffed at a patch between them until it was roughly smooth.

Eliza crouched. "Each vial contains the chemical diluted with water. The fifty percent solution – it's half-water, half-chemical."

Will nodded. "So we need to mix enough from each vial such that the chemical amount in the two separate solutions is the same as in the mixture afterwards."

Eliza nodded. "And the amount afterwards has to

be at ten percent dilution." She scratched in the dirt.

$$0.5C + 0.02D = 0.1C + 0.1D$$

"Total chemical before," she said, pointing at the left. "And total after in the mixed solution at ten percent concentration." She looked up at Will. If there was anything she trusted, it was her ability to solve an algebraic equation. But this wasn't class, where the stakes were measured in letter grades. This was... way more dangerous.

Will nodded. "Looks right."

"So we need..." She scribed a few more lines.

$$0.5C - 0.1C = 0.1D - 0.02D$$
$$0.4C = 0.08D$$
$$5C = D$$

"Five times as much of the dilute vial as the concentrated one."

Will nodded again.

"Are you sure?" Drake said. He was leaning back against the tyre of the ute, and his eyes were closed.

"Yeah," Eliza said, standing. Her eyes flicked over the calculation. She met Will's gaze. "Here goes nothing."

She passed him the light blue vial, then unscrewed the dark blue one. She took a deep breath, then tipped the bottle sideways. The blue liquid trickled out in a thin stream onto the dust.

She stopped when there was only enough liquid in the bottle to reach the bottom marker. Will opened the dilute solution, and with trembling hands, he topped up the bottle until the mixture reached the sixth marker.

Tentatively, Eliza screwed the lid back on. The liquids roiled for a few seconds before settling to an azure blue colour.

Drake opened his eyes blearily. "Drink it quick, before it goes unstable."

*

Eliza's arms burned as she heaved another barrel out of the shipping container. It pitched over the edge and clanged into the barrels already lying in the dust, then there was a second clang as the one Drake was heaving out of the container beside hers collided with it.

He leaned against the door. Eliza frowned. His chest was heaving and his hand was pressed tight against his stomach. He looked up and saw her gaze, and straightened, his lips tugging into a lop-sided smile as he turned and disappeared back into the container.

She sighed, and flexed her arms as she retreated back inside her container. She started to tip the next barrel onto its side and then froze.

There was a small plastic box wired to a metal cylinder attached to the side of it.

"I think I found one," she shouted, backing away. Moments later, Will and then Drake hauled themselves into the container.

"Radio transmitter and detonator," Drake said, shifting awkwardly to peer at the underside of the box. "But luckily, a simple one. As long as you know what to cut." With steady movements, he clipped the wires joining the box to the cylinder with a pocket knife. Then he ripped the box from the barrel and crushed it under his boot.

"That's the easy part," he said. He slowly slid the cylinder out of its holder and stood up.

"Are you going to crush it too?" Eliza said.

Drake wobbled down to the ground again. "The detonator's packed with explosives, and ultra-sensitive. If I stomped on it, it would blow my leg off." Instead he carried it to a concrete pipe lying on the ground by the bridge pylon. "That'll contain it for now. We need to find more, though."

Eliza glanced at her watch. "Drake, you sit. Will and I will search."

Again, he didn't protest. The fact filled her with an urgent, panicky fear. Will met her gaze, his face tense.

An hour later, Eliza jumped from the fourth container, as Will emerged from the middle one.

"Another one," he said, holding up a detonator cylinder.

Eliza nodded. She glanced towards Drake. He was slumped on the ground by the ute, eyes closed.

"Drake," she called, but he didn't move. "Drake!"

He opened his eyes, and relief washed through her. Will finished adding his cylinder to the other three in the concrete pipe then joined her crouching beside him.

"How many?" Drake said.

"One per container," Will said.

"They're consistent then, at least," Drake said. "One container to go?"

Eliza nodded.

"Good," Drake said, and frowned. On his lap was the remnants of one of the plastic transmitters stripped from the detonator. He was rolling the wiring through his fingers.

"Are you okay? You'll make it until we finish the last container?" Eliza said.

Drake waved his hand. "I'm fine," he said. "It's just... this is all a little too easy."

Will scoffed. "Easy like the six guys you took down?"

Drake stared at the containers. "Why is there no failsafe to stop us doing exactly what we just did?"

"Maybe they thought they were in the clear," Eliza said. "If they have someone on the inside, then maybe they're underestimating the police force's ability to stop them."

"They've been thorough so far," Drake said. "This doesn't match up."

"How many guys were at the port?" Will said.

"More than six," Drake said quietly.

Eliza's eyes flicked over the bodies still lying where they'd landed on the dusty ground. She swallowed hard.

"Then we should finish the last container," she said, fighting to keep the tremor from her voice. "Before the rest of them show up."

Chapter 27.

2 hours and 44 minutes left

Eight storeys up, Adam watched the construction site through a handheld scope, his elbows resting on the sill of the smashed window he'd discovered on this floor. There was movement down there. But it wasn't the six men Danial had said would be there.

Ayman was dead. On finding out, Danial had sent Adam instead to act as backup at the site. The damn fool had blown himself up in the explosion at the analyst's house. Ayman had always been too prone to grand displays of violence. And this was how Danial's trust in him had played out.

It didn't matter now. Adam was the right choice for Danial's new number two. He always stayed calm. He always got the job done.

He reached for the sniper rifle leaning against the wall beside him and screwed the scope into its bracket. He raised it to the window and sighted along it, but whoever was in the site had disappeared, obscured by a building.

Something was wrong. That much was obvious. The container doors were open, and there were barrels on the ground in front of all the containers but one.

A gust of wind blew in through the window, stirring up the rubbish on the floor around Adam. He leaned out, and placed the rifle on the concrete ledge outside. Then he stepped through the frame. The ledge was just wide enough to fit his feet side by side.

Another gust of wind whooshed past and he swayed before grabbing the frame. Right on the broken glass. A burning sting lanced through his palm, but he swallowed the pain, his face a mask.

He slipped easily into a prone position on the ledge, then, after grabbing the rifle, started to crawl.

When he reached the end of the ledge, he shuffled until the rifle was wedged into his shoulder. Now the entire site was visible.

He swung the rifle, his eye to the scope.

His heart thudded in his throat. A man in a fluorescent vest was lying face-down, dark red turning the dust to mud around him. Adam's eyes flicked over the shock of blond hair.

Phineas. Danial had left him in charge of the guards.

Adam swallowed a curse.

Suddenly, two figures appeared, jumping from two of the middle containers. He swung the scope over them.

Kids. It was two bloody *kids*.

They walked towards the ute. And then Adam saw another form, sprawled against the tyre, his body limp but moving as the kids approached.

Adam's eyes narrowed. "You are supposed to be dead," he said under his breath.

It was the cop. The one who Ayman had, supposedly, blown up. As the kids crouched beside him, it clicked. The boy: it was the analyst's nephew.

He pulled back from the scope. The shot was not an easy one at this distance. It would be preferable to engage the man at close range. But this cop was not to be underestimated. The port fiasco had shown that. Most of Danial's team had made it out, but only because they had the element of surprise.

He returned to the scope and flicked the rifle's safety switch. The kids were on either side of the cop; the girl was getting up while the boy still crouched. He swung the scope sideways until he could see the closest shipping container and lined up the scope's mil dots with the edges of the container. 2.59 metres in height exactly.

Moving carefully so as not to dislodge himself from the narrow ledge, he tugged a card from his breast pocket and ran down the column of numbers. It was 265 metres to the shipping container. So a couple less to the cop. He dialled in the range.

And he lined up the reticle on the cop's head.

He breathed in, then out.

In, then out.

When his lungs were empty, he froze. And his

knuckle whitened, as he pulled the trigger.

*

Will felt a hot splatter on his cheek. His hand whipped to his face.

Red.

Blood. His?

No. No pain.

Movement at his side. Drake was crumpling to the side in the dirt, his eyes rolling back into his head.

Will's heart froze.

"What was that?" Eliza's voice shattered the silence. There was a clang, and then she screamed.

"Get down!" Will yelled, launching his body onto Drake's. He grabbed him under the armpits, and heaved.

He was too heavy! Will gasped, and there was another metallic crack as something – a bullet, it was a bullet, they were being shot at – collided with the ute behind him.

Then Eliza was there and grabbing Drake too and finally he started to shift.

"Is he dead? Is he dead?" She was shouting it over and over.

Will couldn't answer. Everything he had was going into dragging Drake towards the closest container.

CRACK!

A puff of dust.

"Get him inside!" Eliza yelled.

Grunting, shaking, every muscle in his body screaming, Will heaved Drake onto the container floor. Eliza scrambled up behind, shoving Drake's legs inside and then hauling the door closed.

It shut with a resounding clang. There was darkness, and silence, broken only by the sounds of their ragged breathing.

"Is he dead?"

"I don't know," Will panted.

He heard a half-sob, half-curse in the pitch black. There was another metallic clang on the outside of the container, and Will flinched, grabbing for Eliza.

"Are you okay? Did you get hit?"

"No," she said, her voice breathless. He heard her suck in a deep, shuddering breath. "There's a light switch in here somewhere." The warm presence of her beside him disappeared.

A moment later, Will blinked as the container was flooded with light. He hauled himself up, and crouched over Drake.

"He's breathing," he said, relief washing through him in a hot wave. "But unconscious."

Eliza kneeled at his head, her fingers gingerly poking at his hair. Her fingers came away bloody. "It's skimmed the top of his head. There's a gash. But that's it."

"Holy crap." Will sank back. "That's so lucky."

Eliza glanced at him, her face tense. "I don't know. He's unconscious. Imagine the pounding his brain's taken even from a glancing hit." With jerky movements, she ripped off a strip of fabric from the bottom of her shirt and wadded it against Drake's head.

"Here," she said, grabbing Will's hand and pushing it to the wound. "We need to stop the bleeding."

She pulled her phone from her pocket and swiped the screen on.

"Wait." Will grabbed her hand. "You can't."

"We have to. Drake needs medical help, *now*."

"There's still a detonator in the fifth container. You don't think whoever's shooting at us has a remote to set it off?"

Eliza's face twisted. "We can't deal with this on our own, Will. We need... professionals. Back-up. People who know what they're *doing*."

"As soon as the sniper sees cops and ambulances showing up, he'll set off the bomb," Will whispered. She had to see that. "While there's still a detonator in there, we can't call anyone."

Eliza was silent for a long moment. She looked to the closed door then back at Will. "So what do we do? We can't leave him like this – "

"We're not going to," Will said. "The shots must have come from that derelict building. It's the only one tall enough to see the site. You stay here, and stop him bleeding as best you can." He paused. He couldn't believe what he was about to say. But what choice did they have? "I'm going to go get the sniper."

"*What?*"

"We don't have a choice – "

"You're assuming it's *one guy*. What if it's not? And even if it is! You're going to get yourself killed! No, Will, we need to find that last detonator and then call the cops!"

"There's no time. I'll be careful. I'll sneak up; he won't even know I'm coming."

"And what are you going to do once you get there?" she snapped. Her face was flushing red. "What, just attack him like you're Arnold Schwarzenegger?"

"I don't know. I'll work something out." His pulse raced. What indeed? She was right. He wasn't a cop, wasn't a superhero. He was just... Will.

He stood, his hands clenching into fists. If he didn't do this, neither of them were going to get out of here alive. His eyes flicked over Eliza's strained face, the tousled mess of her half-unwoven plait.

If he didn't go, then she would die here.

"I'll be fine. I promise." He forced confidence into his voice, to convince himself, as much as her.

She stood too, her face still twisted in some combination of anger and fear that sent a pang of pain through the core of him.

"If you don't come back, I'm calling the cops," she said.

He shook his head. "No. Run, down to the river. Swim as far as you can. Drake said the water would absorb the energy from the blast."

She glanced down at Drake, and he saw the thought flicker across her face as if she'd spoken it aloud. She wouldn't leave Drake, or Will, behind.

He reached out, taking her hand in his. "Please. Promise you'll run."

She nodded, but he could see the lie in it. The placation. She was not the kind of person who would leave a wounded man behind, whether it cost her life or not.

He pulled her tightly to him, his arms wrapping around her, and buried his face in her hair. She hugged him tightly back.

"See you soon," he said, drawing back.

She nodded again. And before he could lose his nerve entirely, he slipped from the container door and ran.

Chapter 28.

2 hours and 36 minutes left

Will ran.

A bullet hissed into the dirt at his heels. Ahead he glimpsed his target: a drainage ditch running beneath the fence.

He dove. He flew through the air and landed heavily, every bone in his body jarring. Without stopping to think, he scrambled forwards, wedging his body through the narrow space beneath the fence. The fence scraped along his bare back, but he ignored the pain and forced himself through.

He crawled out, covered in mud, elbows, belly and back grazed and stinging, everything hurting. The building was ahead of him, but only the base was visible: the top was hidden by the awning of an empty coffee shop.

If the sniper couldn't see him, surely he'd stop shooting? As he got up and charged forwards, snippets of movies and comic books flashed through his head. Run in a zigzag. That was how you confused shooters, right?

The shattered glass door was just metres away now. He forced every ounce of energy into his legs, and then he was inside, skidding on the broken glass and grabbing the doorhandle of the stairwell to yank himself in.

He ran up the first few flights of stairs, every echoing footstep a shot of burning fear through his spine. At the fifth floor he paused and listened.

Silence.

He took the next flight at a tiptoeing run. Listened again.

Still silence.

Another flight, and another.

Now there was a breeze, whistling through the stairwell door, jammed slightly ajar.

He stepped from the landing into the corridor. Immediately he recognised the floor he'd gone to with Drake and Eliza. The construction site was on the right.

He swallowed and tiptoed forwards. He could hear nothing but his heart thudding in his ears. Was it possible there was only the single sniper?

When he reached the office, he could feel the breeze whistling in through the shattered window.

There was a crack, followed by a distant metallic clang.

Will flattened himself against the wall. The sniper was in there, somewhere. Outside the window? Hadn't there been a ledge?

He needed a weapon. His eyes darted, then stuck on a fire extinguisher mounted to the corridor wall. He hefted it from its hook and swung it experimentally. It could work. It was heavy, at least.

He took one step into the office. The breeze picked up, and dust swirled into the air from the abandoned desks and filing cabinets.

Will froze.

A red line had appeared in the dust in front of his chest. His eyes followed it to a black box attached to the wall. And to another, identical, on the opposite wall.

Gingerly, he looked down. There was another red line reflecting off the dust at waist height, and another at his ankles.

A light gate. Some kind of warning trigger, for whoever was out there.

He stepped back into the corridor and sucked a deep breath. So much for sneaking up on them from behind.

The laser beams were growing fainter as the dust settled back down. Within moments they were invisible, as the last of the dust fell.

Will gripped the fire extinguisher. Gravity. That was his only other option.

He turned and paced back to the stairwell.

By the time he reached the fifteenth floor, he was panting. He heaved the extinguisher out of the stairwell and onto the rooftop. Then, steeling himself, he jogged for the concrete barrier at the edge of the roof.

He peered over the edge.

Seven storeys down, a man clad in black was lying prone on the thin ledge encircling the side of the building. A sniper rifle was nestled at his shoulder, and he had his eye to the scope.

Will's eyes flicked along the ledge. At the other end, he could see broken glass from the window. And something small, and black, like a television remote.

His heart thudded. Was that a remote for the detonator?

He turned, and ignoring the burn in his arms, hauled the fire extinguisher to the top of the barrier. With both hands, he held it out in the air.

Above the sniper's head.

"Drop the gun!" Will bellowed, as loud and deep as his voice could manage. His arms were already shaking.

The sniper jerked, and he craned his neck upwards. Will saw the twist of a snarl on his lips.

"Drop the gun or I'll drop you!" he yelled again.

The man looked back towards the broken window, then back at Will. "I don't think so," he shouted.

Suddenly, the rifle was pointing up.

Will yelped, and jerked backwards as something hissed past him. He toppled to the roof, the extinguisher on top of him.

He shoved it off and scrambled up. The man was crawling along the ledge towards the broken window, pushing the rifle in front of him.

"Stop!" Will yelled. "I'm not joking. I'll drop it!" He hauled the extinguisher back to the barrier.

The sniper glanced up at him, then turned back to his slow progress along the ledge.

"Please," Will said, softer now. Under his breath. The ground swam below him. It was so far down. The man wouldn't stay on that ledge for long with an extinguisher to the head. "Stop!" he yelled. "Freeze, or I'm dropping it!"

The sniper looked up again. "I'm going to kill them first," he called. His voice was chillingly cold. Flat. Lifeless. "And then I'm going to kill you."

He kept crawling. He was halfway back to the window already.

Frantically, Will looked back to the stairwell. He'd never make it back down before the man cut him off. And then his eyes were drawn to the construction site. Eliza would be still inside the container with Drake. But what difference would that make once this guy got there with his rifle?

He gritted his teeth. "Last chance! Please, stop!"

The sniper didn't even bother to look up.

Damn it. *Damn* the stupid idiot. Will clenched his teeth, then heaved the extinguisher along the barrier as he drew level with, then overtook, the man's slow crawl below.

Seven storeys.

Three metres a storey.

Twenty-one metres.

Five metres in the first second.

Fifteen metres in the second after that.

He slowed, until he was leading the gunman by a couple of seconds. The extinguisher dangled over the edge, swinging gently.

"Please," he said, but his voice cracked this time and he couldn't tell if the guy even heard him. "Stop."

The sniper was almost at the end. His hand opened, and he reached for the black remote.

Will shut his eyes. And opened his fingers.

The extinguisher dropped silently through the air.

The man's fingers closed on the remote. He lifted it, and turned as if to look at Will.

The extinguisher crunched into the side of his head. Blood spurted, splattering across the ledge.

There was a garbled scream, and the remote dropped, bouncing on the ledge. The rifle skidded and fell, end over end, chasing the extinguisher as it continued its journey to the ground.

The man clawed at his head, struggling to his knees on the narrow ledge. Blood poured from between his fingers.

BOOOOOOM!

An explosion rattled the windows. Will ducked instinctively, then lurched forwards. The remote? Had he pressed it?

The man twisted on the ledge towards the site, and his knee shot out over the edge. As it went, it knocked the remote flying into the air.

For a moment the man swayed.

His arms windmilled.

And he began to tip backwards.

He looked up. His face was stuck in a confused, blank rictus.

And he fell.

The remote fell through the air beside him. A second, passed, and then another.

And then he thudded into the ground.

Will's stomach heaved, and he retched, his vision blurring with burning, stinging tears.

The crumpled form on the ground didn't move.

And then a scream drew his eyes upwards to the construction site.

Smoke was billowing from the fifth container.

Chapter 29.

2 hours and 24 minutes left

For a second Will was frozen. Was that it? The bomb, blown by the last detonator?

But no: he could see the container still, through the smoke. The barrels on the ground. Surely it'd all go up at once, if the sniper had hit the button?

And if not, what had happened?

Will, we need to find that last detonator.

Eliza's voice echoed in his ears, and cold flooded his body.

What if she'd gone in there, alone, and found it? Drake said they were ultra-sensitive. What if she'd tried to disarm it… and failed?

He turned and ran, almost dislocating his shoulder as he smashed the stairwell door open. Down the stairwell and out the shattered door.

Past the bloodied, twisted body of the shooter. As he pelted past, he thought he heard a groan, but he didn't slow. No time to think about that now.

He reached the gate and vaulted over it, his hands

and feet finding footholds faster than conscious thought.

The door to Drake's container was open, and Drake was slumped against the wall. Will's chest lurched but he saw that Drake's eyes were open.

"Will – " Drake's voice was hoarse. "Explosion. Last container. Eliza – "

Will didn't wait to hear the end. He kept running, towards the smoking door of the fifth container. He jumped for the door, but his feet slipped in the loose dust and he pitched sideways into the dirt instead.

"Will?" He heard Eliza's voice, weak, from inside.

She was alive! He pushed himself off the ground. As he did, his hand hit something hard. A thick black cable, half-buried in the ground. It was coming from a hole in the floor of the container, and trailed to one of the black cylinders elevating the container off the ground.

He hauled himself through the door. "Eliza?"

It was shadowed inside, the light swimming murkily through the slowly dissipating smoke. There was a crack and a flash, and he ducked, as the smashed overhead light sent a shower of sparks over him.

"Will," she repeated. Her voice was coming from beyond the barrels. The barrels that were criss-crossed with a dense web of black wires. Black wires which were each attached to a detonator cap.

One on every barrel.

Will's heart froze. The other shipping

containers... there had been only one. There was only meant to be *one* detonator in each container.

He pushed through the wires, searching for Eliza. There must be hundreds of detonators in here. How would they defuse them all in time?

Then suddenly, there she was. Huddled on the floor, her back to him.

He twisted between the barrels to get to her. "What happened? Are you okay?"

She turned, looking up at him. Her face was milk-white beneath tiny tracks of red that streamed from a dozen tiny cuts all over her face. All over her neck and throat.

"No," she whimpered. "None of us are okay."

He realised she was curled around her left hand.

"Let me see,' he said, but she just sat there, shaking. "Eliza, let me see," he repeated, more forcefully.

She squeezed her eyes shut. With tiny, pained gasps, she pulled her left hand from her lap.

Will chocked back a gasp. Her hand was limp and flopping, and bleeding from a myriad of little gashes. She cradled it in her right hand like it was a dying animal.

"It's broken," Will said. Distantly, he was shocked at how even his voice sounded. Like it was totally normal that her hand suddenly appeared to be devoid of bones and cartilage. "You'll be okay. Come on. You need to get out of here."

She shook her head.

"You're in shock." He tried to get his arm behind her, to lever her out of the tiny space, but was terrified of hurting her more. "Come on."

"No time," she said softly, her voice flat.

She was staring ahead into space. No, not into space: at the barrel in front of her.

Where a tiny computer screen was counting down.

5:58.

5:57.

5:56.

Will closed his eyes. The world seemed to stop for a moment, everything silent, but for the almost-inaudible *beep*, *beep*, *beep*, of the seconds passing.

Then he opened his eyes. "Tell me what happened," he said.

She swayed, and he grabbed her around the waist, holding her up. "I was trying to find the last detonator," she said. "But there's…" Her eyes flicked around the room. "I pulled one," she said. "I thought if I started ripping them off the barrels maybe I'd get all of them in time…"

"But it went off in your hand?"

Eliza nodded, her eyes slipping closed. "I realised a second before it went and jerked my hand away, but…"

Will gritted his teeth. "Drake!" he bellowed, at the top of his lungs. His voice echoed and bounced off the metal walls, and Eliza flinched, her body curling around her hand again. "If you can move, we could use some god damn help!"

234

He tightened his arm around Eliza's waist. "I'm sorry," he said, and steeled himself. "We've got to get you out of here."

He pulled her to her feet. She cried out, her whole body tensing, but managed to stay upright.

"So there was a fail-safe circuit." Drake's voice, strained and rough, came from the door.

Will glanced up. Drake, pale and shaking, had his hand clamped on the doorframe, and with a great shudder, hauled himself inside. Will saw his eyes fix on the glowing red display on the barrel. "Remove a detonator from here and it sets off the timer. Then this container sets off the other five."

Will focussed on dragging Eliza back into the wider space before the door. "Yeah," he grunted, as he helped her to sit again, her back against the wall. "So what do we do about it?"

Drake leaned over the display, his fingers running over the numeric keypad below it. "It's lucky you didn't set everything off," he said.

"I don't feel lucky," Eliza murmured. Her head listed back against the wall. Will swallowed. Her skin was clammy. She was in shock. She needed a doctor.

"We need to run," Will said. "Get as many people away from the site as we can – "

Drake shook his head. "No point. This'll take out half the city, and irradiate the rest. We're not getting anyone far enough away in five minutes."

"Then you disarm it!" Will's voice cracked.

"There's a passcode input," Drake said, frowning

235

at the display, which now read *4:54… 4:53*. Will tore his eyes away.

"It's a four digit code," Eliza whispered. "There's ten thousand combinations. You'll never get close."

"Start at the start, I guess," Drake said, and he typed *0000* on the keypad. There was a discouraging beep and the four zeros disappeared, replaced by the time. He typed *0001*.

Beep.

4.48.

"That's not going to work," Will said. His voice grew louder. "Drake. We have to run."

Drake ignored him, punching *0002* on the keypad.

"Drake!"

"You two get out. Drive away anyone you can find. This is our only chance," Drake said, without looking up.

Will shook his head, his teeth gritted, but turned and hauled Eliza to her feet, his arm around her back as she cradled her hand to her chest.

"What about you?" Eliza said.

Drake turned, and his eyes flicked between her and Will. Something flickered across his face, clear as if he'd spoken the words aloud.

It didn't matter.

None of them would get far enough away anyway. If Drake failed to guess the code, then it was all over.

"Come on," Will grunted. He hauled Eliza out of the door. They couldn't just give up now. He had to at least try.

236

She yelped as they hit the dirt, then stumbled, her foot catching the cable Will had fallen on before.

"What's that?" she panted.

Will tightened his arm around her and pushed her towards the gate. "There are wires attached to the supports under the container," he said, brusquely. He counted in his head, matching pace to the timer that Drake toiled worthlessly over behind them.

"Why?"

"I don't know! Come on, we need to – "

But Eliza jerked from his arm and turned back towards the container. She was on her knees beside the support cylinder before he could grab her again.

"Eliza, we need to – "

"Look!" she exclaimed, her fingernails tearing at the black cylinder. Beneath the black paint, the barrel was green.

Like the barrels that littered the ground around them, and filled the container above.

"Fertiliser!" she said, rocking back on her heels. "It's more fertiliser. Drake!"

He appeared at the door.

"Drake. The supports are more explosives. We're at a low point here, next to the river," Eliza said, her breath coming fast. She waved her hand around at the mangrove trees that bordered the site, and then at the bridge. "And it's uphill the other way." She waved her hand inland. "If the bomb goes off down here, then the explosion gets wasted on the hill and the trees."

Drake jumped down, his face tense. "So they've

rigged the supports to pop the bomb up into the air."

"Like a landmine?" Will said.

Drake nodded. "The largest landmine the world's ever seen. Ready to rain down destruction from the sky." He glanced at Will. "How much time left?"

Will scrambled inside. "Three minutes!" He launched himself back down onto the dirt.

"Okay. Okay," Drake said, his eyes darting around. "There!"

He started half-limping, half-running towards a wooden crate with an explosives symbol stencilled on the side. Will ran to follow, grabbing Drake's arm over his shoulder and half-carrying him the rest of the way.

"Tell me what you're thinking!"

"Excavation explosives," Drake said, tugging a yellow box from the crate. Inside, nestled in foam padding, were two clear plastic tubes, one filled with a bright blue liquid, the other red. "Mix them, pour them into a drill hole, make the drill hole bigger."

He held the two cylinders and looked at Will. "We're going to blow up the bomb with another bomb."

*

"We need exactly eight parts red to one part blue," Drake said. He was kneeling beside the container. In Will's lap was a copper pipe he'd dragged from a pile, the same length as the gap between the two rear supports.

"So you're going to use this little bomb to blow

238

the big bomb *up* and into the river?" Eliza said.

Drake nodded. "A bomb this size: we're talking a fireball with a radius of thirty metres. In the river it'll detonate safely. It won't set off the other four." He stuffed foam padding into the end of Will's pipe, then held the red liquid up.

"Wait," Eliza snapped. "You need to measure it."

"Running out of time, here," Drake said, his voice terse. "How?"

"You need to add the exact right amount of blue once you're measured the red."

"I'll just add it bit by bit until it blows," Drake said grimly. Then he paused, and looked at Will and Eliza. "You two should go. Now."

"No," Will said. "We just need something we can fill up eight times. Like a bottle. Or a can, or something. There'll be something here!"

He jumped to his feet, and Eliza copied him. He ran, eyes scanning the ground. How was this the world's tidiest construction site? Didn't these bastards drink water, or anything?

"There's no time!" Drake's voice bellowed after him. "You two need to get out of here!"

"We're not leaving you!" Will yelled back. He reached the ute.

And saw the construction cones in the back.

"Here!" he said, grabbing one. "Hold on!"

He skidded to his knees beside Drake.

"This will work," he said. "Quick."

Drake tipped the tube up and emptied it into the

239

cone. Will held the cone up against the sun and scratched a mark at the liquid level.

"I need something to measure halfway between my scratch and the tip of the cone," Will said.

"Here," Eliza said. She was tugging at her shoe and in a moment had the shoelace out. As she handed it to him, Will tipped the red liquid carefully from the cone into the copper pipe, then dropped the cone onto its side. Glancing at Eliza first, he stretched the shoelace from the tip of the cone to his first mark. Then he doubled it back and scratched a second mark.

Eliza nodded. "That's it."

"I think we're about to have company," Drake said, tilting his head. Will paused.

Sirens.

And they were getting louder.

"Then even more reason to hurry," Will said grimly, and held the cone upright again, letting the sun shine through the coloured plastic.

He grabbed the blue liquid from Drake and started to tip it into the cone.

"Slowly," Eliza said.

Will let the stream die down to a thin trickle, until it reached the halfway mark he'd scribed.

"Okay," he said softly, and lowered the cone. "That's the right amount."

Drake took it from him. "Start running," he said, his eyes meeting first Will and then Eliza's. "Head for the gate."

Will nodded, and pulled Eliza up beside him. "See

you outside," he said, his voice shaking.

Drake nodded. "I'll be right behind you. Now go."

They ran.

Eliza yelped and stumbled, and Will hauled her upright, his arm locked around her middle. He glanced back. Drake was tipping the cone into the pipe, his body poised to thrust it between the two supports of the container.

"Go!" Drake's voice chased them as Will hit the gate. He and Eliza threw their combined weight against the sliding metal frame.

It wouldn't budge.

"Harder!" Eliza gasped.

Then Drake was there, and he catapulted against the frame, and suddenly it was moving and all three of them were tumbling through.

"There!" Drake boomed, charging forwards, pushing both of them towards a concrete bench seat. He shoved them both behind it then collapsed to his knees beside Will.

"It didn't go off – " Will started.

CARUMPHHH!

Two jets of fire erupted from beneath the container, throwing the end up into the air. For a split second the container flexed in the middle, before the far end lifted off.

The container rose into the air, spinning end over end towards the river. Then it fell, smacking flat on the river with a crack that echoed off the bridge and buildings.

For a long, silent moment, it floated.

Then one end pitched, sinking into the water. The far end followed.

And a few seconds later, all that was left were bubbles.

"Oh my god," Eliza was gasping, over and over, under her breath. Will went to stand, but Drake grabbed him.

"Don't move!"

The river surface flashed white, the light spreading outward from the rising bubbles.

An enormous ball of roiling water burst into the air. It rose ten, twenty, thirty metres, then paused. Then, like a breaking bubble, it collapsed, great globules cascading back into the river.

There was a beat of silence. Mist rose into the air.

"We did it," Drake said, his voice low, barely more than a whisper.

"We did it?" Eliza said, turning first to him and then to Will.

"We did it!" Will stared at her, and then he bellowed, everything exploding out of him in a great cry of victory that made Drake wince and Eliza break into great breathless sobbing laughs.

"Down on the ground, now!"

Will froze, his arms above his head like a victorious gymnast. Drake stood slowly, turning.

Two police officers were in combat stance behind the open doors of their squad car. And their pistols were aimed right at them.

"Wait a second," Drake said, and reached into his pocket. "I'm an officer – "

He grunted as something thwacked into his chest. Slowly, he collapsed to his knees.

Without thought, Will grabbed Eliza, darting in front of her.

Fire exploded in his ribs, smashing the breath out of him. He gasped, folding, his legs crumpling from beneath him. A black fabric blob bounced onto the ground in front of his eyes.

"Don't move!"

He heard Eliza keening out in pain, the sound almost inhuman. And then someone grabbed his wrists and wrenched them back. Cold handcuffs clicked shut, pinching and biting.

"Her hand's broken!" Will gasped. "Don't hurt – "

"You are under arrest!" A gruff voice cut him off. "You are not obliged to say or do anything unless you wish to do so, but whatever you say or do may be used in evidence. Do you understand?"

"Under arrest for what?" he managed through the dirt and grass jammed into his face.

"National security," the voice said. "And if I were you, I'd keep my mouth shut."

Chapter 30.

2 hours and 8 minutes left

Ten minutes later Will was frog-marched from the squad car and into the looming police headquarters. He twisted, trying to see Eliza. At the bottom of the stairs, she was being hauled out of the second car. On her hand was a thick splint, secured with wide Velcro straps up to her elbow.

"Eliza!" he called, but the two officers straightjacketing him shoved him forwards.

"Eliza's hand's broken," he said, stumbling. Fear shot through him. Her face was still pasty white, and she was wobbling even between the two officers holding her. "And Drake's been shot. They need a doctor."

"Worry about yourself, kid," one of the officers said, a middle-aged man with a close-cropped steel grey beard.

Several floors on the lift and two windowless corridors later, Will was shoved into a tiny room. The door slammed shut.

Will sucked in a breath and then another. There was nothing in the room except a grey metal table and a few chairs. His hands were still cuffed behind him. Awkwardly, he tried the doorhandle.

Nothing. He was locked in.

Where had they taken Drake and Eliza? He slid down the corner of the wall and tried to find a position where his shoulders didn't feel like they were being dislocated, and closed his eyes.

He shivered, the smooth rendered wall sucking the heat from his bare, grazed back. He saw the face of the sniper, turning upwards. The extinguisher slamming into him. The slow topple of the man off the ledge... the twisted form on the ground.

He scrunched his eyes shut and rocked his forehead onto his knees. Nausea roiled and he struggled against it. After a moment he got control of himself again. He felt like he was vacillating back and forth: all at once horribly, horribly aware of what he'd had to do, but at the same time, like he was a player, controlled by someone else, outside of him. Because how could any of this really have happened? Had he really just stopped a bomb from destroying Brisbane? Had he really just... *killed* someone?

This kind of thing didn't happen to people like him. It didn't happen to anyone. Not here.

There was a click, and the door swung open. A young officer stepped through, her brown hair in a neat ponytail. She set a bag of fast food on the table.

"Here," she said brusquely, beckoning him. When

he got up, she spun him quickly and removed the cuffs, then waved at the table. "Eat." She slapped a folded white t-shirt on the table.

Will tugged the shirt on, wincing as it slid over the grazes on his stomach and shoulder blades. "Where are my friends?"

"The feds will be in to question you shortly," she said in clipped tones, and stepped back out through the door.

Will gritted his teeth. He wrung his hands around his wrists, massaging the bite of the cold metal away. After a long moment, he sighed, and sat, pulling a burger and chips from the bag.

When he was done, the door opened again. Two officers with AFP logos on their uniforms entered. One, a middle-aged woman with a shock of curly red hair, was holding a thick pile of papers, and the other, an older man with a scar above his eye, was holding a laptop.

"You are William Roberts, of 13 Park Place?" the ginger-haired woman said.

"Yes," Will said.

"Formerly in the care of Jeffrey Roberts, deceased?" the scarred man said.

Will nodded. "Where are Eliza and Drake?"

Ginger peeled the top page off her stack and slid it across the desk. "How about you tell us what this is all about?"

It was the aerial map from the mystery drive on his computer.

"One of the circles is located right where we found you," Ginger said. "You, plus about eighty tonnes of explosives."

"My friends need medical attention," Will said. His voice was hard. "Where are they?"

Ginger suddenly banged her fist on the table. "You need to realise the seriousness of the trouble you're in here, William," she said. "*You're* the one you should be worrying about."

Scar made a placating movement with his hand. "Paramedics have assessed Eliza Carrolson's injuries and stabilised them sufficiently for questioning."

"So start talking," Ginger said, her voice sharp. She tapped her fingers against the piece of paper. "Tell us about the map."

"You realise we're the good guys, right?" Will snapped. "We just disarmed a bomb that was going to kill thousands of people. Ask Drake. He'll tell you."

"Sergeant Wessley has been sedated and is on route to the hospital for surgery," Scar said.

Will glanced down at the map then back at Ginger. "The bad guys are still out there," he said, struggling to keep his voice even. "You're wasting your time with me."

"A dead cop and six dead construction workers were found at the scene," Ginger said sharply. "Shot by Drake's gun."

"They attacked us – "

"Because you were trying to set off the bomb?"

"No! We had to – " He stopped, heart racing.

"Look. Drake's wounds didn't come from *construction* workers. Those men shot at us. And there was a sniper. In one of the buildings. I knocked him off the ledge."

Ginger glanced at Scar then back at Will. "Blood was found near the building, but there was no body," she said.

"No," Will shook his head. "There had to be. The guy was on the ground... all twisted up." The image flashed painfully again. Burnt into his memory forever.

"William," Scar said, his voice firm. "How about you start at the beginning. Tell us everything you know. Leave nothing out, and let's straighten out what exactly is going on here."

Will was silent for a moment, looking between them. Then, he sighed. "Fine." He stared Ginger in the eye. "Three days ago, someone murdered my uncle."

He told them about Jeff's disappearance. About Drake and Melissa showing up. At first, Ginger wrote notes, her hand moving quick over the page as Will spoke. But when Will told them of the attack at Jeff's house, she sighed, and put her pen down, crossing her arms.

After about ten minutes, he stopped talking. For a few seconds there was silence.

"Well. That's quite a story," Scar said. He scratched the side of his mouth, then picked up the notepad. "So why... call this bomb the *Bravo* bomb?

248

Why'd you think these terrorists didn't call it Alpha, for example?"

"I don't know," Will snapped. "Alpha, bravo, omega – whatever. They probably just needed a name."

"And the disappearance of the sniper you killed? Any theories on that?" Ginger said.

"I don't know!" Will exploded. "He got up and walked away? Isn't that your job to find out? You should be out there searching for him, instead of wasting time here. The only reason we had to do *any* of this is because of the traitors in *your* police force!"

Ginger's face reddened. "Don't presume to know what we are and are not doing. Techs have taken the electronic signature of your hard drive and are running traces right now. There are dozens of officers in the field rounding up hundreds of suspects – "

"Right," Will said. He felt hot all over, and sick. "What sort of tests are you running then? You guys are *always* up to date with the hackers, obviously."

"The department here is state-of-the-art – "

"You're probably running an off-the-shelf tracker," Will said. "Probably paid ten times as much as you should have, for software that was already three years out of date when you bought it. I bet the company that sold it to you showed you some pretty amazing performance figures. What is it, ninety-eight, ninety-nine percent accurate?"

Scar raised an eyebrow. "99.9%, actually."

"Great," Will said. "That's the sort of irrelevant

figure the software companies pitch to make your IT departments feel good."

"The suspects we're rounding up right now says otherwise," Ginger snapped.

"Uh-huh," said Will. "So you ran a 99.9% accurate test on what, a million computers in Brisbane? You know what 99.9% accuracy gets on a million people who are almost all completely innocent? A thousand innocent people. But hey. Good luck with that, while the real terrorists slip through your fingers."

Ginger opened her mouth but Scar put a hand on her shoulder, murmuring something. She sat back with a huff of breath, her arms crossed tight across her chest.

"Let's talk about these earthquake readings that Eliza and…" He squinted at the page of notes between him and Ginger.

"Melissa," Will snapped.

"Yes, Melissa. That Eliza and Melissa were given at the embassy."

Scar tugged a slip of paper from the stack. "Based on these aftershock readings, you and your friends decided that this training camp was testing bombs." He slid the paper across the desk. Will recognised the seismology graph Eliza and Melissa had brought back with them. "Is that because one of you is a qualified seismologist?" Scar spoke overly-politely, the sarcasm barely hidden.

Will stabbed his finger on two spikes of the graph. "These aren't aftershocks. They're occurring too frequently. The 2.8 was a fifty tonne test explosion."

"So you said," Scar said. "And the bigger spike, the 5.3, that was one hundred tonnes. About the size of the bomb we found *you* with."

Will ground his teeth at Scar's tone. "Look, Eliza's been obsessed with earthquakes forever. They're not aftershocks. Get a scientist in here if you don't believe me."

Scar just raised an eyebrow. "Let's skip ahead to how you found the bomb. You went out with a couple of Geiger counters and got a reading on its location? You somehow managed to narrow down the location to *the exact spot* the bomb was located, in the whole of Brisbane city, just with two old counters?"

"Geiger counters don't work that way," Ginger snapped, before Scar raised a hand to quiet her again.

"We didn't just go out and wander around with them, if that's what you mean," Will said.

"Humour me," Scar said. "And talk us through it."

Will sighed roughly. "I need the tablet that was with all this." He waved his hand at the paper from the embassy and the circled map.

Scar nodded at Ginger, who left before reappearing a moment later with the tablet in a bag labelled *EVIDENCE*. Will navigated to the map screen with the readings, and spun it to face the officers. Quickly he explained how they'd identified the bridge.

Ginger scoffed. "Conveniently works out just right, doesn't it."

251

Scar was frowning down at the screen. "These numbers aren't *just right*, actually." He glanced at Ginger. "I used to be a teacher. I could always tell who was cheating, who'd made it all up, because their numbers were always perfect." He leaned back, and tapped one side of the circle, his eyes on Will. "But these numbers aren't perfect. They look like real noisy sensor readings."

"What?" Ginger said, leaning to peer at the tablet.

"All the readings are a little bigger on this side of the circle," Scar said. "If he was faking it, the numbers on each side would be the same. All neat." His eyes, dark and piercing, studied Will's face.

"Well, he's obviously practiced at faking it well," Ginger said.

Will ignored her, and grabbed the tablet. Scar was right. The numbers were all slightly bigger on one side. They'd seen that before. But assumed it was the sensor being inaccurate. No one had noticed that they were *uniformly* larger on one side of the line than the other.

Ginger was speaking to Scar but the words became a drone as Will hunched over the tablet. His brain started to whirl, the confusing swirl of everything that had happened fading away as his mind clicked into gear.

Why call this bomb the Bravo bomb?

Will grabbed the seismology graph. The squiggles flashed across his mind. The two small 2.8 readings, and the 5.3.

Double the reading, double the bomb size, Eliza had said, when she'd shown Drake and Will this graph.

But it wasn't. The Richter scale was a *logarithmic scale*. She'd gotten it wrong. Suddenly, a flood of earthquake videos, watched over and over when they were kids, rushed through Will's mind. It had been Eliza's thing – she'd been obsessed – but she'd loved the geology of it, while he'd connected with the numbers.

On the Richter scale a 3.0 earthquake wasn't fifty percent more powerful than a 2.0 earthquake.

It was *ten times* more powerful.

He looked at the 2.8 reading. They knew it was a fifty tonne bomb. Then the 5.3 reading...

It was more than a hundred times more powerful than the 2.8. Equivalent to at least *five thousand tonnes* of explosives.

He grabbed the aerial map that they'd found on Jeff's hard drive. The tiny yellow circles were scattered across the city. The one over the bridge had *100* written next to it.

Five containers, each holding twenty tonnes of explosive. The bomb planted to target the fireworks festival on the river bank.

His eyes slowly panned to the giant yellow circle that covered the entire city. And his finger stopped on the number written next to it.

The number *15*.

The room had gone silent. Will glanced up to see Ginger and Scar looking at him.

"What is it, Will?" Scar said.

Will sucked in a shaking breath.

The Bravo bomb is located at the bridge. Detonate early if revealed. 7 PM the lights go up.

"What time is it?" he said, his voice coming out like he was being strangled.

"5:45 PM," said Ginger.

Will's hand, on the map, started to shake. He'd thought the largest circle meant something else. But it didn't. It was a bomb target too.

But the number next to it wasn't measuring yield in tonnes.

It was measured in *kilotonnes*.

A fifteen kilotonne bomb.

The fifteen kilotonne *Alpha* bomb.

Chapter 31.

2 hours and 5 minutes left

Danial watched as two of his men heaved the artillery shell off the trolley and onto the floor. It landed with a solid, metallic thud.

"Careful," he snapped, as the shell listed to the side. One of the two caught it before it toppled, shooting a tense look his way.

He huffed, and strode to the edge of the building to look down at the ground, eighty storeys below. No windows or barriers had been installed yet on this rooftop garden, so he had an unrestricted 360-degree view of the city, bathed in golden late-afternoon light.

"Danial, still not getting anything," Harris, a short and wiry man who had always reminded Danial of some kind of reptile, slithered up to his shoulder.

"Call them again."

"I've been hitting redial for the last half an hour. Still no answer."

Danial squinted at the bend in the river where the bridge crossed over.

"Maybe they've been delayed," Harris said.

"No," Danial said, his voice terse. "Something has gone wrong." He glanced at the man crouched beside the artillery shell, pressing buttons on a black remote. "We'll know in five minutes."

"Should we shift our plans forwards?" Harris said.

Danial shook his head. "Everyone must be here."

"Perhaps they were captured. They could be being interrogated."

Danial scoffed. "You would fall asleep in an interrogation here, my friend."

He turned and strode back to the empty garden bed, where three more men stood ready with shovels at a large hole in the centre of the dirt. The man with the remote passed it to Danial, then joined his companions in burying the shell in the rich, dark dirt. When they were done, the burial site was indistinguishable from the rest of the garden bed.

"It's one minute to five, Danial," Harris called from the edge of the building.

Danial nodded, his gaze flicking around to his men gathered, waiting. Together, they joined Harris.

"Ten seconds." Harris was looking at his watch.

Danial stared towards the river, his eyes locked on the bridge. This was it. The start of everything they'd worked for.

"Five. Four. Three. Two… one."

Silence.

No explosive boom.

No smoke, rising from the university buildings.

Danial sucked in a breath. No explosion.

No explosion.

His fists clenched. The air hissed with tension, and he was aware of his men drawing back, silently, as if he, Danial, were the bomb.

Then the lift chimed.

As one, his men turned, swinging their rifles to point at the door.

Slowly, the lift slid open. A man stumbled forth, his high visibility jacket splattered with blood.

Adam.

"Lower your weapons," Danial snapped. He strode towards Adam. He half-collapsed into Danial's arms.

"Where is the rest of the team?" Danial said, his voice caustic, as he hauled Adam to a bench. "Why has the bomb not detonated?"

Adam listed to the side. His face was a mess of purple and red, and one eye was swollen completely shut. Gritting his teeth, Danial grabbed Adam's shoulders and shook him. "Answer me!"

"The team was attacked," Adam slurred. "A cop shot them all."

Danial sucked in a breath. First Ayman and his brutish brother at the analyst's house. Now Phineas and his entire team too. "How many cops? How was the location revealed?"

Adam shook his head. "Not *cops*. One. One cop." A shudder rippled through his body.

"*One?*"

Adam said nothing, his body curled in on itself.

"And please enlighten me, then, how did *you* manage to escape this *one* cop?"

"I shot him," Adam said. "But…"

"But what?"

"There were two kids as well."

"Two *kids?*"

"One of them got the jump on me. Knocked me off the building. And then the rest of the police showed up. I managed to hide before they found me."

"And the bomb?"

"They disarmed it," Adam said flatly, closing his one good eye.

Danial released him and Adam's head flicked backwards, colliding with the wall behind him. He groaned, slumping over sideways. Danial stood, pacing back and forth. The cop, and the two kids. He would bet anything that the cop's name was Senior Sergeant Drake Wessley. And that the children were those Riley had marked sniffing around the analyst's death.

Ayman had failed. No doubt the journalist was still alive too. Danial struggled against the snarl that threatened to burst forth. At least his *failure* had already been paid for.

"There's something else," Adam said.

"What?"

"The rest of the police: they went in hot. Took the cop and the kids down with beanbags. Handcuffed them and hauled them off in the back of their squad cars."

Danial stilled. "They didn't come as backup?"

Adam shook his head, a tiny, pained movement.

"It matters not," Danial said shortly. "The cop and the children found the Bravo. If they worked that out, then it's only a matter of time before they work the rest out too. We cannot afford to let them find this location. Not for the next two hours."

"I will lead an attack on the station," Harris said, his voice swelling with zeal. He stepped forwards, his rifle clenched tight in his fist. "I will personally ensure that the cop and the two brats do not leave that station alive."

As soon as he finished talking, another of Danial's men stepped forwards, and then another, echoing Harris' pledge. In moments, the rooftop echoed with the vehement declarations of his men.

"Enough," Danial said, raising his hand. "The whole force will be on high alert after finding what's left of the Bravo. A large group will stand out."

He paced to the edge of the building. They must take action. That much was certain. This was no time for waiting and hoping that all went as they had planned.

He crossed his arms and stared out at the darkening sky. Helicopters were buzzing over the river and the bridge, searchlights dancing over the gathering crowds on the banks of the river.

His eyes caught on one of the choppers. Or rather, on the bold Channel Eleven logo emblazoned on the side. He turned, scanning the city quickly.

Aha. There. His eyes locked on a skyscraper bearing the same logo.

"The journalist," he murmured, under his breath. "Perhaps her failure to die can work for us after all."

"Danial?" Harris said, again hovering like the toad he was at Danial's shoulder.

"The journalist," Danial repeated. "She works at Channel Eleven."

He turned. His men stared at him, their faces blank, nonplussed.

"Right," Danial said. "I need six men."

Chapter 32.

1 hour and 23 minutes left

Melissa rapped her fingers against the desk and looked at her watch again. Then she snatched her phone up again and dialled Drake.

After four rings it went to voicemail.

She hung up. Where was he?

She clicked the news feed on her computer. More reports flooding in about the explosion that had sent a container full of explosives into the river. But nothing more than a few sentences and some helicopter footage of the three suspects who had been taken into custody.

She clicked on a video she'd already watched a dozen times in the last hour. Drake, his form hunched over as he was bundled into the back of an ambulance. Will's sandy brown head being pushed into the back of a cop car. And Eliza into another.

Was it over? Had the three of them defused it, once and for all?

"Still here?"

Melissa turned. Her boss, Dereck, was at her office doorway.

"Yeah. Following the developments," she said, nodding to the screen.

"I'd have thought you'd be out there. Getting interviews. Your kind of story, right?" He tilted his head quizzically.

She shrugged noncommittally. Her fingernails rapped on the desk.

Dereck's phone rang in his pocket, and he held up a hand apologetically to Melissa, half-turning away to answer. "What? A foreign press delegation?" he said.

Melissa looked up. Foreign... from where?

"Have they gotten clearance... oh. Right. Okay. I'll come down." He hung up and raised his eyebrows at her, appearing exasperated. "Fun never stops."

"Who are they?" she said quickly.

"Don't know. They're here about the show-down at the bridge. Not sure what they've got to do with it." Looking at his phone, he flashed her a quick smile and then disappeared down the corridor towards the lift.

Melissa hit the redial button on her phone again. Damn Drake. Why wouldn't he pick up? Unable to sit still any longer, she darted into the corridor and into a darkened room.

Ralph, one of the station's production editors, was hunched at a bank of widescreen monitors, a pizza box balanced on his crossed knee.

"Oh, hi, Melissa," he mumbled through a mouthful of food, as she burst in.

"Is there any new footage coming in from the chopper at the bridge site?"

He swallowed and tilted a hand back and forth in the air. "Yes, but it's all crap." He opened a series of windows. She glimpsed police tape around the four containers that remained beside the bridge, shots of the gathering fireworks festival crowd from above, battalions of police cordoning off the area, experts in puffy white suits picking through the scattering of barrels that littered the construction site around the containers, and police boats moving in on the now-still water where by all reports a fifth container had landed and detonated in the river.

Ralph frowned and looked back at the open door as she leaned over him, studying the footage for any clue as to what was going on. "Did you hear that?"

"What?" Melissa said, her eyes on the screen.

"I thought I heard something. Like, people shouting."

She turned and followed his eyes to the door. Drifts of conversation, little more than murmuring.

And then a definite, loud, thud. Like something being slammed into a wall.

She froze. Ralph half-rose from his chair, the pizza slipping to the floor. She waved at him to stay still, and slipped to the door.

She peeked out, looking back towards her office and the lift in the station foyer beyond.

And something cold and hard jammed into the side of her head.

"Don't move."

The voice was cold, smooth, and male.

Melissa turned into ice.

"Hands up. Slowly."

She did as he said, and squeezed her eyes shut briefly as he grabbed her roughly, dragging her into the hall and shifting the gun barrel to between her shoulder blades.

"Whoa, whoa!"

She heard Ralph exclaim as another gunman dragged him out into the corridor behind her.

"Walk," her captor said.

Ahead of her, in front of her boss' office, another man stood. He was clad in black and glared at her, his eyes fiery. She trembled. He was wearing identical clothes to the man she'd killed at Jeff's house. His jacket was open, over magazines of ammunition strapped to his chest. Grenades hung from his belt.

A woman with plaited red hair and wearing a black suit was kneeling just inside Dereck's office door, her hands behind her head. She looked up as Melissa entered, and Melissa recognised her as the Channel Eleven head of security. Judith? Julie? Her brain felt like it was filled with cotton wool.

Dereck was kneeling beside his desk, sobbing. Blood streamed from his nose.

Sitting behind Dereck's desk, in his prized leather chair, was a tall, middle-aged man. He was flanked by two more men armed with rifles.

His hands were steepled in front of him. His eyes

narrowed as her captor pushed her forwards, his gaze tracking her movements.

"What is your name?" he said, in clear but accented English, as the man behind her shoved her into a chair before the desk.

"Melissa – " she started, automatically.

"Don't – " Dereck squawked as she spoke, but the man beside him smashed the butt of his rifle into Dereck's side, and he yelped, buckling over.

Melissa cried out, her hands jerking, and the rifle barrel jabbed harder into her spine.

"Melissa…" the man in the chair said, savouring the word. "Melissa *Green*, I'll warrant." He paused, his eyes like oil sliding over her. "Funny. Your boss assured us that you'd left for the day."

Her blood turned to ice.

"What a pleasant coincidence that he is *wrong*." The man turned and looked at Dereck.

Dereck started to shake. He met Melissa's eyes, and she choked back tears. What had she done?

"Who are you?" she said, her voice thick. "What do you want?"

"You can call me… *Ben*," he said, his lip curling in a sneer. He rose from the chair and stepped lithely around Dereck, coming to the front of the desk. Then he leaned against it, facing her, and she shifted in her chair, her body yearning to put as much distance between them as she could. "And you are going to provide us with some assistance."

"I'm just a journalist," Melissa said. She pushed

every ounce of her years of journalistic training and experience into her voice to keep it smooth, steady and in control. "What possible help could I provide?"

Ben reached forwards, and despite herself, she flinched, but he simply plucked her media badge from her shirt.

"We need to go somewhere that you can take us," he said, turning the badge over in his fingers.

"Why?"

"The why is not your concern," he said, reaching back and taking the lapel of her shirt between his fingers. Gently, he affixed the media badge back in position. Her skin crawled as his fingers brushed against her collarbone. "You are going to escort my men to the police station," he said, leaning back again and waving his hand around at the armed men crowding the room. "As television crew members."

"And if I refuse?" she said, raising her chin.

"Then your colleagues will die." Ben smiled, as if this were both obvious and every-day, as normal as discussing the weather. He nodded to the back of the room and Melissa twisted.

Ralph was being pushed into the room. His shirt was gone, replaced with a black vest. Wires protruded from a padded area at the front. Dereck – or Judith-Julie, she couldn't see which – let out a whimper.

"He is wearing enough explosives to kill everyone in this room," Ben said. Then, bizarrely, he laughed. "What am I saying. The whole *floor.*"

Chortles rattled from one or two of the gunmen as

well. Melissa sucked in a shaking breath.

"One button press is all it will take," Ben said, holding up a black remote, before handing it to the man behind Melissa. "You do what we need, and no one here gets hurt. Simple."

He smiled at Melissa, waiting. There was a long, fraught silence.

"I help you, and no one gets hurt?" she said, finally. "No shooting. No explosions?"

"As I said," Ben held up his hands. "You do as we ask, and no one here gets hurt."

"Okay," she said, her voice soft. "I'll do it."

Ben smiled broader.

"You want me to take these four?"

Ben nodded.

"You'll need to leave your guns. Carry sound and camera equipment, boom mikes, that kind of thing. I need to get it from the production room."

Ben tilted his head. "The guns stay. They will go into the camera cases."

Melissa stilled, her heart thudding hard in her throat. "You said no one was going to get hurt."

Ben leaned forwards, and placed a slim hand on her shoulder. "Worry about keeping your friends safe," he whispered, gesturing to Dereck, Judith-Julie and Ralph. "And don't concern yourself with things that are far bigger than you understand."

Chapter 33.

1 hour and 12 minutes left

"Yes, Lord Mayor. Yes, sir, I understand. Yes, I know. I realise that, sir." Ronnie's eyes flicked up, his phone to his ear. "Yes, I know how important it is. But the event needs to be cancelled. Surely you – "

Drake gritted his teeth as the Mayor interrupted Ronnie yet again. His head felt thick with fading drugs and the room swam when he moved too quickly. Or, at all.

"Yes, suspects were arrested," Ronnie continued. "But as I said already, I don't believe they are the guys we're after. Yes, Senior Sergeant Drake Wessley. I'm with him now. He's just come out of surgery and – "

Another diatribe from the Mayor. Ronnie shook his head at Drake and made a rolling motion with his hand as the Mayor continued.

"Of course sir, you'll be the first one I update. I'll call as soon as I have more information." Finally, he hung up. "Bloody useless bureaucrat," he said, tossing the phone down on the bed as if it were too hot to hold.

"What the hell is going on, Ronnie?" Drake croaked. "They think we did this?" He jerked his hand, and the handcuffs attaching him to the bedframe clanked loudly. The two officers stationed at the door to his room turned and glared at him.

"Stop moving. You'll rip out your drip," Ronnie said, collapsing into the chair beside Drake.

Drake closed his eyes briefly, ignoring the growing pounding in his bandaged-swathed head. "Just get me the hell out of this bed," he snapped.

"Listen." Ronnie said. He glanced at the officers. They were facing the hallway again. "I don't know how long we've got. The feds are on their way. You're going to have to go along with their interrogations so that we can get you cleared."

"I need to be out there, getting the guys who did this – "

"You've done a good enough job of that already," Ronnie said. "It's a shame you didn't leave any of them alive, though."

"There was no room for finesse," Drake snapped. "I had to shoot the six who were guarding the site. And Will took out the seventh."

Ronnie frowned. "And Detective Riley? How did he play into this?"

"Riley?"

"Seven bodies were found at the site," Ronnie said. "And one of them was Riley."

Drake's eyes narrowed. "No. Six guys dressed like

construction workers, and a sniper. That's who winged me in the head. Will knocked him off the building."

"No Riley?"

"If he was there, I never saw him."

Ronnie leaned back and pursed his lips. "Well. Forensics will determine if he was killed before you got there or not. But the sniper. If he got up and walked away, that's at least one terrorist still on the loose."

"There were more than a dozen guys at the port," Drake said. "One injured sniper is the least of our problems. The whole city needs to be locked down."

Ronnie shook his head. "The Mayor won't approve it. I've got a team heading to his office to argue with him in person. But as far as he's concerned, the problem's over. The bombing failed. Suspects in custody. All I've been able to do is pull in everyone who's off shift, and pump as much security into the city centre as possible."

"With the festival visitors, they'll blend in and be long gone before anyone can do anything."

"I know. I've tried to tell him."

"And the kids? Where's Will and Eliza?"

"They were taken to headquarters," Ronnie said.

"What?" Drake jerked, the cuffs rattling. "Eliza's hand is broken. She was practically holding a detonator when it went off."

"She was treated by paramedics," Ronnie said. "They're being held for questioning." He held up his hands against Drake's furious glare. "Nothing I could do about it. The feds are flipping out. At this stage, Drake, it's my word against a whole bank of evidence that they were acting to help the situation, not avoid it."

"How long before they're released?" Drake said, through gritted teeth.

"A day, maybe two, as long as they cooperate." Ronnie stood, scooping his discarded phone back up. "And nothing's going to happen to them. They're perfectly safe. There's a hundred cops in the building."

Chapter 34.

1 hour and 9 minutes left

Will grabbed a printout of a Brisbane map from the pile of paperwork and snatched up Ginger's pen. He marked out Eliza's circle then copied the readings from the tablet to the paper, marking in the line splitting the circle from weakest to strongest.

"If you're wasting our time…" Ginger said. She glared at Will. "You can't get yourself out of this by pretending there's a phantom bomb out there."

Will ignored her and hit the calculator buttons on his phone. He crossed out the first reading, *43*, and wrote *5* instead, then started on the second point.

"Talk us through this," Scar said, waving a hand at the paper.

"We missed something when we found where the first bomb was," Will said, fingers flying over the keypad. "I'm removing its readings, and seeing what's left."

A few minutes later, he'd rewritten all the numbers around the circle. With trembling fingers, he drew a second line, from the new smallest value to the new biggest one.

It ran directly across the centre of the city.

He looked up at Scar. "There's a bomb on this line somewhere," he said.

Scar studied the page, then met Will's gaze. "Where?"

"I don't know," Will said, leaning back in the chair, his fingers rapping spasmodically against its steel frame. "The readings are too noisy. It's a faint signature. I can't work out the distance like we did with the Bravo."

"Convenient," Ginger said with a scoffing laugh. She turned to Scar. "He's playing with us. Making out like he's here to save the day – "

Scar cut her off. "The Bravo had a huge output."

"I don't think this is the same type of bomb," Will said. "I think it's a – "

"Sir, he's wasting our time! He either knows *exactly* where there's a second bomb because he helped his friends plant it, or he knows nothing and he's toying with us for fun – "

The lights went out.

For a moment the room was enveloped in complete darkness. Then a dim light flickered on outside, glowing in through the small window in the top of the door.

"Check it out," Scar said, his face shadowed in the gloom.

Ginger rose and opened the door. "What's going

on?" Her voice echoed hollowly down the hall.

Another female voice replied from outside the room. "The bloody toaster's probably tripped the safety switch again."

"The recording equipment's down until the power's back on." Scar stood, and glanced at Will. "We'll be back when they get it sorted."

He followed Ginger through the door, closing it tight behind him.

Will jumped up, scooting around the table to try the handle. Locked.

He grabbed the paper with his new circle on it. He had to get out of here. If the Alpha bomb was in the city, then everyone was going to die.

BOOOOOOM!

Will's body slammed against the door as the floor bucked. He gasped, staggering upright. What now?

Muffled shouting came from beyond the door. Shadows flitted past the tiny window, heading right.

BANGBANGBANG!

Rapid gunfire from below. Getting louder.

More screams. Shouting. More shadows running past.

Will's breath caught, his heart hammering. Desperately, he yanked at the door handle. Nothing.

CARUMPHHH!

Another shudder rattled the building.

Will turned and grabbed Ginger's chair. He heaved it above his head and slammed it into the window. It rebounded, clocking him in the face.

He yelped as pain exploded from his nose. Clenching his teeth, he hauled the chair back up and twisted it until it was wedged behind the door handle.

Then he yanked, as hard as he could.

The handle screeched, bent outwards, then popped off, sending Will flying back. He scrambled up and put his fingers into the hole, tugging as hard as he could.

The door didn't budge.

The gunfire was getting louder. There was another muted *BOOM* and then another.

Will shoved the door. Maybe it would open outwards. As he did, two figures ran past the window. One paused and raised a handgun, firing once, twice, three times, back the way they'd come.

Will flinched as automatic gunfire exploded right outside.

The figure with the handgun fell.

Will's legs shook. He stepped back, his muscles almost giving out beneath him. He had to get out of here. Find Eliza. Get out of this building.

The room flashed white and shuddered. Will ducked, his hands flying over his head.

He coughed. Smoke was billowing into the room.

The door. The explosion had stoved it inwards.

He fought against the smoke, yanking his shirt up over his nose and mouth. He grabbed the door and pulled, the metal frame protesting with a piercing shriek before the door slammed into his body, finally free of its frame.

He froze, his heart hammering in his ears, and listened. Outside, someone was firing single, spaced-out shots.

There was a burst of automatic gunfire. Close.

He flattened himself behind the buckled door as two shadowy figures with rifles jogged past the door, the smoke swirling in their wake.

More gunfire. Getting quieter through the thick walls of the station.

He sucked in a slow breath through his shirt. He had to find Eliza.

Steeling himself, he shoved the door out of the way and slipped into the corridor. Towards the lifts he'd been brought up in, he could see only smoke. In the opposite direction, the corridor was empty.

He flinched as another barrage of automatic gunfire popped and cracked. But it was further away now. He forced himself forwards.

And tripped, on a body lying on the floor.

He grunted as his hands, thrown forwards to catch himself, landed on the woman's bloodied stomach. Fighting back the urge to scream, he scrambled backwards until his spine slammed into the wall.

For a moment he just gasped, the smoke burning his throat and eyes, his gaze locked on the dead officer's body. It was the young woman who'd brought him food. Her brown ponytail was splayed behind her head, and her eyes were open, staring at the ceiling as if slightly puzzled by what had happened to her. Her arms and legs were splayed at awkward angles, one arm across her chest, the other flung out beside her.

Shaking, Will looked at his hands. They were red with blood. The image of the sniper, body bent and broken on the ground, far, far below, flashed across his mind again. And the burnt, twisted corpse of the man at Jeff's house.

With jerking movements, he wiped his hands on his jeans. Faster and faster. But the blood wouldn't come off. It just smeared in great blotchy streaks. His vision blurred as tears burned and then fell.

How had it come to this?

He sank back against the wall, sucking one heaving breath after another, until the tears stopped.

Eliza. She was what mattered now. He hadn't had a choice. And he didn't have a choice now. She was locked in one of these rooms, as he had been. He was her only chance.

He rocked forwards onto his knees, and scanned the woman's body. He let his eyes slide over the red-black pool in her belly.

There. On her belt. A ring of keys.

His fingers trembled as he struggled to unhook it from her belt. He tugged, and her arm flopped from her chest, thwacking him in the thigh.

He jerked, biting back a yelp. And felt the cold metal keychain disengage.

He scrambled to his feet, backing away from the officer's body, the keys hanging from his hand. And he ran.

The corridor was lined with more interrogation rooms like the one he'd been in. Most of them were dark, empty, the doors with their tiny rectangular windows pinned neatly back against the wall. But ahead, through the smoke ghosting down the corridor, he saw one that was closed.

Will skidded to a stop. Inside, he glimpsed Eliza's huddled form sitting at the table. He fumbled with the keys until he found the one that opened the door.

She looked up as Will burst in.

"Will," she said, dully. She was hunched around her broken arm, which was still encased in the thick temporary splint. She was visibly shaking, and her face was bone white.

"Are you okay?" He shoved past the table, its legs screeching on the concrete floor.

"What's happening out there?" Her pupils were huge, great pools of black ringed by brown.

"The station's being attacked. We have to get out of here." Gingerly, he pulled her to her feet. She wobbled, and he slipped an arm around her waist. She held onto him with her good arm, the other still clenched to her chest.

He poked his head into the corridor. Still nothing but smoke. Smoke, and the dead woman's body.

He headed away from the lifts, where the smoke was thinner.

Then shouts echoed from behind them.

"Quick," Will said, his arm tightening around Eliza's waist. At the end of the corridor there was a heavy door marked *FIRE EVACUATION*. He yanked it open, pushing her inside, as the shouts were joined by the thudding of footfalls.

Then gunfire cracked. Close. In the corridor.

He slammed the door closed. "Go! Up!"

Eliza stumbled forwards, and Will grabbed her, hauling her to her feet. They hit the stairs running. After the first few flights, Eliza pulled herself free from his grip.

"I'm okay," she panted. Her face was flushing pink, the blood chasing away the pallid white.

When they'd made it up half a dozen flights, she held up her hand. "Stop. Do you hear that?"

Will struggled to fill his lungs with air. Eliza was leaning over the edge of the stairs looking down the centre well, her hair shrouding her face.

A door slammed, far below.

"Damn it!" she hissed, and jerked her head back. "Run!"

She shoved him forwards, and down the well, he glimpsed the men dressed in black hustling onto the stairs, far below. A face appeared, peering up the well.

Shouts in another language echoed.

"They've seen us!" Will gasped, pumping his legs after Eliza. She didn't answer.

"The roof," he said, minutes later, as they reached the top of the stairwell. Eliza nodded, and shoved through the door onto the rooftop. As soon as Will was through, they both threw themselves against it, and it clanged shut with a resounding bang.

"We need to jam it with something," Eliza panted.

"Stay away from me!" A shrill voice came from behind them.

Will turned. There was a thin young man in a suit, backing away. Beyond him, the sky was darkening. Only the tips of the tallest buildings were still in sunlight.

"We're not the bad guys," Eliza snapped, striding past Will. She was making for a flimsy metal table with three mismatched chairs around it, topped with a full ashtray. She glanced back at Will. "Come on. Help me with this."

"Oh," the man said. As Will joined Eliza in dragging the table, the suited man tentatively approached, finally grabbing the other side of the table and pushing once they were metres from the door.

"Upend it," Eliza ordered.

As they did, there was another volley of automatic gunfire. Then shouts, this time in English, but indistinguishable through the walls.

The suit yelped, and backed away from the door. "You led them up here!"

Will ignored him, running for the edge of the building.

Black trucks were pulling up on the ground. Police in tactical gear jumped out and ran into the building.

"We need to hide!" he said, as Eliza joined him.

"Where?" Eliza said, flinging her arm around at the flat concrete space, punctuated only by low air-conditioning units and the odd piece of old, broken furniture.

"Look, the police are getting the upper hand." The suit said, now at Will's other side. "The SWAT teams are here."

"We don't have SWAT in Australia," Eliza snapped at him. "Will, we need to get off the roof. They're driving them up here."

"We should sit tight until the cops come!" the suit interjected, his voice increasingly shrill.

"They're coming *towards us*." Eliza's face was flinty. The man swore.

Will nodded. "If we can't hide, then we have to get down somehow."

All three of them ducked as an explosion shook the stairwell door.

"Quick – check over the edge," Will said, pointing to the opposite side of the roof. Eliza met his gaze, swallowed, then ran for the back of the building. Will ran to the left edge and peered over. Nothing. No fire escape, no pipes, no ledges. Just concrete and bitumen, twenty storeys below.

He sprinted to the other side. There was a swimming pool, far below, built on the roof of the station's enlarged base. Quickly, his eyes scanned down the side of the building. Fifteen storeys down to the pool. Along the front edge of the station, he counted the car parks between where he stood and the pool.

Ten spaces. Twenty-five metres from the roof

edge to the pool.

"There's a rooftop carpark on this side!" Eliza yelled, and Will ran over to her at the rear of the building. Peering over, he could see the top of the multi-storey carpark, covered in stretched fabric sunshades, about seven storeys down.

But between the multi-storey carpark and the station building was a ground-level carpark. Six car spaces separated the two buildings.

"Will, I know what you're thinking," Eliza said, turning to him, her face stricken. "It can't be done. We won't make it."

"Won't make what?" The suit yelped from behind them.

"We have to jump," Will said, turning so he could see them both.

"We can take our chances here," Eliza said. "Wait for the cops to come – "

"There's another bomb," Will said.

Eliza broke off with a small sucked-in breath.

Will waved his hand at a giant digital clock on the side of a nearby building. It read *5:58*. "That's what's going to go off at 7:00 PM. Not the Bravo. The *Alpha*."

"Oh god," Eliza breathed.

"We have to get off this roof to stop it," Will said. "Otherwise we, and every other person in this city, are dead."

He stepped forwards, and put his hands on Eliza's forearms. "We can do this," he said, softly. Tears were welling in her eyes, and one spilled over. He reached up, and wiped it away. "Are you with me?"

She was motionless for a moment, and then she nodded. "I'm in."

Will pulled her into a hug. She squeezed him hard with her good arm.

"You're nuts!" The suit squeaked.

Will pulled away from Eliza. "I need you to keep watch at the door," he said firmly, turning to the man. "Tell us how many floors before they get up here."

The suit paled. "I ain't jumping off no roof," he said.

"What's on that side?" Eliza said. Her breathing was steadying, and he could see her mind clicking into gear.

"A pool. Fifteen storeys down. So forty-five metres…" Will scrunched his eyes shut.

There was another burst of automatic fire.

"The door!" Eliza snapped at the suit, and finally, he moved, jerking the table back and opening the door a crack.

"Four floors and closing fast!" he called.

"Three seconds…" Will continued, his mind whirring. "At least twenty-five metres… eight and a bit metres a second." He opened his eyes and met Eliza's gaze. "Damn it."

"Three storeys! No, two!" The suit's voice rose, panicked.

"The carpark," Will said flatly. "We've got a better chance of making it."

Eliza nodded, her face white.

"Come on," Will shouted to the man. "We're going over the back." He ran towards the front edge of the building.

"But you said there's a pool on that side!" the man yelled, pointing, as he ran towards them.

"We won't make it. We can make the carpark!"

"Are you sure?" Eliza said, coming to a stop beside him, their backs to the front of the building.

He met her gaze. "Trust me," he said.

Gunfire peppered the stairwell door.

The suit shrieked and changed direction, running towards the pool side.

"Stop!" Will yelled. "Don't! We need to go over the back!"

It was too late. The man reached the edge and jumped, his scream ripping through the silence. As he disappeared, the stairwell door exploded open.

"Run!" Eliza screamed. She broke into a sprint, and Will slammed his legs into gear. They passed the stairwell door as two men in black backed onto the roof, firing back into the building.

Time seemed to slow. Will glimpsed the look on one of the men's faces as he turned, and saw Will and Eliza running.

The rifle swung to follow them, as they approached the edge.

Three steps left.

Two.

One.

Please, please, let him be right.

Will jumped.

Chapter 35.

1 hour left

There was a volley of cracks as bullets snapped through the air over Will's head. His arms windmilled, as he tried to stay vertical, but he pitched forwards into a spin.

Eliza was screaming, the sound whipping through the rushing air.

Will got a glimpse of the encroaching roof. He wrapped his arms over his head.

The impact crushed the air out of his body and his vision went black. There was a rending rip, and then he kept falling.

Another bone-numbing impact, a metallic bouncing.

Then silence.

Silence, darkness, and pain.

A groan. Belatedly, Will realised he'd made the noise. He opened his eyes. Blackness swam, slowly clearing to sparkling white and then to normal vision.

He was on his back, on the roof of a car. Above

him, the sunshade awning was ripped and fluttering weakly in the wind.

There was another moan.

"Eliza?" he said, struggling to sit. His body screamed in protest, but obeyed, although his vision filled with light again.

More moans. He blinked through the sparkles and saw her hammocked in the next awning.

"Are you okay?"

"No!" she said, and cursed. "I just jumped off a damn building!"

He grinned in relief, and heaved himself to the ground.

Shouting and gunfire echoed from the rooftop, and he flinched, as an explosion boomed. Then another, and another.

"Get me down," Eliza said, her voice slipping back into panic. He could see her shifting, scrambling for the edge.

"I'm coming," he said, hauling himself up onto the car parked beneath her.

The sound of the explosions reverberated for a moment, then gunfire broke out again.

As Eliza slipped awkwardly down into his waiting grip, the shots stopped. Together, they backed away from the car, looking up to the twenty-storey rooftop that only moments ago, they had been standing on.

There was silence. Smoke drifted through darkening sky.

Then a man's voice echoed down. "Clear!"

"Whatever painkillers they gave me are wearing off," Eliza said, her voice tight. She was leaning against the car. There was a long gash on her leg from where she'd hit one of the metal pinions holding the awning in place. Will had ripped off the bottom of his shirt to bandage it, but the blood was still soaking through it.

Will pursed his lips, his phone to his ear. "We'll get you help," he said, then looked away as a man answered. "I need to speak to Drake Wessley," he said, deepening his voice. "It's extremely urgent and a matter of national security."

Eliza raised her eyebrows.

"Hold please," the man said.

Will jittered his fingers on his folded arms as there was a long pause filled with call-waiting music.

"Hello?"

"Drake," he said, relief washing through him like warm water. He hit the speaker button. "It's me. Eliza's here too. The police station was attacked."

"What?" Drake's voice cleared, filling with anger.

"They have guns, explosives – "

"Did you get out? Are you in a safe location?"

"We're safe, for now," Will said, glancing at Eliza. "But Drake – that's not all. There's another bomb. Somewhere in the city centre."

"No," Drake said flatly.

"We missed it. But everything points to it being there."

For a moment no-one said anything.

"You're sure?" Drake said.

"One hundred percent," Will said.

"Okay. Okay." Will could hear Drake's breathing speeding up through the speaker. "So we evacuate the city centre. Buildings should be pretty empty by now, after hours on a Friday night…"

"No," Will said. His heart hammered in his chest and he looked at Eliza as he said it. "It's a nuke, Drake. Not a dirty bomb. A full-on, proper nuke."

Eliza's eyes widened, and her whole body tensed. There was another long pause.

"How do you know?" Drake said softly.

Quickly, Will explained. The big spike on the graph, what he'd remembered about the Richter scale, how they'd missed the bigger readings on one side of Eliza's circle. "The Bravo was always just the first drop in the ocean," he finished. "Maybe to get everyone's attention for the real show, I don't know. But this bomb – the Alpha – this has always been their main plan. That's what they meant when they wrote *the lights go up*."

"Then we don't have much time," Drake said. "You said it's on a line southeast from the readings we took?"

"Yeah."

"Then if they're smart, it'll be somewhere high."

"The professor said the Hiroshima bomb went off six hundred metres above the city," Will said. "But they can't have it in a plane or helicopter. It was here when we took the readings."

"The only thing close to six hundred metres tall is that new high rise," Eliza said. She had her phone out, a map open on the screen.

"The Skyfeller Centre," Drake said quickly. "Yes. Is it on the line?"

"Yeah," Eliza said. "Smack bang on it." She held up the map to Will and he could see the rough sketch she'd recreated of their earlier readings.

"That'll be it," Drake said. "It's still under construction, and everyone will have knocked off hours ago." He paused. "Hang on. My boss is here. I need to speak to him for a minute."

"How are they going to clear enough of the city to save everyone?" Eliza said quietly, while they waited.

"I don't know," Will said, his chest tight.

"The station's out of action," Drake's voice returned. "Ronnie's sending the nearest suburban squad. They'll go to the Skyfeller and deal with it." His voice became more urgent. "You two need to get out of the city, as quick as you can. As far away from the Skyfeller, and from the police station, as you can." He cleared his throat. "I've told Ronnie everything. But as far as anyone out there's concerned: you two busting out coincides with the attack. It's going to look like your terrorist buddies came in to get you out. Until everything can be straightened out, you need to stay away from cops, flat out. And I don't want you detained anywhere near the city centre until we know this nuke's been deactivated. You got it?"

Will glanced at Eliza. He could see in the clench of

290

her jaw and the tense way she held herself that she was in pain, and a lot of it. "I get it. But Eliza's arm – and she's cut her leg – she needs medical help," he said.

"I'll be fine," she said, but her voice was strained.

"There's an all-night medical centre on George Street," Drake said. "It's far enough away from the station that you might miss getting picked up. Get what you need then get out of the city."

"Okay. We'll go there now."

Eliza didn't protest, just gritted her teeth together.

"Will, Eliza – be careful," Drake said, his voice solemn.

"We will. You too," Will said, and he hung up the phone.

Eliza was shaking again by the time they got to the bottom of the carpark and out into the mostly-empty streets. They walked and jogged as Eliza could manage it, directly away from the station for half a kilometre, then turned onto George Street.

Sirens wailed in the distance. Will kept his eyes on the street, searching for the medical centre.

"Look," he said, finally. "Almost there. Painkillers on the way."

"Awesome," Eliza said flatly. She was limping heavily now, with almost all her weight on Will.

The sirens got louder. Then a police car burst onto the street, its lights flashing.

"Damn it," Will muttered, angling his body away from the street and tightening his arm around Eliza's waist. He picked up the pace until they were almost running.

A black truck screeched around the corner, tailing the squad car, followed by another the same. All three roared past Will and Eliza.

"There's the Skyfeller Centre," Eliza said, her voice tight. "They're heading for it."

At the end of the road, the convoy skidded to a stop before a towering building clad in scaffolding. The truck doors burst open and a flood of black figures bundled out. They spread out into the street, and faint shouting drifted towards them. Police started moving back down the street, shouting instructions to the pedestrians who'd frozen when the convoy passed by.

"Quick," Will said, hurrying Eliza the last few metres to the medical centre. He glanced up as they passed through the sliding glass doors. The final rays of sunset illuminated the top of the Skyfeller Centre. Then it was gone, and they were inside the white glossy reception of the medical centre.

Inside, a doctor was standing with her back to them at the reception desk, writing something on a clipboard. She turned as the door slid shut behind them.

"Oh – oh dear," she said. Will saw her eyes flick over their torn and smoke-stained clothing, their grimy faces, and the bloodied rag tied around Eliza's leg. "What has happened here?"

"Uh," Will said, unsure where to start. But the

doctor wasn't listening. Instead she bustled them through the empty waiting room and into the clinic.

"Sit down," she commanded, and Eliza slumped into a chair. "I'm Doctor Bryde," she said briskly, kneeling to unwind the cloth from Eliza's leg.

"Eliza," Eliza said weakly.

"And Will," Will added. "She's in a lot of pain."

"I can see that," Doctor Bryde said. She was whisking needles, vials, bandages and padded dressings from a metal trolley. "This is a bad cut, Eliza," she said, her voice taking on an authoritative, slightly over-loud doctor tone. "It's going to need a lot of stitches. And a broken arm?" The doctor's eyes narrowed as she touched Eliza's arm, and Will saw her glancing back and forth between the obviously-medical splint and Will's attempt at makeshift bandaging.

"They splinted it after the explosion," Eliza said.

"Explosion?" Doctor Bryde looked between Will and Eliza sharply.

"It's a long story," Will said quickly. His heart was suddenly thudding in his chest. Had they made the right call coming here? They looked so suspicious, in their filthy, ripped clothes.

"I going to call an ambulance to get you to the hospital," Doctor Bryde said. She glanced between the two of them again, then briskly, she swabbed Eliza's leg with disinfectant. She slapped a thick pad of cottony stuff onto it then began to bandage. "You need x-rays and the bone to be set properly."

Will's heart skipped. None of the hospitals met Drake's criteria of *get out of the city*. And that was *if* the doctor didn't just call the police on them. He looked at her face, and as she finished the bandaging she looked quickly up at him again. He could see the tension in her, the jutting out of tendons in her neck. She knew something wasn't right.

He glanced back towards the front door. Had the police squad gotten the Alpha under their control?

"Wait here," the doctor said, standing up.

"Wait," Will said quickly. Maybe they could make a run for it, if Eliza could walk. He could break into a car, hotwire it – get both of them out. "What about her pain? Can't you give her something?"

The doctor hesitated. "I only have adult painkillers here. You'll have to wait until the ambulance arrives – "

"She needs it now," Will said, trying to keep his voice steady. He lowered his tone, tried to sound reasonable and not like a criminal. "Please. I practically had to carry her here."

The doctor glanced back towards the reception area, then back at Eliza. She had her eyes closed and her head was leaning back against the wall, her face pallid. "Okay. Let's get you more comfortable," she said, letting out her breath in a rush. She hurried to another cabinet and pulled out a small vial. She jabbed it with a needle and drew back the plunger. "How much do you weigh, Eliza?"

"Forty-five kilograms," Eliza murmured.

"Fifteen milligrams for an adult, so eight milligrams for you," the doctor muttered. She glanced at Will before tucking the vial with the remaining liquid into her pocket. "Wouldn't want your heart to stop."

She stabbed the needle into Eliza's arm, who flinched.

"I'm calling the ambulance now," the doctor said brusquely, leaving the door open as she left.

Will hurried to sit beside Eliza. He took her good hand and squeezed. "Eliza. We need to go. She's going to call the cops on us."

Eliza opened her eyes. "Whoa."

"You feel like you can walk?"

She flexed her foot up and down and then a goofy smile broke over her face. "I feel... awesome."

"Come on then," Will said, smiling tightly back. "We need to move."

He hauled her up, worried that she might not be able to stand if whatever the doctor had given her was that strong. But she stood easily, putting her weight casually on her injured leg.

Will hustled her through the door, every inch of him on high alert for the doctor coming back. He froze when he saw her, standing with her back to them, at the reception, talking quietly to the young man at the receptionist desk. The receptionist had the phone to his ear.

Doctor Bryde turned.

"Wait – " she started, her face twisted in a frown.

Then the entire glass shopfront of the centre exploded.

The building shook, and Will's ears wailed with a high-pitched squealing. Car alarms blared outside.

He realised he was on the floor, Eliza's limbs tangled in his.

"You okay?" she gasped, and he nodded.

Slowly, he raised his head. The doctor and receptionist were on the floor too. Holding each other up, he and Eliza struggled to their feet. The doctor stirred, and started to get up, her face white.

"Wait – " she said, but Will ignored her. Something had gone wrong. That wasn't the Alpha going off. If it had been the Alpha, none of them would be here now; they'd be nothing but clouds of vaporised atoms. But he didn't need a betting bot to win him money on the odds that Drake's police team had not been responsible for the blast.

With Eliza at his side, he climbed through the shattered glass. A roiling cloud of black smoke was coming from the direction of the Skyfeller Centre.

"The cops didn't set that off," Eliza said, jumping to the same conclusion as he had.

He shook his head grimly. The smoke was drifting apart in clumps now, and he could see that the police car, and one of the trucks, was burning furiously.

"Bodies," Eliza whispered. He followed her gaze, and saw the unmoving figures on the ground.

Will's heart felt stuck in his chest. "I'm going to check it out," he said, woodenly. "Stay here."

"No way," she protested. "You're not going in there alone."

He opened his mouth to argue, but she cut him off.

"Will. Come on. Together, right?" Without waiting for an answer, she broke into a barely-limping run.

He followed, quickly catching up to run beside her. He slowed only when she did, as they reached the first body.

The remnants of a police uniform smouldered on the stiffened corpse.

"Oh god," she breathed through her panting breaths.

They passed another, and another. By the time they'd reached the blazing truck, he'd counted five dead cops.

The inside of the truck was gutted and roaring with too-hot flames. He shielded his face with his arm.

"There's someone alive in there!" Eliza exclaimed, pointing towards the second truck, beyond the also-burning squad car.

He jogged beside her past the car, trying to see what she'd seen. All he could see was fire and smoke. They reached the second truck. One of the back doors was open, and now they were close enough, Will glimpsed the shape of a figure, sitting inside.

Eliza yanked the other door open. There was a click, and then all Will could see was the barrel of a handgun pointed at her head.

"Eliza – get back!"

"Are you okay?" Eliza was saying.

"Who are you?" The cop inside was slumped against the side wall of the truck, the gun still aimed at Eliza's skull. Beyond him, there were panels of electronics, computer displays and what looked like miniature flying drones.

"I'm Eliza," she said, and gestured behind her. "And this is Will. We've been helping Drake Wessley."

The man's hand shuddered, the gun almost falling, but then he strengthened his grip, steading his aim on Eliza's head. Will saw there were two bloody holes in his shirt, just above the belt.

"I know Drake," the officer said dully. "But for all I know, you're with *them*."

"The terrorists killed my uncle," Will said. "We disarmed the first bomb."

"And Will's the one who worked out there's a nuke in that building," Eliza added. "Don't you think that if we were with them, we wouldn't have bothered telling any cops that it was there?"

The man sighed, and the gun collapsed to his lap. "I was doing comms when the team went in." He coughed, and blood flecked his lips. "They waited until the whole team was inside. They never had a chance." He struggled to prop himself up straighter against the wall, his face twisted. "I went in after the bomb went off. But they're all dead. They shot me. I ran. The smoke... I guess they couldn't see me. Or didn't care about finishing me off quick."

"They're on a clock," Will said. "They only need to keep everyone out for another…" He paused, glancing at his watch. "Forty-five minutes. Have you called for back-up?"

The man's face whitened. "There is no back-up. Not in the next forty-five minutes. The station's in chaos. The rest of the districts are out rounding up suspects!"

Will clenched his teeth and sucked in a breath. He looked at Eliza. Her face was stricken.

"Then we have to stop them," she whispered. She tore her eyes from Will, back to the cop. "Do you have any guns?"

"I can't give you my gun," the cop spluttered.

"They're going to wipe out the entire *city*," Will said. "I don't think you have a choice."

"Have you ever fired a gun before?"

Will shook his head, and Eliza did the same.

"Then you're more likely to shoot each other or yourselves than a terrorist," the officer said, some of the characteristic authority coming back into his voice that Will recognised from Drake's mannerisms. Then he sighed. "And I've got no ammo left anyway. But I've got an alternative. Get me one of those." He pointed to the drones shelved behind him.

Will scrambled up into the truck. The drone was heavier than he expected, about the size of a large pizza, with four struts leading out to black propellers. The central metallic latticework was festooned with cameras and antennas. As he handed it over he saw a short black cylinder protruding from the underside.

"The quadrotors will be your back-up," the officer said, flicking a switch on the underside of the drone. He tossed Will a yellow and red armband. "The armband carries an electronic ID. The quad will neutralise anything it perceives to be threatening the person wearing the band."

He chucked the drone out the door of the truck into the air. The propellers spun, and it hovered in the air.

"How long will it last?" Will said, tugging the arm band on. He grabbed another drone and passed it out to Eliza, before jumping down himself.

"Ten minutes."

Will glanced at the officer. "Ten minutes? That's it?"

"You said they're on a clock anyway," the officer said grimly. "This is better than nothing."

"Did your team have these when they went in?" Eliza said. She was struggling with the band, and Will took it from her, slipping it up over her splint to her bicep before tightening it.

"Uh." The officer hesitated. "They're… experimental. There was an… incident in testing."

Will froze with Eliza's drone belly-up in his hand. "And?"

"It shot an officer by mistake. But look. They're working fine now. They can aim far better than you and – "

"Come on," Eliza said. She reached over the drone and flicked the switch, then tossed the drone up beside Will's. "He's right: it's better than nothing. We're wasting time."

Will pursed his lips, his eyes on the quads hovering benignly above their heads. "Fine." He turned back to the cop. "There's a medical centre half a kilometre up the road. Get yourself there and call Drake. Tell him what's happening. Can you do that?"

The cop nodded, his hand clamping over his wounded stomach. He twisted himself towards the door and Will caught him as he slipped out, helping the man stabilise himself, leaning against the truck.

"What are you going to do if you find the nuke?" the officer gasped, through tight, pained breaths. "My bomb disposal guy's dead."

"I don't know," Will said, his gaze turning to the Skyfeller building, towering above them. "We'll have to work it out when we get there."

Chapter 36.

39 minutes left

Will hesitated at the shattered doorway to the Skyfeller building. He glanced at Eliza. "Ready?"

She nodded. Above her, the drones hovered, swaying slightly, blades whirring.

He went to step forwards, but she caught his arm.

"Will," she said softly. "We're not going to get out of this alive, are we."

He swallowed. Left a long, blank silence hanging between them, saying everything he couldn't. Because she was right. They were about to charge into a building filled with men who'd just taken out a team of highly trained professionals, to try and find a nuclear bomb and somehow disarm it before it went off in... just over half an hour.

"But if we don't, there's no one else," she continued, after the silence grew too loud. "So we do this. Together."

"Together," he echoed, and he forced a smile.

She nodded. And side by side, they stepped

302

through the shattered glass.

Inside, smouldering debris masked the foyer with wavering black smoke. Beyond, Will glimpsed movement in the shadows at the back of the foyer.

"Quick," Eliza hissed, and ran crouching towards the remains of the expansive reception desk.

There was a shout. A figure emerged from the smoke, holding a walkie-talkie and aiming a rifle at Will as he scrambled to follow Eliza. Above him, he heard the buzz of the drone increase in pitch, like an angry wasp.

He collapsed to the ground beside Eliza, the desk giving them cover.

"The drone didn't go for him," he panted. "He was pointing the gun right at me and the drone didn't go for him. The cop said they'd neutralise threats."

"They must have made them less trigger-happy after one shot the cop," Eliza said, her brow furrowed.

"Hey!" A shout rang through the foyer, in heavily-accented English. "Children! Our boss wants to speak with you!"

Eliza's eyes were wide and disbelieving. "That's a trick, right?" she hissed.

Will popped his head above the desk. There were two men now, both with rifles hanging loosely in their hands, pointed at the ground. The first man he'd seen was holding up the walkie, as they picked through the debris towards Will and Eliza.

"They're coming," he whispered, dropping back

down.

"What do we do?"

"We have to force the drones to attack."

"How?"

"Follow my lead," he said, steeling himself. He grabbed a piece of twisted metal piping from the floor. Eliza caught up a splintered hunk of timber and hefted it like a club.

"Ready?"

She nodded.

"Charge!" Will ran towards the two men, pipe hoisted over his head. The men looked startled, then swung their rifles up, as Will screamed what he hoped sounded like a battle cry, and swung the pipe.

A high pitched whine bloomed above him.

CRACK!

The sound came from over Will's head, and the head of the man closest to Will snapped backwards.

CRACK!

The other gunman followed his companion in collapsing to the floor.

Will skidded to a stop. Smoke was drifting in tiny tendrils from the drones.

"Oh god," Eliza gasped, almost colliding with him. "They're dead. Oh god. It shot them."

"Come on," Will said, adrenaline coursing hard and fast through his veins. Trying not to look at the blood pooling under the man's head, he grabbed a rifle, slinging it over his shoulder. No matter what the cop in the truck said: he felt safer with it. Eliza gingerly took the other rifle.

"Lifts," Will said, pointing, and he jogged through the debris towards them. But nothing happened when he pressed the call button.

"The explosion will have shut them down," Eliza said breathlessly. "But there could be a freight lift from the basement carpark."

Will nodded, and followed her as she jogged down the corridor towards the fire stairs. They went down two flights to a door marked LOADING BAY.

The bay was empty apart from a black ute. A shattered wooden crate was sprawled over the tray.

"There," Eliza pointed. Beyond the ute, huge industrial-looking lift doors were marked MAINTENANCE LIFT. Will hit the button, and a distant hum echoed down the shaft.

There was a series of rapid beeps from above him. The drone was flashing red lights, and he grabbed it, the blades slowing. A battery display on the bottom was blinking red.

"Almost out of juice," he said, flicking the switch off.

"Mine too."

He tucked the drone under his arm and helped Eliza switch hers off. "At least we've got these," he said grimly, tapping the rifle.

The lift arrived. Above the hundred and two floor buttons was a button labelled *Rooftop Garden*.

"Rooftop?" Eliza said, and Will nodded.

"That's our best shot for where they'd be, I

guess."

"I don't want to shoot anyone," Eliza said softly into the humming quiet of the lift's ascent.

"I don't either," Will said. "But we may have to make them think we will."

The lift chimed. When the door opened, Will stepped out onto an unlit pathway surrounded on both sides by fern-filled garden beds. Gravel crunched below his feet.

Up ahead, the path split around a water feature. Beyond, there was a vast bed of dirt, dotted with trees and piles of turf, lit from temporary lighting hanging from the open arbour roof.

Will ducked back behind the fountain. "Three guys," he whispered. "Sitting on the benches. They've got rifles. And shovels, for some reason."

"Maybe the bomb is buried."

Will nodded. "Would make sense to hide it."

"So, charge them and let the drones take... um, care of them?" Eliza's face was tight as she spoke.

"Yeah," Will said softly. "Ready?"

She nodded. Will flipped his drone, and got ready to flick the switch back on.

"On three," he said. "One. Two. Three."

Simultaneously, they tossed the drones into the air, and burst from behind the water feature, their rifles raised and aimed, bouncing madly, at the seated men.

One of the men exclaimed something in another language, and all three of them leapt up, grabbing the rifles leaning against the bench.

CRACK! CRACK!

Both drones fired, and as if in slow motion, the two men closest Will and Eliza collapsed, crumpling into the dirt.

BANGBANGBANG!

There was a sharp retort of automatic fire and a burning sting in Will's bicep. He yelped.

"Go right! Zig-zag!" Eliza yelled.

Will dashed for one of the trees. Eliza was still running erratically, one of the drones sluggishly following her. As he dove behind a tree-trunk, her drone gave a panicked bleating of beeps and then ploughed into the dirt.

His back slammed into the tree and he panted. He clamped his hand against his bicep, twisting to see. The bullet had just clipped him. A red channel through his flesh was soaking his sleeve with blood.

Then the drone over his head exploded.

Will squawked, crouching down as shattered metal and plastic rained over him.

"Let go of me!"

He froze. Eliza!

"Come out, or your friend dies."

The man's voice was cool, steady. Will stood, his heart hammering.

A fourth man – he'd missed him before, where had he come from? – was standing with his arm around Eliza's chest.

And he was holding a knife to her throat.

"Let her go!" Will said, his voice shaking.

"Drop the rifle." The man's eyes locked onto Will's, shadowed beneath the sickly yellow lighting. He tightened his grip on Eliza, and her eyes widened. A thin trickle of red ran down her neck.

Will's fingers were numb. He opened them, let the rifle fall to the dirt. "Don't hurt her."

Immediately, the third remaining gunman limped towards him, jabbed his rifle into Will's side and grabbed his arm to manhandle him forwards. "Not so tough without a fire extinguisher in your hands, are you," he snapped.

Will started. Instantly, he took in the cuts and bruises all over the man. The awkward way he was limping, and the stiff, strapped arm he held the rifle with.

The sniper. It was the sniper from the construction site.

The sniper stepped over Eliza's drone as he dragged Will towards Eliza and her captor. The propellers were motionless, two of them buried in the dirt. But some of the lights on its underside still pulsed.

"The police are coming," Will said, as he and the sniper reached Eliza. "You should surrender now, and they may go easy on you."

Knife Man smiled, a slow, deadly smile like a lion might give before eating a particularly helpless antelope. "I am in control here, child, not you."

With a sudden, sharp movement, he grabbed Eliza's bandaged arm, and wrenched on it.

She screamed, a wretched, gasping wail. Will dove for her. But her eyes rolled up, and then she sagged, the knife sawing against her throat and drawing out another thin line of red.

THUD!

Will collapsed to the ground, his head screeching in red-hot pain. There was another thud, and this time agony exploded across his ribs and chest.

He struggled to breathe, but sucked in dirt and coughed, spluttering, the movement sending further torturous swords through his body.

"I shall kill him for you, Danial." He heard the sniper spit out. "Wipe them both from this life."

"Patience, Adam," Knife Man – Danial – said.

Something smashed jerkily into Will's side, and he rolled. Eliza was slumped on the ground beside Danial's feet, one of which had just ploughed into Will's kidney. His eyes locked on her. She was breathing. The knife had left only thin slices across her neck, nothing more.

"You and your friends have been quite the thorn in my side," Danial said, crouching down and putting a hand gently on Will's shoulder. "Though if you two are here alone, I do wonder what has happened to your police friend."

Will spat out dirt. "He'll be here any second."

"I think not," Danial said. He gazed out over the city lights. "What a pity that he shall miss the show."

"You can stop the bomb," Will said. "You still

have time. You can escape. Leave the city."

Danial smiled. "There is no escape for any of us. You, or me."

"Please," Will said, his voice pitching. "Just walk away. Go home. See your family – "

"What did you say?" Suddenly, the calm on Danial's face disappeared, his features twisting, and he snapped his hand forwards, grabbing Will's throat.

"See… your… family…" Will croaked. He struggled to heave a breath past the man's death-grip.

"You stupid, stupid child," Danial snarled, and his fingers tightened.

Will panicked. Air gone. He thrashed, his hands clawing up to pull at Danial's.

"I cannot go back." Danial's voice drifted, as if from a hundred metres away. Will's vision started to sparkle white and black at the edges. "None of us can."

There was a sudden electronic ringing.

Danial's fingers loosened, and Will gasped. Oxygen, precious oxygen, rushed into his lungs.

Danial rocked back on his heels, tugging a phone from his pocket. Adam lurched forwards, his rifle jabbing into Will's chest, pinioning him.

"What?" Danial's voice was terse.

"The inner city's being evacuated." Danial was close enough that Will could hear the tinny whine of the voice on the other end. "The streets around the Skyfeller have been locked down. Police are everywhere!"

Danial's face tensed in annoyance. "It matters not," he snapped. "They will all be dead soon."

"We cannot get out of the city," the voice continued. "We are running out of time to get outside the blast radius!"

Will saw Adam flinch, saw him glance quickly at the watch on his wrist, before increasing the force on Will's chest with the gun.

"That is not our mission," Danial snarled. "Our mission is justice, you fool. Nothing else matters."

"But – "

Danial stood abruptly, and whatever else the man said on the other end became inaudible. Danial started speaking very fast in another language, his voice rising angrily. After a moment, he hung up.

"I must deal with this before one of them does something terribly stupid," he snarled at Adam, striding towards the lift.

"Sir – " Adam started.

Danial cut him off with a wave of his hand, without turning back. "Do not let anyone but I onto this rooftop," he snapped. "And kill them both."

Chapter 37.

31 minutes left

Will's eyes darted. There had to be something he could use as a weapon.

But there was nothing but dirt and stones.

The barrel was jerked away from his chest.

"I think I will shoot her first," Adam said softly. He walked over to Eliza's unconscious form.

Will flinched, and immediately the rifle was pointed at him again.

"Have you ever seen a child die, boy?"

Will didn't answer. His eyes landed on his rifle, far beyond the sniper and Eliza.

Adam followed his gaze. "Optimistic, aren't you." He steadily aimed the rifle at Will's forehead.

"Mmph." Eliza moaned and shifted at Adam's feet, her legs curling up awkwardly towards her belly where her broken arm was cradled. And as she did, Will saw behind her legs, the drained drone, half-buried in the dirt.

Too flat to fly. But lights still blinked on its

underside.

Adam started, and jerked the rifle to point at Eliza. As he glanced away, Will shoved himself to his feet, his arms and legs pumping like pistons.

"Get back – " Adam shouted.

Will dove, ploughing into the dirt at Eliza's feet. He stretched, stretched, and his fingers wrapped around the drone.

He twisted, and pointed the drone at Adam.

"Your toy is dead," Adam said.

The rifle was aimed squarely at Will again. And Adam pulled the trigger.

CRACKCRACKCRACK!

Man and machine fired simultaneously.

There was a piercing scream. The drone exploded in Will's hands, shards of slicing material ripping through his shirt. Belatedly, Will realised the scream had come from his own mouth.

And then there was silence.

Adam was staring down at him, the rifle hanging loosely by his side. He swayed. And a red stain spread slowly across his stomach. Another matched it on his gun arm, just below the elbow.

"Will!" Eliza's voice was thick and panicked. She was struggling to sit up, her eyes on Adam's wobbling form above her.

Adam tried to lift the rifle, but it fell from limp fingers, spearing into the dirt. Heart screaming in his ears, Will scrambled up and charged, hitting the sniper with his shoulder.

Adam flew backwards, toppling into the dirt, as Will grabbed the rifle.

"Stay down!" Will yelled, his voice tearing raggedly at his throat. He grabbed Eliza's outstretched hand, hauling her to her feet and shoving her behind him. They backed away from Adam, Will's hands shaking on the gun aimed at the sniper's chest.

Adam groaned, then rolled onto his hands and knees.

"I'm warning you," Will said. "Don't move! I'll shoot!"

Adam looked up at him, freezing half-erect.

Will tightened his grip on the rifle, but it shook in his hands. "Don't," he said, softly.

A slow, rageful smile broke over Adam's face. "You are weak. Every person in this forsaken country is weak. You hide behind your technology and your advanced weaponry. But when that moment comes, when you must take a man's life *yourself*, you falter and weep. You let the weapons do the dirty work for you, because you trick yourself into believing that it removes the guilt from *your hands*."

He took a step, and Will jerked backwards, pushing Eliza further back behind him.

"But you are all at fault. The guilt cannot be wiped clean by your decadent denial." He waved a hand around, encompassing the glimmering city lights of Brisbane around them. His eyes, dark pools, locked onto Will. "Only fire can do that."

He charged.

Will shouted, the words lost even to him, and jerked the rifle. But Adam wasn't running for him and Eliza. Before Will could swing the rifle to aim again, Adam had dived behind the water feature.

Will followed, his feet pumping in the dirt. But before he made the fountain, a door slammed, echoing loud across the rooftop.

Will skidded to a stop, panting.

"He's gone down the stairwell," Eliza gasped, at his back.

Will turned, and dropped the rifle, grabbing her. He pushed her tangled, dirt-filled hair back from her face. "Are you okay?" His eyes flicked, scanning for injuries.

She nodded, wincing as he stroked her hair back over the lump on her skull.

"Sorry," he whispered, his hand freezing.

She looked up at him, her eyes wide and glistening, her face streaked with grime.

"It's okay," she said. "I'm okay."

Something inside him clenched too tight for him to breathe, and he pulled her tight to his chest. For a second, they stood there, breathing hard in synchronicity.

"This is so messed up," he murmured into the brown tangles of her hair.

She nodded, and pulled away. "No time to chase him down," she said softly. "If the nuke's up here, we need to find it."

Cool air rushed in against Will's body, the feeling

amplified by the lack of her heat against him. "They left shovels," he said. He scanned the wide garden bed, his stomach sinking.

"If we had one of the Geiger counters…" Eliza wobbled as she spoke, and he caught her arm, guiding her to the bench abandoned by Adam, Danial and the other two men. Carefully, they avoided the corpses sprawled on the dirt.

"Yeah. I guess I just have to start digging." He handed her the rifle, catching her eye grimly. "Cover me. They'll be back."

"We've got twenty-five minutes. We don't have time to dig up the whole garden." She glanced around and then set the rifle down, hauling herself up to grab a thick metal stake attached to one of the many saplings dotting the garden.

"You need to rest," he protested.

"We don't have time for that," she snapped. "Help me with this."

Together they rocked it back and forth until it slid easily from the soft dirt.

"We do a search grid," Eliza said. "Like in a crime show. How big do you think the nuke is?"

"A metre? Maybe?"

She nodded. "Okay. So ram the stake into the dirt as deep as you can."

Will hoisted it, then flung it down. The shaft thudded into the dirt, half of it disappearing below the surface.

"Now take a step, and repeat."

He heaved against the stake, pulling it out. As he did, she hurried to another tree, swinging back and forth on its stake until it came out.

"Ten seconds," she said, as she came back and jammed the stake in with her good hand beside him. "We need to go faster."

He nodded. Lift, throw, thud. Take a step.

"Eight seconds, better."

Lift, throw, thud. Take a step.

"Six seconds, awesome."

Lift, throw, thud. Take a step.

"Six seconds, keep it up."

Lift, throw, thud. Take a step.

"Six seconds. Take two steps this time."

"We might miss it." He was panting, his arms burning. He leaned against the stake.

She glanced at him. "We're going to run out of time otherwise." She took two wide steps, and rammed her stake down.

Lift. Throw. Thud. Two steps.

The silence of the rooftop was punctuated by nothing else but the dull thudding of the stakes entering the ground. They reached the end of the bed and turned, then again at the other end. By the time Will turned for the third time, his hands were raw and blistered.

Lift. Throw. Thud. Two steps.

Lift. Throw. Thud. Two steps.

Lift. Throw.

CLANG!

Will froze. Had he imagined it? But no, the jarring through the stake was still shaking up into his arm and shoulder. And Eliza had dropped her stake.

"Shovel!" he panted, and she grabbed it as she passed the bench, tossing it as she reached him.

He jammed it into the dirt, over and over.

Then: *CLANG!*

Eliza knelt, scooping with her good hand. Something green appeared amidst the dirt.

"That's it," she breathed. She looked up at him. "We found it."

"Hop back," he said, and jammed the shovel in beside it, digging quickly, but carefully. Moments later, he dropped the shovel.

Sitting in the hole was a drab green cylinder. It was about thirty centimetres in diameter, and a metre and a half long. One end was flat; the other tapered to a blunt point.

"It looks like an artillery shell," Eliza whispered.

Will crouched beside it. Tentatively, he ran his hand over the cold metal. A chill ran up his spine, popping goose bumps out all over him. Such a small thing, ready to kill millions of people. He swallowed. "There's no screws. No control panel or anything."

"How are we going to dismantle it?"

Will stood, staring at the shell. "I have no idea."

Eliza pulled her phone from her pocket and one-handed, typed something.

"The three Ds of bomb disposal," she read after a moment. "Defuse?"

Will shook his head. "I don't think so."

"Destroy, then." She glanced at the edge of the building. "We could roll it off. A hundred storeys onto concrete might break it."

"Or it sets it off," Will said.

"Then that leaves only one option."

He looked at her. Her face was tense.

"Detonate," she said.

There was a long, fraught silence.

"So we take it somewhere," Will murmured. "Somewhere safe, and let it go off."

She nodded.

"But where? Where can we take it that's *safe*?"

Eliza swallowed. "We can at least get it away from the city centre," she whispered. "The further we are from the centre, the more lives will be saved."

He looked down at the bomb. Then back at Eliza. And he nodded. This was the only way.

He jumped into the hole.

"Here," she said, handing him one of the stakes.

He wedged it under the bomb and pivoted it on the edge of the hole, heaving down on the free end with all his weight. The shell edged upwards, then rolled back down.

"You need a longer lever arm," Eliza said. She was hugging her broken arm to her chest again, her face pale. And Will saw that she was keeping her weight off her injured leg.

He nodded, grabbed the shovel, and wedged it under the stake as the pivot so that he had a longer handle to push on. He threw his weight down.

Ponderously, the shell lifted. Eliza pulled with her good arm and it stopped, teetering on the edge. Will jumped into the hole it had left and shoved, until it rolled slowly onto the flat dirt at Eliza's feet.

"I think I can roll it to the lift," he said, panting, as he climbed out. Eliza nodded, hefting the rifle.

A few minutes later, the shell sat in the centre of the industrial lift. Will stood, his back and arms aching, and glanced back. Eliza was hurrying down the gravel path towards him.

"I found these," she said, her voice tight. She held up a set of keys as she got in. The door pinged and closed, and the lift started to descend. "On... one of the bodies. If we're lucky, they're for the ute we saw downstairs."

The magnitude of what they were trying to do was rising up in Will's chest. He sucked in a shuddering breath. "Even if they are the ute keys, where can we take a fifteen kilotonne bomb in..." He glanced at his wrist. "Twenty-three minutes?"

Eliza passed him the keys then cradled her broken arm again. "Open water might work. The river's too shallow. But we wouldn't make it in time."

"Road tunnels?"

Her face screwed up. "Maybe. I think they get down to, like, a hundred metres deep under the city."

"And if that's not deep enough, then we're just going to blast millions of tonnes of radioactive rock all over Brisbane."

320

"How deep do we have to go?" She leaned against the wall of the elevator.

Will frowned. She was shaking again. The painkiller the doctor had given her was wearing off, he could see it. "Drake said that the fireball from the Bravo would have had a radius of thirty metres. But the nuke's a hundred and fifty times more powerful."

"A nine kilometre fireball," Eliza said tersely. "How the hell – "

"No," Will said, shaking his head. "It follows the cube law. So not one hundred and fifty times bigger. More like five times. But that's still a three hundred metre wide fireball."

"Not to mention the fallout," Eliza said.

The lift shuddered to a halt. Eliza leaned out, her hand tensing on the rifle. "It's clear," she whispered. "And the ute's still here."

Will breathed out, a great huff of relief. That was something, at least. He watched, as she slipped out, turning back to hold her arm across the sliding doors to keep them open. Her hair swung, tangled, around her face.

He swallowed, and bent to roll the bomb forwards. This was it. He could do this. He *had* to do this.

The shell rasped against the concrete, the sound echoing against the floor and walls of the loading dock. The ute was backed against the dock, so all he had to do was roll the bomb onto the open tray. The suspension screeched and the tray lowered several centimetres.

"Close it while I check the keys work," he said quickly, glancing at Eliza and jumping down to the front of the ute. She nodded, crouching to fiddle with the back tray flap.

The second key he tried was the right one. The locks on both front doors clicked open. Hand shaking, he tugged the driver's door open and slipped inside, jamming the key into the ignition.

He could see in the rear view mirror that Eliza was climbing awkwardly down from the tray, her injured leg stiff. His eyes scanned the dash. CB radio, cigarette lighter, stereo...

There.

He saw the button he needed as she flanked the passenger door.

He hit it. The central locking button. The doors locked again with a soft snick, and he sucked in a long, shuddering breath.

Eliza grabbed the passenger handle and tugged.

Nothing happened.

"The door's locked," she said.

He met her gaze steadily, though everything in him was shaking. It felt like even his blood was vibrating.

"Will, unlock the door," she said, her voice urgent.

He tore his eyes away, and turned the key in the ignition. The engine roared to life.

"Will!" Her voice rose, and she banged on the window. Her expression slipped from tense to confused, panicked.

He clenched his teeth together. "I'm sorry," he said. But it came out no more than a whisper.

"Open the door!"

He pressed the power window button for a fraction of a second, letting it slide down a few centimetres. Far enough for sound. But not for her to get her arm inside to unlock it herself.

"I'm sorry," he repeated. "I have to do this." His eyes lingered over her, taking in every last detail. The deep pools of brown, that were welling now with tears. The tiny upturned flick of her nose at the end. The tiny, thin scar on her left cheek, almost invisible after all these years. She gotten it falling – or jumping, rather – from the swing set in her backyard, when they were seven years old.

She'd wanted to fly.

"You can't do this alone," she said, and her voice pitched, cracking. "I'm coming with you!"

He shook his head. He had to protect her.

"There's only twenty minutes left! Where will you go?" Her voice became shrill.

"I'll work something out," he said. "Run. You have to run, as far as you can. Then find a basement, something solid. Lots of concrete. It'll protect you." He hoped with everything he had that the movies and television shows were right. That he was right in telling her that.

"No, Will, don't," she said, and now a sob cut through her words. "You'll... you'll die."

Her eyes were full of tears now, and they spilled over, thin, pale tracks through the grime coating her cheeks.

"I know," he whispered, tearing his eyes away from her. He reached down, pushing the automatic stick into drive. "But you won't."

And he hit the accelerator.

She yelled, and he heard the metallic clang of her fists beating against the side of the car.

He clenched his teeth together, fighting against the tight, strangling feeling in his chest. He could do this, at least. Get the bomb as far away from the city as he could.

Tears stung, as he glanced up, and caught sight of her tiny form, fading smaller and smaller, in the rear-view mirror.

He had nothing left to lose.

Just her.

Chapter 38.

19 minutes left

Danial hung up the phone with a fierce jab of his finger. It had taken too long to placate the idiots.

But now they were moving in on the Skyfeller building, ready to stand by him for the end, as they had vowed.

He strode back towards the destroyed foyer. As he stepped through the shattered glass, he almost tripped on a shadowed figure, crumpled on the ground.

"Danial," the figure moaned, as Danial stopped.

He frowned. "Adam?"

"I was looking for you." The man's voice was weak, and Danial crouched, trying to see in the dim, flickering light from the last remaining fluorescent tubes in the building's foyer.

Adam shifted, and Danial saw the dark stain soaking across the man's belly. Adam had one hand clamped over the wound.

"The children?" Danial barked, grabbing Adam by the shoulders. Adam flinched, his head lolling back.

"I was looking for you, but I fell… the bullet… my stomach – " Adam broke off, coughing in a wet, wracking hack.

"You left the bomb?" Danial shook the injured man hard.

"They overpowered me. I was wounded – they had the gun – "

"You *fool!*" Rage bubbled up inside Danial. Was every man he'd brought to this forsaken country as useless as the next?

"It's buried!" Adam spluttered. His eyes were listing unevenly closed. "It is safe!"

Danial stood abruptly, ripping out his phone. He tapped the screen and then cursed. "It's safe, is it?" He held the screen in front of Adam's face. On it, a flashing red dot moved slowly across an aerial map of the city.

"I – I – " Adam spluttered, his face draining white.

Danial backhanded him, hard, and Adam's head flicked into the floor with a sickening crack.

Danial's jaw clenched, and he punched the phone's call icon. In a moment, Harris answered. "The Alpha has been taken," Danial spat.

"What?" Harris' voice squeaked.

Danial jerked back from the smashed doorway as a spotlight swept over the building's entrance. A helicopter was passing overhead, the beam of light swinging methodically from side to side. "You will see the co-ordinates on your phone. Follow it. Kill the children. Bring the bomb back here." He looked

326

down at Adam, who lay, white-faced, watching him. "Adam will be... waiting to help you get it back in position."

He hung up.

"You're not going after it yourself?" Adam said thickly.

Danial pulled a media pass from his pocket and clipped it to his shirt. He glanced up at the sky. "I did not say that. I am taking matters into my own hands."

"But – "

He cut Adam off with a kick to the ribs. The man groaned, crumpling. "Because not a one of you can be trusted to do what needs to be done," he snarled.

And leaving Adam curled, moaning, on the floor, Danial stalked out into the smoke-filled street.

*

Will drove from the Skyfeller Centre, his heart thudding hard.

Police block ahead. Flashing lights. Concrete barriers.

He slammed on the brakes, and swung the ute around, wincing as he heard the groan of metal in the tray as the bomb shifted.

Moments later, he had to turn again. And again. And again.

He was trapped.

He jumped as his phone rang, blaring over the grumble of the engine. He tugged it out, and saw Drake's number.

"Where are you?"

"I'm stuck in the city," Will said tersely. "The cops have locked down the streets around the Skyfeller."

"I told you to get out of the city! There's a shoot-on-sight order for you and Eliza. Don't you get what that means?"

"It's too late for that," Will cut him off. "I've got the Alpha in the back of a ute. I'm trying to get it as far away as I can before it goes off."

There was a long, fraught pause. *"What?"*

Will sighed impatiently. "What I said. They wiped out the team you sent in."

Drake audibly ground his teeth. "They just told me that. But they're sending in another team. They'll still have time to disarm – "

"It's an artillery shell, welded shut. I don't think it can be disarmed."

"Bomb disposal guys are trained for this, Will: they'll disarm it!"

Will's mind flickered. "So I take it to the nearest cops, then. They'll shoot me, but the team will get to it in time to disarm it in… seventeen minutes?"

Drake was silent again for a long moment. "I don't want you getting shot," he said stiffly.

"I won't survive a bomb blast, either way." Will flinched as a jet roared overhead, its afterburner on full. It pitched upwards and streaked high into the blue-black sky, passing over Mount Coot-tha.

Something clicked.

"Drake," he said sharply. "How far is it to Coot-tha from the city? And how tall is it?"

"Eight or nine kilometres. And about three hundred metres. Why?"

Will slammed on the accelerator. "Three hundred metres."

"Tell me what you're thinking, Will. You get it up there, the nuke's still going to take out the Western suburbs."

"Not up," Will said. He glimpsed the flash of lights in his mirror and swore under his breath. A cop car was accelerating behind him. "*Under.* There's a quarry there. And tunnels, going under the mountain." His phone beeped, and he risked a glance at the screen. The low battery indicator was flashing. "Damn it," he grunted. "Drake – I'm running out of time. And the cops have just realised I'm here."

Static clicked on the phone. He heard Drake say something, but couldn't make it out. Behind him, a siren started wailing.

Will yanked the steering wheel, flying around a corner, and clamped his foot down hard on the accelerator.

"Drake? Do you hear me?"

"… get yourself to… chopper… what I can…" Static almost totally overwhelmed Drake's voice.

"If you can still hear me, I'm going for Coot-tha," Will said, his voice rising.

"… try… road…"

The phone died in a fitful burst of beeps. Will swore, and swung the wheel again. A roadblock loomed from the darkness ahead.

There was a gap. The squad car chasing him had left a space – not wide enough for the ute, but a space nonetheless – in the blockage.

Will clenched his jaw. If he could get through, without getting shot: maybe he could make it to the mountain.

He floored it.

Officers flooded into the road. Guns rose to aim at the ute. Someone with a megaphone blared something. Will steeled himself. They were probably telling him to stop or they'd shoot.

Fractions of a second later, the windshield starred. He was metres from the narrow gap between the cars when the windshield shattered completely, and bullets smacked into the rear cabin wall.

He ducked. Blind, he kept his foot clamped to the accelerator.

And hoped he'd still be alive on the other side.

The impact jerked the steering wheel from his hands as the ute funnelled between the cars. The screech of metal, screams and crackling yells over the megaphone filled the air.

Pain lanced through Will, as his body was thrown against the seatbelt. And then the piercing tear of metal stopped, and the ute was still careening forwards.

He grabbed the steering wheel. He was through.

He was through!

In the mirror, he could see the squad cars flung out where he'd ploughed through. Cops were running

330

after him. He yelped and ducked again at the crack of bullets thwacking into the back of the cab.

But nothing pierced the metal cab wall.

He focussed on the road ahead, his foot still flat to the metal. He wove between the few cars on the road, slamming the brake only when he had to. The wind howled through the smashed windscreen, stinging his eyes.

Behind him, the drone of sirens rose. And then the flash of lights appeared in his mirror.

They were catching back up.

A sign appeared ahead. Five kilometres to the mountain. Will sucked in a breath. Could he make it?

The lights grew behind him, the sirens a whining roar. The ute crested a slight rise.

And a semi-trailer appeared in front of him, chugging slowly up the hill, as the ute catapulted straight for the back of it.

"Crap!" Will slammed the brakes and yanked the steering wheel. The ute spun sideways, and Will swung the wheel back the other way, trying to regain control.

But it was too late. The ute lost all grip on the road and just kept spinning. There was a bone-shaking crunch as it hit the raised median strip between the lanes of traffic. Blood exploded in Will's mouth as he bit down on his tongue, the car bouncing him into the door.

The ute spluttered, and stalled.

A stunned fragment of time. The air filled with the

harsh pants of his breath.

And then the sirens broke through the silence.

Will struggled upright, and with shaking fingers, twisted the key in the ignition.

Nothing happened.

"Come on, come on," he muttered, the taste of metal filling his mouth. In the mirror, the squad cars were seconds away.

Will twisted the key again. Nothing.

He swore, and smashed his fist against the dashboard. The handpiece of the CB radio popped off and clocked him in the knee before swinging on its curly cord.

He risked another look back. The squad cars were screeching to a stop behind the ute.

"Start, damn it!" He twisted the key so hard he thought it might snap off in his hand.

"Come out with your hands up!" A voice boomed through a megaphone. "You have five seconds before we open fire!"

Will closed his eyes briefly. Shot by cops. At least it was a dramatic way to die.

He looked out the window. The closest cop was poised behind her open car door, a pistol trained on his head.

Will shook his head. "Don't," he whispered.

She lowered her head, sighting along the top of the gun.

Will looked at the car's dash clock. Hopefully Drake's bomb team would get here in time. Maybe they could disarm the bomb, after all. Maybe he'd gotten far enough away that Eliza would survive the blast.

Maybe. Maybe. Maybe. It was too late now.

There was a bright trace of something very hot and moving very fast zapping towards the closest squad car.

And then an incandescent fireball exploded, encompassing the squad car and the officer.

Will screamed, ducking as the ute's remaining side windows shattered, raining safety glass over him. When he raised his head again, a smoky fireball was rising, the gutted skeleton of the car left in its wake.

Cops were screaming and running, rearranging themselves with their guns pointed backwards now, away from Will.

Towards a white van, pulled up fifty metres behind Will's ute. Men hung out the open door, one holding what looked like a rocket launcher. The others held rifles.

They, and the cops, opened fire simultaneously.

"Crap!" Will, heart hammering, tried the key again. The car spluttered, almost starting, but failed. "Come on!"

He heard the pulsing beat of a helicopter. Then:
BOOM!

The rocket launcher bucked, and the other cop car exploded. Burning fragments rained down on the ute's bonnet.

Then there was silence.

"Boy!" The voice came from the van, again through a megaphone, but it was a strongly accented voice now. "Get out of the car, and we will let you walk away!"

Will glanced in the mirror. Black-clad men were spilling from the van, rifles raised. As he watched, a cop shifted on the ground, and one of the men shot the figure calmly in the head. A casual movement, as if exterminating an annoying pest.

Will gritted his teeth, and forced himself to slowly turn the key in the ignition again. He jiggled the wheel as he'd seen Jeff do a thousand times.

The ute backfired, coughed, then roared.

"Yes!" Will floored the accelerator, and the ute took off, the wheels spinning in the gravelly edges of the median strip. There was a bump as the rear wheels got over the concrete divider, and then he was charging forwards, on the wrong side of the road but *moving*, moving again, towards the mountain.

In the mirror he saw the men piling back into the van. It took off after him, thudding over the median strip behind him.

And then a helicopter swooped down in front of him, the tail spinning until the chopper was side-on to the front of the ute.

Will cursed, and slammed the brakes again, but the chopper was manoeuvring quickly out of his way, swinging off until it was next to the still-charging ute. Will glanced over, his hands clamped on the wheel.

It was a medivac chopper. The huge red cross on

the side flashed across his vision.

And through the open cabin: was that… was that *Drake*, flying it?

Will gaped, and then yanked on the wheel as cars emerged in front of him, blaring their horns. The ute thudded over the median strip again, and he was back on the right side of the road. The chopper disappeared behind him, the blades tilting down as it zoomed towards the white van.

Mount Coot-tha: 3 km.

The sign flashed past Will. He swung the wheel, getting the ute off onto a side street. Where hopefully there'd be less traffic. With his peripheral vision he watched the mirror, counting.

One one thousand.

Two one thousand.

Three one thousand.

Four one thousand.

Five one thousand.

And then the van burst around the corner onto the road behind him.

The chopper – Drake – if it was him – had gained him a hundred metres. Will turned sharply again. And the CB radio handset smacked him in the leg again, swinging from its cord.

The radio.

Will grabbed it. The chopper had to have an emergency frequency it could be reached on, right?

He held down the button. "Drake!"

Nothing.

335

Without taking his eyes from the road, he twisted the CB frequency dial a click. Then shouted Drake's name again. And again. And again.

"Will? Holy hell! That you?"

Will would have gone limp with relief if he hadn't been holding onto the wheel and the CB handpiece so hard.

"Are you in a chopper?" he yelled.

"I've got eyes on you! I'm on your back!"

The beat of the chopper's blades droned through again, and Will could have cried.

"I can't shake them," he said, his voice cracking.

"They're not going to shoot you with the bomb in the back," Drake said grimly. "They're just following you. You can do this."

"Shoot them!"

"It's a hospital chopper, not an army one," Drake said grimly. "But I'll charge them again. Slow them down. Will, you're coming up on the roundabout that leads to the base of Coot-tha. When you get to the quarry, you drive down the main tunnel. It's decommissioned but you should be able to get in. Go in as far as you can. Roll the bomb off. Then get the hell out of there. I'll be waiting in the quarry to pick you up."

"Okay," Will said, hope filling his chest like a puffy balloon. "I can get it done."

"I'm going to charge them again. Try to get them off your tail."

The drone of the chopper died off. In the mirror,

Drake angled the chopper down, zooming towards the van. It swerved, and then Will lost sight of it as the roundabout appeared in front of him.

He shot through at eighty kilometres an hour, scraping past the solitary car already making the turn.

"Will!" Drake's voice crackled through the CB. Simultaneously, there was a colossal bang, and the ute swung and shook. "They're trying to take out your tyres!"

The ute jerked, and then spun completely around. Bullets hissed past Will into the car's bonnet. As the ute came to a stop facing the wrong way, he saw the van skidding down the road towards him, men with rifles hanging out the side.

Drake's chopper swarmed down again, and the van swerved, but straightened and kept coming.

Will cursed and hit the accelerator, spinning the wheel around. The ute moved sluggishly, and a rubbery limping sound on one side told him at least one tyre had been blown out.

"What the – " Drake's voice cracked through again.

Will glanced up. Drake was keeping pace with him in the air, periodically swooping down towards the van.

But now something else emerged from the darkened sky. There was a pulsing overlaying the drone from Drake's chopper.

And a *second* chopper appeared behind Drake.

It was flying so low, the streetlights cast enough

light over it for Will to glimpse the Channel Eleven logo.

Melissa. The news station she worked for?

A flash of flame lit up the side of the media chopper. Sparks exploded from the rotor blades of Drake's.

"They're shooting on me!" Drake's voice was panicked through the CB.

Will tore his eyes away from the firefight, swerving along the curving road. "Drake – it's Melissa's chopper. From Channel Eleven."

"It ain't Melissa in it," Drake ground out. "Keep your eyes on the road. You've got a job to do – "

The sky flashed, and Will yelped. An explosion of flame burst in Will's mirrors. Drake's chopper emerged from the flame.

The tail boom was on fire. Will glimpsed the mangled twist of the tail rotor. Then Drake's chopper wavered, and started to spin.

"Drake!" he yelled into the CB.

"Will – get to the quarry," Drake's voice cracked. "I'm going to buy you some time."

Will saw the medivac chopper list sideways, as if Drake was trying to get it back under control. It drifted, its spin increasing, towards the van.

"No, Drake, don't – " Will shouted.

"Get the bomb into the tunnel – "

And then Drake's voice cut off, as the chopper ploughed into the van.

There was a *WHOOMPF* that rattled the ute as the

338

van and chopper collided in a great, glowing fireball.

"No," Will said, his voice cracking into a sob, his finger still pressed down hard on the CB handset.

And the fireball rose into the dark behind him, the trail of smoke left in its wake lit yellow by the streetlights.

The ute sped towards the mountain. Will's fingers were white as he clutched the steering wheel.

And his eyes were slick with tears.

Chapter 39.

14 minutes left

Wind howled through the smashed windows of the cab. In moments, the tears had stopped. What was the point of crying now? Drake was gone. But so was Jeff. So were his parents.

So was he.

Will felt a cold, numb calm descending over him.

Get to the mountain.

Drive into the tunnel.

Let the bomb go off, underground.

Dimly, over the whip of the wind, he heard the pulse of the media chopper. It was following him. Whatever gunman it contained: they were not giving up yet.

It didn't matter. What could they do from a chopper? It couldn't fly after him into the tunnel.

He just had to get there.

Drive under.

Let it go off.

Mount Coot-tha was looming on the skyline ahead

of him. Then, half-hidden behind overgrown bushes, he saw the red sign with the word *QUARRY* emblazoned on it.

He swung the wheel. The back end of the ute slid out as the bitumen gave way to gravel. The road curved in a large arc around the side of the mountain, threading its way between the mountainside and a fenced-off lake, before opening up into the bottom of a huge open-cut quarry.

In the moonlight Will could see the sloped quarry walls, cutting deep into the side of the mountain. Each wall was covered with an enormous tarpaulin held down with cables.

He was suddenly sucked back to a time long, long ago. Before his parents had died. Back when Uncle Jeff had still been... Uncle Jeff, and not a person scarred by the death of his brother and struggling under the pressure of raising a kid that wasn't his, alone. His Dad had set up a slip-and-slide in the backyard. Eliza had been there – of course, because she had always been there. They'd squirted dishwashing detergent all over it, pinned the hose down with a brick at the top of the slide and then thrown themselves down the tarp, over and over, sloshing into the well of muddy water at the end.

When had that been? How old had he been then? No more than five, and yet he remembered it so clearly.

He was inside the quarry now, passing mining trucks, bulldozers and white demountable offices.

And then his headlights flashed over the boarded-up tunnels, leading under the mountain. He took his foot off the accelerator, letting the ute slow under its own weight.

He glanced at his watch. 6:47 PM.

The beating drone of the helicopter rose. Will glanced back and saw it descending to the road between two trucks a fair distance behind him, cutting off the way back out.

No matter. He wasn't getting out of here anyway.

The ute had rolled to a stop. He followed the headlights ahead again. The road curved, then seemingly ended at the quarry wall a hundred metres or so ahead, at a heavy-looking wooden door.

Drake's tunnel.

Will glimpsed movement in the mirror. A man was jumping down from the chopper. He paused in the centre of the road, his face, invisible across the distance, turned towards the ute. Then he jogged back past the helicopter, towards a bulldozer parked behind the trucks.

Will gunned the engine again, and the ute sprung forwards, kicking up gravel. In the mirror he saw the dozer's lights flash on. Then it was moving forwards. Distantly, Will registered the shriek of tortured metal. And then the helicopter was crumpling, as the bulldozer pushed it off the road.

Cold trickled down Will's spine. Whoever it was: they'd just cut off their own escape route too. Will swallowed, and floored the accelerator.

The tunnel got closer. Will glimpsed the biggest padlock and chain he'd ever seen holding the door shut, flashing in the ute's headlights.

And then he squeezed his eyes shut, as the ute ploughed through the timber.

The steering wheel wrenched at his hands as the ute's bull-bar splintered the door. An explosion of wood and metal showered through the broken windows and he screamed, ducking and covering his head with his hands. There was a tearing roar of metal on stone, and sparks showered him, burning tiny holes wherever his flesh wasn't already covered by debris.

As the pelting shards stopped, he grabbed the steering wheel and yanked, and then the ute was roaring along free of the wall, charging into the dark. One headlight was still working. He glimpsed wooden support struts flashing past in the shadows. The tunnel was about five metres wide but less than half that tall.

BANG!

The car jerked, and swung into the other wall. Will yelped, hauling on the wheel as the ute shuddered and screamed along the rough stone wall. He managed to get it back in the middle of the tunnel, but it was shaking up and down now, a dull thwacking sound coming from the back.

Another tyre out.

The ute slowed, the engine making a weird rhythmic groaning. Will pumped the accelerator, but nothing happened. In moments, he was going only thirty kilometres an hour, no matter the force he jammed onto the accelerator.

How far under was he? Was it far enough?

He started to count, and pleaded with the car to hang in there, as long as the tunnel lasted. They limped on in the darkness for another full minute.

Then the tunnel walls disappeared.

A spike of panic flushed Will and he slammed the brake. The ute started to spin, the headlights glancing around an open cavern, about four times the width of the tunnel. He glimpsed fallen trestle tables and rusted metal lockers before the pitch darkness swallowed them again.

Finally, the ute stopped spinning. The engine spluttered. And then it died.

Will panted. All-encompassing silence blanketed him. He sucked in a long, shaking breath, and then looked at his watch. Eleven minutes to go.

The ute had come to a stop with the lights pointing across the cavern. At the far side, cables snaked up into the darkness, above a metal cage sitting beside a black hole in the ground.

With shaking hands, Will pushed the driver's door open. It jammed, the metal twisted and buckled, and he had to kick it with both feet before it would let him free. Finally, he slipped out onto the hard stone floor.

A strong breeze was rushing towards the tunnel, swirling his sweat-damp hair off his forehead. How far had he come under the mountain? A minute at thirty kilometres… about five hundred metres.

Far enough to contain the explosion? Hopefully. Maybe.

The silence was broken by the dim echoing of a dull, roaring rumble. Will's heart jumped into his throat. He peered down the tunnel. Was that… light growing in the distance?

The dozer. It was coming.

He swallowed hard, and scrambled for the back of the ute. Get it off the tray. Then there'd be no chance of driving it back out of here. For better or worse, this is where it would detonate.

After the third kick the mangled rear door on the tray came loose. Will clambered up, and shoved at the nuke.

Nothing happened.

"Damn it!" He wedged himself between the cab and the shell, and heaved.

As he did, an incandescent beam of light lit up the tunnel. The mechanical rumble grew to a roar.

Will swore, and threw every ounce of effort he could at the shell. Ponderously, it shifted, and then started to roll. He heaved again, and it tipped off the end of the tray, thudding onto the dirty stone, and kept rolling, coming to a stop a few metres away.

Will jumped, throwing himself back into the shadows beyond the ute, as the bulldozer burst into the cavern. It didn't slow down. Instead, it ploughed into the ute.

The ute crumpled, crushed under the huge bulk of

the earthmoving machine. Will dove out of the way, rolling to a pained stop with his arms over his head, as the dozer ploughed the smashed ute across the cavern.

Then finally, it stopped, and the engine cut out. There was aching, ear-splitting silence, broken only by Will's harried gasps.

The door opened, and a man climbed down slowly, his face lit eerily by the glow from the twisted ute's remaining headlight.

It was the leader of the group from the rooftop.

Danial.

The knife that he'd held against Eliza's throat glinted in his hand. His dark eyes scanned the cavern. And then his face twisted into some semblance of a smile, as he saw Will, curled on the ground.

"What a shame you weren't in the ute," he sneered.

Will climbed to his feet. "It doesn't matter if you kill me," he said. His voice came out steady. Calm. He was going to die down here, with this maniac on a bulldozer, every one of his atoms obliterated in the most fundamental of all energy reactions. "We're both dead now, no matter what you do."

Danial's eyes flicked around the cavern, a brief flicker of frustrated anger passing across his features. Will held still. The bomb was in the dark, back behind the dozer now, practically still in the tunnel.

"You must think you've won," Danial said. "Saved the day."

"Not won," Will said. His hands clenched and unclenched in fists. "But a whole lot less people are going to die now, at least."

"You haven't changed anything." Danial took a step closer. The knife glinted in the pallid yellow light. "You will die. And I will die. But nothing has changed."

"You deserve to die," Will said softly. "You murdered my uncle. And all those police."

"I brought murderers to *justice*," Danial spat.

There was a sudden burst of stronger wind, and Will frowned. The cables beyond the crumpled ute were wavering slightly. He glanced back at Danial, registered what he'd said. "What are you talking about? Jeff never hurt anyone."

"I was a farmer once," Danial said. His voice grew cold, flat. "I grew my crops, sold them at the market, provided for my family. I had a son and daughter, a few years younger than you. And then a bomb landed on our home. I watched from my field as it destroyed everything I loved."

Will swallowed. He shifted, slowly, his eyes on Danial. The cage sprawled on the ground in front of the mangled ute was below a shaft. A shaft that went up, into the mountain. And was letting air in, to rush through the chamber as a breeze.

"I went to my village elder and they gave me four hundred dollars and said there was nothing else they could do. So I went to the city and the American embassy and after months and months I could talk to them. But they refused to tell me anything. And the French embassy. And the British." Danial was staring blankly into space, as if Will wasn't even there.

A rushing burst of adrenaline flushed through Will, a pulsing, swamping energy that burnt through his resigned, numb calm.

Maybe there was a way out of here.

"I'm sorry your family was killed," Will said, into the tense silence. He shifted closer to the cage. "But that's not the fault of anyone *here*."

Danial's cold eyes locked onto him. "I went back to my home, and I searched until I found a fragment of the bomb, and I took it to the local fighters. It was an older bomb, only in use by a few countries. And they showed me their surveillance for that day. It was an Australian plane that bombed my home. An Australian pilot who murdered my wife and my children."

Will stilled. "Australian pilots?" His heart beat hard, every nerve alive and buzzing.

Danial's face twisted. "You didn't know your troops were in my country?" he spat. "You didn't see them, paraded around, waving your flag? Did you ever think about what they were actually doing over there?" Danial's hands were shaking, the knuckles white around the knife handle.

"They were there to help you," Will said. His voice cracked.

"You ignorant fool," Danial hissed. "They were there to kill my family."

"It must have been a mistake." Will took another edging step towards the cage. His mind split. He was raking over what Danial was saying; he needed to keep the man talking, keep him distracted. But now he was close enough to the cage to see how the cables all interlaced. And that calm, rational part of his mind shoved its way to the front, taking over.

This was a puzzle.

He just had to solve it.

The cables snaked down from above, attaching to eyebolts on the top of the cage. One bypassed the cage, and was attached to an empty metal basket, inset in the black hole in the floor of the cavern.

Beside it, was a neatly stacked pile of hefty stones.

"There was no mistake," Danial's voice pitched louder. "Our village had no terrorists in it. They knew that and they bombed us anyway. And then covered it up, so your reporters wouldn't have to talk about how your country was responsible for killing innocent children."

Will was behind the pile of stones now. Could he get enough into the counterweight basket before Danial was on him?

Danial raised the knife. "I saw my children murdered in front of me. To lose your family, outlive your children is the most horrible of things. You have denied me my revenge…"

Will moved.

He threw all of his weight against the pile of rocks. There was a grinding scrape, and the pile tumbled into the basket.

The basket sank into the hole, and simultaneously, the cage shuddered and dust puffed as it started to lift off the ground. The basket disappeared completely below the ground, as Will launched himself at the cage, already at head-height.

Both hands locked on the caged base, and he was sucked up into the air.

And then a searing pain tore through his right side.

Danial's knife skittered away to the ground below, as blood spurted from below Will's ribs. He cried out, the wound like a blade of fire lancing through him. His grip slipped, his right hand going limp as the cage rattled and shook.

The cage stopped dead.

Will tightened his left hand on the cage, his right dangling heavily by his side. He tried to heave it back up, but the pain sent a blinding red haze across his vision.

"You are quick." Danial's voice drifted from below.

Will fought the haze, twisting to look down.

Danial was ten metres below, both hands clamped on the counterweight cable.

"I didn't realise there was a way out, until you moved," Danial said, his voice strained. He lifted one hand from the rope. There was a bright, bloodied stripe across his palm where the rope had ripped into the flesh.

Will clenched his teeth. The muscles in his left arm were burning, the feeling coming through in dull waves between the blinding throb in his side.

"I wonder…" Danial said softly. "Will you fall, or bleed out? Or will you last, until the explosion?"

Will's mind darted. Even if he survived the fall, and somehow managed to take out Danial, he'd have seconds, if that, to grab the counterweight rope himself, before the cage disappeared completely into the darkness above.

Taking with it his only chance of escape.

He'd shoved at least fifty or sixty kilograms of rock into the basket. But by the way Danial was holding the cable, with one hand, it looked like he was hardly lifting anything at all.

The cage jiggled slightly, and his left hand slipped.

"Come down, child."

With a mammoth effort, Will threw his right hand up, grinding his teeth through the pain. A cry tore out of him, but then he'd done it, his right hand was back on the cage again.

He clamped his fingers, locking them tight.

He had to make Danial let go of the cable. Or make the cage lighter. Then the cage would rise.

But how? Jump off? Pointless.

The cage jiggled again and then rose. Below, Danial stepped backwards, still holding the cable, towards his knife.

Will's blood froze. If Danial cut the counterweight cable and let go… Will would fall ten metres to the

351

ground, before being crushed by several hundred kilos of metal cage a fraction of a second later.

Several hundred kilos of metal cage...

Bingo.

Will heaved, with everything his muscles had left, and swung his legs up. His body screamed, the pain lancing through him like molten fire. He missed the cage and his legs swung back down, sending a whole new level of pain raging through him.

He gasped, struggling for breath. No time. Do it now!

Again he swung. Again his legs missed, and yanked down again on the wound.

Again.

And this time, he wedged one foot between the vertical bars of the cage.

He hauled himself up, as Danial reached the knife below. The man's eyes were on the ground. Not on Will, struggling, bleeding, heaving himself onto the top of the cage like a half-dead seal.

The cable was wound in a complex knot around a rusting ring bolt welded to the top of the cage. There was a release mechanism like a rock climbing carabiner. Will's hands shook as he shoved at the release prong.

It didn't budge.

The cage lurched. Through the cage, Will saw Danial lift the knife.

And he started to saw.

Will tugged at the knot. But the fibres were

melded together by the tension.

"Damn it," he said, his voice cracking. Hot, stinging tears of pain and frustration made his vision swim. Desperately, he hauled himself up, until he was standing on the cage. And he kicked the ring bolt.

Rust flaked off in dingy fragments. He kicked again, and again.

And finally, the clasp screeched open.

He collapsed back to his knees, clinging to the cable as the cage swung wildly. The rope was wrapped tight against the top of the ring. And it wouldn't move.

The cage lurched suddenly, the cable whiplashing wildly in the air above him. The tension relieved around the ring bolt for a fraction of a second, before gravity pulled it taut again.

Clinging to the top of the cage, Will saw that strands of the thick cable were unravelling as Danial sawed through it.

And every time a strand snapped, the cage lurched again.

Everything seemed to slow. Will wound his left hand around the cable above the cage. Then he grabbed the ring bolt with his right, and he watched Danial sawing, back and forth.

His side throbbed. His pulse raced, beating loud and hard in his ears.

Another strand of the cable snapped with a loud crack. The cage fell. Will ripped the cable down and sideways.

And it popped out of the ring.

The cage started, ponderously, to fall.

The rope jerked, tearing into Will's hand. His grip slipped, and burning pain seared through his forearm. He got his right hand onto the cable and then his whole body was snatched upwards, his feet waving, dangling, in the air.

He heard Danial's scream, as the cage collapsed towards the ground, and the counterweight was snatched from the man's hands, no longer balanced against the cage.

He got one last glimpse of the man's twisted, rage-filled face, a macabre mask in the stark light from the bulldozer, before he was sucked into the shaft above.

And into endless, fathomless blackness.

Chapter 40.

The air rushed past, the breeze morphing into a gale whipping past his ears. He had no idea how fast he was moving. He scrunched his eyes shut but it made no difference: the dark was total and absolute.

He forced his eyes open long enough to look down. The cavern was a tiny yellow dot, dwindling fast. With a ragged gasp, he tightened his hands on the cable. Falling... would not be fun.

How far up did this elevator shaft go? He suddenly had visions of the cogs and gears and pulleys that the cable was flying through, counterweighted by the heavy basket of rock falling into the depths of the earth, far below. He pictured his body, thrown upwards at high speed, mangled and torn up by the ancient rusted machinery.

Right before the bomb blast blew him to smithereens, anyway.

Then, with gasping relief, he saw a slight lessening in the dark above.

The top was open, after all. The breeze hadn't lied. He was going to come out of this great column of stone into open air, on top of the mountain.

And then he realised that he would fall.

Straight. Back. Down.

He was hurtling towards the open top of the shaft at breakneck speed. He would shoot out into the air, gradually slow to a stop... right before gravity pulled him smoothly right back into the shaft.

He kicked out frantically. The dim patch of open sky above was growing fast. His body swung in reaction to the kick but he hit nothing.

He kicked again. This time his foot hit the shaft wall. Spasms of pain ricocheted up his leg and burned across his torso.

He gritted his teeth, and kept kicking. Above, he could see now that the cable ran over a thick beam, which bisected the opening of the shaft. Moonlight spilled into the shaft, lighting up the walls as if it were day, compared to the blackness below.

Thirty metres to the top.

Twenty.

Ten.

Five metres from the top, he let go of the rope, mid-swing.

The rope shot ahead, and his body continued its trajectory behind it. He catapulted from the hole, his feet clipping the edge. He pitched forwards, still sailing through the air, arms and legs windmilling, desperately trying to find land, or anything that would slow his crazed flight.

And then he arced downwards and ploughed into the ground, sliding face-first to a stop in the dew-damp grass.

*

For several long seconds, he just panted, great huffing breaths that blew dirt and grit up into his face.

Then he forced himself to his feet, wincing as his side protested with a great torrent of slicing pain.

He held his arm tight to the wound. His shirt was thick and wet with blood. But at least it didn't seem to be spurting out anymore.

He looked around. He was in an open grassy area surrounded by trees. A dirt path led out of the clearing. He hobbled towards the path, glancing down the shaft as he passed it, half-expecting to see Danial's crazed face climbing hand-over-hand up the rope. But there was nothing but darkness. The rope had run through and fallen back down, leaving nothing but a still-turning pulley wheel at the top.

He glanced at his watch.

Five minutes.

Five minutes before the bomb directly below his feet obliterated the mountain and anyone still on top of it.

His hobble turned into a limping run. Five minutes to try and get far enough away that he might survive.

Even as he pushed through the overgrown trees, he knew it was hopeless. Five minutes to get off the mountain? He'd never make it.

But some dogged part of him wouldn't let him give up. And it whispered: *try*.

So he ran.

Fifty metres up the path, the trees opened to another clearing. A chain mesh fence appeared on either side of the path, which ran beside a couple of sheds before heading uphill.

There was a sign on the fence. Beyond it: the distant lights of the city. Higher up loomed television towers, peeking over the tops of the trees.

He squinted at the sign, forcing his eyes to adjust to the dim moonlight.

Only powered flight and hang-glider launches from this point. Wing suit jumpers use Point Smeets: 1500m. Downhill MB course: 300m.

An arrow pointed up the path towards Point Smeets, and down to the mountain biking course.

His mind clicked into gear. A bike. The sheds. He could see now the familiar logo of an energy drink company pasted on the front wall.

He ran for the closest one, and yanked at the door. It was padlocked. The second shed wasn't, but the door was still locked. He backed up, then charged at the door.

Agony exploded as his shoulder hit the metal. There was a taut shrieking as the door buckled, and then he was tumbling onto the concrete floor inside.

A wall-mounted light flickered on. The shed was filled with sporting equipment: skateboards, mountain bikes, roller blades. Colourful bodysuits hung from the walls.

He grabbed the nearest bike.

"Three minutes to the road," he muttered, jerked the bike to untangle it from the other equipment. "Ninety seconds, at full speed, gets me… damn it."

He hauled the bike towards the buckled door. It wasn't going to be enough. Even if he could go at full speed, with his side bleeding out…

As he tried to yank the bike over the bent door, the handle snagged on one of the suits. The fabric flared outwards and unrolled.

Will froze.

What he'd taken for the arm of the suit, was actually a *wing*.

He dropped the bike, and grabbed the suit down from the wall. He ran his bloodied hands over the webbing strung between the arms and legs.

He'd seen such a suit before. But from a long way away. From the bus, with Eliza, when it had been gliding through the air.

He leapt over the broken door, clutching the suit to his stomach, his mind whirring. He'd drop like a stone, for several seconds, until he hit a high enough velocity to start gliding forwards. So he needed to be high. As high as he could get.

His eyes locked on the television tower, rising high above the tree line.

Then at his watch. 6.57 PM.

"Damn it," he muttered, and backtracked into the

shed, hauling the bike one-handed over the door. It clanged, caught, and then finally fell free onto the path.

He threw his leg over the seat and hit the pedals. Gravel spun from the wheels, the bike sprung forwards, and Will took off, towards the tower.

Chapter 41.

0 minutes left

Half a kilometre below, Danial sat on the bulldozer.

A photo rested in his palm. He lifted a hand, and touched the faces that stared back at him. Smiling faces. Relaxed arms around small shoulders.

His fingers smeared blood across the glossy surface. Smeared blood across the last impression left in this world that any of them had ever existed.

A few metres away, deep inside its dull green metal casing, a cylindrical uranium bullet rocketed down a barrel and smashed into a uranium spike at the end.

A millionth of a second later, the bulldozer, Danial and the entire cavern were vaporized in a flash of light.

And then there was nothing but blackness.

Epilogue

No parachute.

Alive, but falling, falling fast, towards an imploding mountainside covered in rocks and trees.

Will fought the rushing wind to suck in a tight breath. He scanned the ground, looking for something, anything, that would mean something other than instant death if he landed on it.

The river? Could the wing suit get him that far? He scanned the horizon.

No chance. He couldn't even see it from here. It was kilometres away.

And then his eyes caught on something pale and expansive, shining dewy-wet in the pale moonlight.

That day, so long ago, flashed across his mind again. The summer slip-and-slide. His parents, alive. Jeff, stress-free and relaxing.

And Eliza.

And with a smile, he twisted his arms and legs to bank sharply through the air, ignoring the pain ricocheting through his injured side, and he headed for the great, taught tarps, spread over the quarry walls.

*

Will opened his eyes.

Dimly, he registered a white ceiling. Muted fluorescent lights. Pale blue concertina curtains, hanging from a suspended rail. A television mounted from the ceiling, switched on but playing aerial footage of Brisbane on mute.

He was in a bed, he realised. He tried to sit, wincing pre-emptively. But there was no tearing pain in his side. Not even an ache. Just a dull, cotton-wool kind of feeling, all over his body.

His eyes drifted to beside his bed. And something warm and choking and beautifully painful welled up inside him.

Eliza.

She was curled in a brown fake-leather chair, her eyes closed. Her hand was in a pale blue fibreglass cast, up to the elbow. A thick white bandage swathed her leg. Her chest rose and fell softly, and her eyelashes fluttered, but she didn't wake.

He slumped back into the bed, and a huge grin spread over his face. His cheeks hurt, like the muscles there hadn't been used for smiling in a long time. Like, a *really* long time. He felt light and floaty, and a high, disbelieving laugh escaped his throat.

"You're awake!" Eliza had catapulted from the chair and was on top of him before he could blink.

He laughed breathlessly, as she wrapped her good arm around his neck and crushed him. He half-sat, curling his arms around her and holding on, burying his face in her hair. She smelled perfect, clean, vaguely like some kind of flower, like *her*.

"I didn't think I'd ever see you again," he whispered.

She stilled in his arms. "I didn't think I'd ever see

you again," she breathed against his neck. And as she pulled back, he saw tears glistening in her eyes.

Then she slapped him hard on the shoulder. "What were you thinking?"

"Hey! Go easy. I'm injured!" he said, with a laugh.

"Trust me, that's the only reason I'm only beating you with *this* hand," she said, her eyes flashing, holding up the arm uncovered by the heavy cast.

He leaned back against the bed. "Well. I guess my luck hasn't run out entirely, then."

She sat on the side of the bed, facing him, and he shuffled his legs to make room for her. "You should buy a lottery ticket. You've had more good luck than any one person deserves."

Will swallowed. The crashing drive into the mountain… the jerking ride up the shaft… the flight and then his skidding, crazed landing on the quarry tarps, flashed through his mind. "It didn't feel like good luck," he said softly.

She leaned forwards, taking his hand in her good one. "You're alive. Right?"

He nodded.

"And you saved Brisbane," she went on. "Because of you, all this is still here." She waved her hand around, taking in the hospital, and the city beyond.

"What about the mountain?"

"Well, it's basically a pile of rubble." She dropped his hand and ran her hand through her hair. "The area's been evacuated. The whole lot's cordoned off, while they mitigate any radiation that was able to

364

escape. But no one else died. Not by the bomb blast, at least. Except…"

"Except Drake," Will said, the man's last ditch dive flashing back suddenly. His throat tightened, and his eyes stung. He swallowed. "He was a grumpy old bastard. But he died to protect me. We have to make sure everyone knows that. He flew the chopper into the van to stop them – "

Eliza was looking at him strangely, and she cut him off suddenly, leaning forwards eagerly. "Will, Drake's not dead."

"What?"

"He's not dead!" The words tumbled from her mouth. "They pulled him from the wreckage. He's got bad burns, and more broken bones than you could count, but he's alive, and he's going to pull through. He's recovering in the ICU, here, in this hospital."

Slowly, as she spoke, a wide smile split over Will's face. "You're kidding? Really?"

"Really." She grinned. "I was going to say *except* the terrorists themselves."

"Holy crap," he breathed. "That is…" He trailed off, the reality of what she'd said sinking in like warm butter into fresh pancakes. "That is really, really awesome."

She nodded, beaming.

"And Melissa. Is she okay?" Will asked after a moment. "Danial – their leader – he had the chopper from her news station. How did he get it?"

"She's okay," Eliza said. "She was here this

morning, but she had to go back to work. They've been run off their feet, reporting what's happening…"

Quickly, Eliza related how Danial had busted into the station, taking Melissa's colleagues hostage in exchange for her getting them into the police station. "That's how the attack started," she said. "The terrorists tried to shoot her, as soon as they'd gotten in. But she managed to get away, barricaded herself and a bunch of other civilians in an office. They held off, like, three gunmen with nothing more than coffee cups and staplers."

Will laughed incredulously.

"Well, not quite, but she's kind of a hero." Eliza grinned. "She's been interviewed almost as many times as I have." She put on a haughty, I'm-famous face.

"Really?"

Eliza nodded. "She's coming back in this afternoon." Her face turned serious. "She's bringing you something. Some photographs, that Jeff gave her, of you and him together." Her voice dropped, becoming soft.

Will's throat caught. "Oh," he said, his voice cracking.

"He gave them to her before he died," Eliza continued.

Will nodded, not trusting himself to speak. Everything else had gone, in the explosion that had destroyed Jeff's house. That there was something left…

Eliza leaned forwards, taking his hand again, interlacing her fingers with his, her brow dipped down in the middle in a tiny crease. "I think she'd like to, maybe, see you occasionally," she said, tentatively. "Like, be friends."

Will swallowed. "I think I'd like that too," he said quietly, and Eliza smiled.

"Mum and Dad were real stoked to find out we weren't dead," she went on, after a moment of silence. Her smile became strained, and her expression darkened. "I explained everything... still feel like crap though."

Will felt the hot wash of guilt rise up his neck. "Yeah. Tell them... I'm really sorry that it had to be that way."

She waved a hand. "It's okay. They understand." She hesitated, looking at him carefully. "And they want to adopt you, you know," she said slowly. "If you want them to, of course."

Yet again tears threatened to spill over. He tightened his grip on her hand.

"I mean, you're old enough to probably not even need legal guardians," she said, quickly, misinterpreting the look on his face. "You'll be eighteen in two years anyway – "

"No," he said, and she fell silent. "I mean, I'd like that. I want them to."

She smiled like the sun rising. "Really?"

He nodded quickly, pushing back the welling up feeling of crazy lightness building in his chest. She

367

slipped her arm back around his neck again and he rose up to hug her, hard.

"We're going to be okay, Will," she whispered, her breath tickling against his neck.

He closed his eyes, and there was nothing but her that mattered in the world.

"I know," he whispered.

Message From the Author

Hello. I hope you enjoyed the story, I sure enjoyed writing it.

Now, did you…notice anything particular about the story? Maybe you did. But for those of you who didn't, I have a surprise to reveal to you.

You've just read the world's first math thriller. That's right, I did mean to say *math*. You've just read a story packed with math, and not just any math. This story contains many mathematical concepts any member of society should understand. Probability. Statistics. Finance. Basic Dynamics.

Perhaps you're wondering why anyone would want to write a math novel? Well, my motivation was very simple. I wanted to find an exciting way for people to learn math. Most teachers attempt to make math more interesting by making it *relevant* to real life, or by having fun examples. For example, they might try and learn about finance and probability by analysing your mobile phone bill, or guessing the outcome of a coin flip.

I decided to try a different approach. I structured

an entire story around about twenty six key mathematical concepts that I (and many others) believe any *mathematically literate* member of society should understand. The concepts that help you avoid getting conned by dodgy politicians spouting dodgy statistics, that help you understand what risks you're facing when you walk into a casino, and that temper your anger when you get a speeding ticket going down a hill.

Instead of illustrating these concepts in "realistic" situations, I deliberately chose the most outrageous stunts, chases, fights you can imagine. Situations you'll never, ever (at least I hope) find yourself in during your lifetime. Hopefully, if you've made it this far, this idea has worked. Because it's hard not to absorb a little bit of math when it means the difference between going splat on the pavement 20 stories below, or successfully defusing a 100 tonne bomb.

Mathematical literacy is critically important in the 21st century, more so now than at any other time. Society is going to have to decide how to deal with fundamental challenges to humanity, including climate change, overcrowding, and the ever present threat of biological and nuclear terrorism and war. The worst, worst thing that can happen is to have poorly educated or even deliberately ignorant loud voices confuse us by exploiting gaps in our understanding of basic mathematical principles and reasoning.

An informed, critically thinking population is a wonderful thing. I hope I can help to get us all there.

Where to Find Out More

I gave a TedX talk on "How Hollywood can save math education" which you can watch on YouTube: https://www.youtube.com/watch?v=m_U7qIjvMJw

Look me up using my twitter handle "maththrills"

www.MathThrills.com

Come visit the Math Thrills website where we offer a range of exciting educational resources including maths fiction, animated tutorials, worksheets and action-packed workshops.

www.ingramcontent.com/pod-product-compliance
Lightning Source LLC
Chambersburg PA
CBHW050614110726
47899CB00001B/107